Nickeled-and-Dimed to Death

Center Point
Large Print

Also by Denise Swanson and available from Center Point Large Print:

Devereaux's Dime Store Mysteries
  Little Shop of Homicide

Scumble River Mysteries
  Murder of the Cat's Meow
  Murder of a Creped Suzette
  Murder of a Bookstore Babe
  Murder of a Wedding Belle

**This Large Print Book carries the
Seal of Approval of N.A.V.H.**

Nickeled-and-Dimed to Death

A Devereaux's Dime Store Mystery

Denise Swanson

CENTER POINT LARGE PRINT
THORNDIKE, MAINE

This Center Point Large Print edition
is published in the year 2013 by arrangement with
NAL Signet, a member of Penguin Group (USA) Inc.

This is a work of fiction.
Names, characters, places, and incidents either are
the product of the author's imagination or are used
fictitiously, and any resemblance to actual persons,
living or dead, business establishments,
events, or locales is entirely coincidental.

The text of this Large Print edition is unabridged.
In other aspects, this book may vary
from the original edition.
Printed in the United States of America
on permanent paper.
Set in 16-point Times New Roman type.

ISBN: 978-1-61173-756-1

Library of Congress Cataloging-in-Publication Data

Swanson, Denise.
  Nickeled-and-dimed to death : a Devereaux's Dime Store Mystery /
Denise Swanson. — Center Point Large Print edition.
  pages cm
  ISBN 978-1-61173-756-1 (Library binding : alk. paper)
  1. Large type books. I. Title.
  PS3619.W36N53 2013
  813'.6—dc23
                                                        2013006509

Thanks to all my Facebook peeps,
who answer my questions,
wade in with their opinions,
and encourage me to write the next book.

CHAPTER 1

I mentally tapped my toe as I waited for Miss Ophelia to make her selection from the glass candy case. As the foremost authority on etiquette in Shadow Bend, Missouri—population 4,028—she'd been whipping the future generations of my hometown into excruciatingly correct behavior for the past fifty years. And since I had bought the dime store ten months ago, it had become her habit to stop in to purchase a single treat for herself every Saturday afternoon. Her last class on the proper way to dine, dance, and flirt with the opposite sex ended promptly at three thirty, and she arrived at my store exactly seven minutes later.

While Miss Ophelia dithered between a hand-dipped dulce de leche truffle and this month's signature candy, a red velvet bonbon, I glanced at the vintage Ingraham schoolhouse regulator hanging on the wall behind the front counter. Although the clock was manufactured in the 1920s, its beautiful carved oak case, convex glass, and brass pendulum still looked brand-new, and it kept perfect time. It was now 3:52.

Eight more minutes and my weekend clerk, Xylia Locke, and I could shoo out the loiterers, flip off the neon OPEN sign, and bolt the door.

Devereaux's Dime Store and Gift Baskets closed at four on Saturday, and today I wasn't letting the customers linger a single second longer. I had smoking-hot plans for the evening, and only ninety minutes to make myself beautiful enough to fulfill them.

After a lengthy verbal debate with herself, Miss Ophelia finally made her choice—completely changing her mind at the last minute and going with the butter crunch toffee. While Xylia was ringing up the older woman's purchase, I began the process of herding the stragglers toward either the register, for those who wanted to make a purchase, or the exit, for those who were sitting at the soda fountain, using the free Wi-Fi and socializing.

My clerk had one foot over the threshold as she said good-bye to me, when an attractive thirty-something brunette carrying a large package rushed past her into the store. I called out that we were closed, but the woman either didn't hear me or ignored my admonishment. Xylia raised a questioning eyebrow, but I waved her away. Whatever the last-minute shopper wanted, she'd have to come back on Monday.

I locked the door behind my assistant, not wanting another eleventh-hour customer to sneak in, then said to the brunette standing near the cash register, "I'm sorry, but we're closed for the day."

"Do you own this store?" the woman demanded, making no move to leave.

"Yes." Considering the cardboard carton in her arms, I wondered if she had a complaint about a previous purchase. "I'm Devereaux Sinclair. And you are . . . ?"

"Elise Whitmore." She thunked the box down on the marble counter, and I heard a metallic clinking sound. "I understand you like old stuff." She scrutinized me, her expression clearly indicating that she found wanting my less-than-fashionable jeans, yellow sweatshirt with DEVEREAUX'S DIME STORE embroidered across the chest, and frizzy cinnamon gold hair scraped into a pony-tail. "Is that true?"

"If you mean vintage and antique items, yes, I am interested in them. I both collect them and use them for the gift baskets I make." When I had purchased the dime store, I had added the basket business.

"Good." Elise unfolded the carton's flaps and reached inside.

My treasure-hunting curiosity was piqued.

"I've got some old chocolate molds I want to sell." Elise pulled out a pair of metal Easter Bunny casts. "What do you think?"

One bunny was close to a foot tall and had a basket attached to his back, and the other bunny, about half the size of the first, was carrying a mushroom. I loved them. They would be perfect for my Easter window display and for the traditional basket orders I had for the holiday. The erotic baskets I made needed a vastly different type of merchandise.

"They seem nice," I answered neutrally, hoping to keep the price within a range I could afford. "How much do you want for them?"

"You can have the whole box for a thousand bucks." Elise put down the ones she was holding, then lined up three more Easter-themed molds— a girl bunny, a set of four eggs, and a rabbit riding a duck.

I didn't know much about these particular collectibles, but I had a hunch this was an extremely good deal. "Can you give me a second?" When she nodded, I slipped into the storeroom, bent over my computer, and typed ANTIQUE CHOCOLATE MOLDS into Bing.com. *Zowie!* According to several of the Web sites I clicked on, the largest rabbit alone was worth 950 dollars.

Suddenly afraid that the woman would leave or change her mind about selling the molds, I hurried back out to the sales floor and, keeping my voice cool, said, "Since they're a seasonal item and there's only three weeks left until Easter, I'll give you seven fifty."

Elise frowned, then shrugged. "Eight hundred, but I want cash."

Since so many people used credit and debit

cards, I wasn't sure I had that much money in the till. "Eight fifty if you'll take a check." I was willing to pay fifty bucks more to cinch the deal.

"No." She shook her head. "Cash, or I take these to the pawn shop at the edge of town."

"Let me see what I have on hand." I went behind the counter and opened the register. As I added up the contents of the drawer, I held my breath. I really wanted those molds.

"I don't have all day." Elise tapped her foot. "Do we have a deal or not?"

"One second." I dug in my jeans pocket and pulled out a twenty, two fives, and a single. "Here you go." Adding them to the stack in front of me, I handed the pile to Elise.

She counted the money, nodded, and stuck it in her Dolce & Gabbana handbag, then turned on her heel and marched toward the exit. I followed her and unlocked it. She hesitated halfway through, and I nearly hit her with the door I was already closing.

Elise took a swift step to avoid the collision, then said over her shoulder, "Do me a favor and don't tell anyone where you got the molds."

"Why?" I called after her. A sinking feeling made my stomach clench. "They were yours to sell, weren't they? You are the owner, right?"

But it was too late; she had already gotten into her red Lexus and was backing into the street. As she sped away, I noticed her license plate read

WUZ HIZ. Damn! I knew that had been too easy. Why hadn't I asked more questions? Had I just committed a felony?

After hastily sticking the chocolate molds into my safe, I finished locking up the store and jumped into my sapphire black Z4. It was one of the few possessions I had kept from my old life —the one where I earned a six-figure salary as a financial consultant employed by Stramp Investments.

I'd allowed myself to hang on to the BMW by rationalizing that in this economy I'd never get what it was worth if I sold it. However, the truth was, I loved that car, and I knew there was more of a chance of me winning the Miss Missouri contest than of ever owning a vehicle like it again.

Chuckling at the thought of being a beauty pageant queen, I put the Z4 in gear and headed home. I lived with my grandma, Birdie, just outside of Shadow Bend on the ten remaining acres of the property my ancestors had settled in the 1860s.

Because of the three generations before me that had produced only one child each, relatives who had moved away, and several Sinclair men who'd died in various wars, Gran and I were the last of our clan in Shadow Bend. My grandfather's death fifteen years ago had forced Gran to begin selling off the land surrounding the old homestead to pay the taxes and support herself and me. Piece by piece, my heritage had been stripped away, and I treasured what we had left. Just as I cherished my grandmother.

It was when Gran had started to have some memory issues that I had quit my job in Kansas City and purchased the dime store. Going from a sixty-hour or more workweek to a little over forty had given me the time I needed to be there for her. As had swapping my two-hour round-trip commute for a twenty-minute drive.

Gran had taken me in thirteen years ago when my parents deserted me. Although my father hadn't had a choice about it—he'd been sent to prison for manslaughter and possession of a controlled substance. My mom didn't have any excuse.

She had dumped me on Birdie's doorstep with a suitcase and a fifty-dollar bill and run off to California. I was sixteen at the time, and even though Gran had showered me with love and attention, I never got over my mother's actions or the feelings of rejection and abandonment they instilled.

Which is why when Gran's doctor had informed me that she needed me to be around more, I hadn't hesitated to find another way to earn a living. I put in my two weeks' notice at Stramp Investment as soon as the deal for the dime store purchase was complete. Some people thought I resigned from my job because I found out my boss, Ronald Stramp, was a crook, and that he paid for my silence. But I'd been as surprised as the rest of the world when his Ponzi scheme was revealed.

Just as my father had claimed he had been set up and was as innocent of committing manslaughter as he was of the bank embezzlement of which he'd also been accused but never convicted, Stramp also maintained his innocence. However, unlike Dad, the jury at my boss's trial acquitted him—a fact that the people Stramp had bilked out of millions still resented.

Unfortunately, most people blamed me for the not-guilty verdict that freed him. I hadn't been able to testify about Stramp's scam because I hadn't been aware of it. I don't know which I felt worse about: that my ignorance allowed him to get away with his crime or that I was so dumb I never noticed what he was doing. My only defense was that Stramp was an extremely secretive and clever man.

All of this was on my mind as I made the short drive home. After both my father's and ex-boss's scandals, I had struggled to rehabilitate my image. As a teenager, I had shunned any and all controversy—never getting so much as a detention at school or a speeding ticket around my hometown.

And having made it through the Stramp disaster, I had pledged to avoid even the hint of dishonesty. Heck, I had solved a murder in which I was the prime suspect in order to escape being tainted by more gossip. Of course, my fear of being sent to prison might have also motivated me to find the real killer.

Now, as I tore down the blacktop toward home, passing farmhouses, fields, and pastures of grazing cows, sheep, and goats, I wondered if my love of collectibles and antiques had led me to commit a crime. If I had, could I make things right before my reputation was damaged beyond all repair?

Hitting the steering wheel, I groaned. *Great!* My good name was on the line again. And this time, it was my own damn fault.

CHAPTER 2

Birdie was waiting for me just inside the front door. Her summer tan was fading, and when she pursed her lips as she was doing now, her wrinkled face looked like a half-baked biscuit.

"Sweet Jesus!" She flipped her long, gray braid over her shoulder and demanded, "Why are you so late? He'll be here in less than an hour, and you're a hot mess." She held her nose. "And you smell." Gran was never one to mince words, especially when she was aggravated.

I discreetly lowered my head and sniffed. *Ew!* Eau de Hard Work wafted from my body. "Thanks so much for the confidence booster." She might be right, but I didn't have to like it.

"You're welcome." Birdie's impatient expression intensified. "Now get your rear in gear while you answer my question."

"Yes, ma'am." I sketched a mocking salute, then, with Gran in hot pursuit, hurried toward my bedroom. While explaining about the woman selling the vintage chocolate molds, I stripped off my jeans, sweatshirt, and underwear. I didn't include the information that those molds might be stolen property. Birdie would be mad enough to spit at my stupidity, so why stir up that hornet's nest?

Gran trailed me into the bathroom and watched as I turned on the shower. Some privacy would be nice, but if I complained, she'd remind me about the diapers she'd changed and the pictures she had of me wearing nothing but Mr. Bubble in the tub.

Instead, while I waited for the water to warm up from frigid to tepid—we really needed a new water heater—I finished up my story about Elise. "So I got the whole boxful, all five molds, for less than what one of them is worth. And they're fabulous."

"You should have told her to come back Monday." Birdie's pale-blue eyes glinted with displeasure. "This could be *the* night. Jake said he has a surprise for you. You have to look your best."

Deputy U.S. Marshal Jake Del Vecchio, the guy I was dating, was the grandnephew of Birdie's old high school flame, Tony. She and Tony were bound and determined to see Jake and me walk down the aisle. I suspected they were trying to consummate their own unfulfilled romance through us, but I'd never had the nerve to say so out loud.

"And you know what Jake said, how?" I asked. It was a purely rhetorical question, because clearly Gran had been reading my text messages again. I needed to remember to lock the screen on my phone.

Especially since I was pretty darn sure that the "surprise" Jake had mentioned had more to do with him finally getting me horizontal and seeing the tiny shooting star tattoo on my hip than with the engagement ring Gran was hoping he had in his pocket, ready to slip on my left hand. Allegedly, we were going into nearby Kansas City for dinner and a show to celebrate our one-month-of-dating anniversary, but I suspected we were really going into the city to find some privacy. A commodity that was difficult to obtain in my hometown.

I stepped into the shower, thinking that maybe Gran would lose interest and leave, but she continued to talk to me through the closed curtain. When she got to the subject of my wardrobe, I cringed. Birdie's taste in clothing was eclectic at best. One day she'd wear a poodle skirt from her teenage years, and the next she'd have on a Jackie Kennedy suit—complete with matching pillbox hat and pumps.

Turning off the water, I answered her clothing inquiry with, "I'm all set. I have a new dress."

"Really?" Birdie's voice held a note of delight. "You spent money on clothes?"

"Well . . ." *Oops!* I hadn't meant to admit that to Gran. It was the first new item of clothing I had purchased since quitting my job and buying the dime store, so she'd know I was excited about this date, too. "It's no big deal. It was on sale on Overstock.com."

"Uh-huh." Gran's expression said she knew this date must be important to me if I was willing to spend hard-earned cash on a new dress.

"It's true." Obviously, my excuses weren't fooling her, but I gave it one more try as I stepped out of the shower. "And I had a coupon and shipping was free."

"No need to explain." Birdie smirked. "I'm thrilled you finally bought something nice for yourself." She paused. "It is nice, right?"

"It's hanging on the inside of my closet door."

I'd toweled off and now picked up my blow dryer, gesturing toward my bedroom. "Go ahead: take a look."

I smiled. Her oohs and aahs were loud enough to be heard over the noise of the turbo stream of hot air I had aimed at my head. If Gran was happy, maybe she'd let me finish getting dressed in peace.

Or not.

As I was winding my hair around hot rollers, Birdie darted back into the bathroom and asked, "What shoes are you wearing?"

"My T-strap peep-toe sandals." Although I had sold most of my designer clothing, especially the suits, when I quit my city job, I had kept the shoes since I was reasonably sure the market for used footwear was fairly limited.

Birdie nodded and disappeared, muttering to herself about sexy heels helping my too-curvy calves.

I hollered after her, "What time is it?"

"Five ten."

Crap! Jake was picking me up in twenty minutes and I still had to put on my face, brush out my hair, and get dressed. I dug through my makeup case, searching for my seldom-used base. It had been so long since I'd applied it, I had almost forgotten the swirl, tap, and buff method that bareMinerals recommended. For a second, I was afraid I would have to dig out the instructional video.

I hadn't bothered with much more than lip gloss for a long time. For special occasions, I slapped on some concealer and brushed on a little bronzer, but I hadn't put on the whole shebang since working in the city. Luckily the technique came back to me, and ten minutes later my eyes were shadowed, my lashes curled and mascaraed, and I was done.

Running into my bedroom, I nearly tripped over Gran's ancient Siamese cat, Banshee, who hissed and clawed at my leg. I loved 99.9 percent of all animals, but not Banshee—and the feeling was mutual. Our war had started when he ate my pet gerbil. Considering his stealth attacks on me from the tops of bookshelves and around corners, there didn't appear to be any truce in sight.

Gran had laid out my best bra and panty set on the bed, along with a pair of sheer, lace-topped, thigh-high nylons. Where had she gotten those stockings? And when had my grandmother turned into my pimp?

On the other hand, as I smoothed on the filmy hose, I had to admit they did wonderful things for my less-than-perfect legs. Taking my new dress from its hanger, I stroked the pale-pink fabric. It was strapless with a sweetheart neckline and had embroidered butterflies scattered randomly on the bodice and the above-the-knee skirt.

After putting on the dress and slipping on my high heels, I turned to look in the mirror.

Surprised, I turned all the way around, then did it again. Yes, the girl in the glass really was me. It took a few seconds for me to realize that I felt young and pretty and hopeful—emotions I hadn't experienced in a very long time.

With my thirtieth birthday looming at the end of the year, I had been feeling old, and I rarely thought of myself as pretty, but the sensation of optimism was what really astonished me. I couldn't remember feeling that way since before my dad went to prison.

Fifteen minutes later, as Gran and I stared out the front window of the living room, I fingered the silky material of my dress and wondered why Jake was so late. He was almost always on time, yet there was still no sign of him. Why hadn't he called?

"Sweet Jesus." Birdie popped out of her recliner. "Where is that boy?"

"I'm sure he'll be here any second," I said, keeping my voice as nonchalant as possible. If Gran knew that I was concerned, she'd leap to the conclusion that I was in love with Jake. And since I'd known him for only six weeks, that couldn't be true. Right?

"Humph." Birdie paced from the sofa to the TV and back again.

"I'll text him and see what's up." While I searched for my cell phone, questions ping-ponged through my mind. Had I misunderstood his original message? Had something happened to him? And although I told myself over and over again that arriving late for a date didn't mean he was dumping me, a little voice in my head kept suggesting that was exactly what was happening.

Just as I located my elusive cell hiding at the very bottom of my purse, the phone in the kitchen started ringing.

Expecting it to be Jake, I hurried into the next room and grabbed the handset on the second ring. "Hello."

"Why aren't you answering your cell?" The irritated voice of Boone St. Onge buzzed in my ear.

Before I could respond, Gran walked into the kitchen, an inquiring look on her face. I mouthed Boone's name, and she retreated to the living room to resume her vigil at the picture window.

"Did you forget to charge it again?" Boone demanded. He, along with Poppy Kincaid, were my two best friends. All three of us grew up together. The only time any of us lived anywhere outside of Shadow Bend was during college, and, in Boone's case, law school.

I checked the small screen of the tiny device I was still clutching and saw that I had accidently muted the ringer. "The battery's fine. I just didn't hear it." Flipping through the missed messages, which were mostly from Boone, I asked, "What's up?"

"Not much right now. Later I've got that thing I told you about." Boone had mentioned that he and a friend were going to an art gallery opening in Kansas City, but those events usually started pretty late.

"What time are you leaving?" I knew it took a good hour to get into the city even without commuter traffic.

"Ten." Boone crunched something in my ear, then explained, "We're going to grab a bite to eat, then go to the gallery. The artist claims to be a vampire, so he only shows his work from midnight until dawn."

"How . . ." I searched for the right word. "Inconvenient for his mortal patrons."

"Hey, at least it's something new to do. Lately, I've been so bored I could scream." Boone chomped again; I was pretty sure he was eating an apple. "How about you? Are you doing anything interesting?"

"Just sitting here with Gran," I answered truthfully. I hadn't mentioned to either Poppy or Boone that Jake and I had a big date. Both of them were already way too interested in my relationship with him.

"You need to get a life." Boone sighed, then added in an discontented tone, "We both do."

"Hey, I tried once, but they were out of stock."

Boone ignored my feeble attempt at humor and said, "On a more positive note, at least you have time to talk to me." I could hear him settling in for a good gossip.

"Uh—"

Boone didn't wait for my answer. "You'll never guess who I saw at Brewfully Yours today." He paused dramatically. "Or what she had on."

As I listened to Boone's description of his encounter at the local coffee shop with Gwen—a woman we both disliked—I continued to scroll through my voice mail. The very last one in the queue was from Jake. I covered the other phone's receiver and pressed the button to listen to the message.

"Devereaux"—Jake's sexy, deep voice swept over me—"I'm sorry to cancel our date at the last minute, but I just got a call. I've been cleared for duty and they have a case they want me on ASAP." He paused, then added, "I'm heading to St. Louis as soon as I hang up. I'll call you when I get a chance, but it may be a while."

For a second I sagged against the kitchen counter. Jake had been injured in the line of duty more than a year and a half ago. He'd been working on his granduncle's ranch while waiting to hear if he'd healed enough to resume working as a deputy U.S. Marshal—an outcome he desperately wanted and that I had mixed feelings about.

While I was glad that Jake's leg was better and he could get back to the job he loved, it meant he'd be living in St. Louis—more than four hours from Shadow Bend. It also meant that he'd be in contact with his ex-wife, Meg, every day, since she was his supervisor. Heck, for all I knew, they'd be spending nights together, too. None of those circumstances held much promise for the future of our relationship.

Finally I straightened, took a deep breath, and forced myself to continue the conversation with Boone, who was saying, "And she was wearing the most hideous gold dress with purple tights and bright aqua stilettoes."

Thank goodness Boone was on a roll and didn't require much more than the occasional, "Oh, my . . . ," "What was she thinking?" and "I can't imagine," because my mind was fully occupied with Jake's news.

Twenty minutes went by and Boone was winding down when the call-waiting tone started bleeping in my ear. Crossing my fingers that it was Jake phoning to say he'd changed his mind, decided to resign from the Marshals, and was staying in Shadow Bend, I said good-bye to Boone and picked up the other call.

"Dev?" A too-familiar voice socked me in the gut. "It's Noah."

I really wished I had looked at the caller ID. Because if I'd known it was my old high school boyfriend, Noah Underwood, I would have ignored the call.

CHAPTER 3

Noah Underwood and I had known each other since birth. Actually, we might have met while still in our mothers' respective wombs. Both women were pregnant at the same time, and they were often together at community events. In fact, considering both women's love of attention, they had probably stood side by side, vying for the limelight.

The Underwoods and the Sinclairs were two of the five founding families of Shadow Bend, which made socializing with one another inevitable. Consequently, when Noah and I hit adolescence, it had seemed natural for us to become sweethearts. And once we started dating, we were inseparable. It hadn't taken long for Noah to become the most important person in my life, and I had thought I was the most important one in his. Regrettably, I had been wrong. Very, very wrong.

Thirteen years ago, before everything changed, the Sinclairs and the Underwoods were social equals. Both families were respected and well regarded. But when my father went to prison, the Sinclairs became the town pariahs, while the Underwoods continued to grow more revered with every year that passed.

Few people blamed Noah for ending our relationship. After all, he was the golden boy, and my family's reputation was tarnished beyond redemption. The fact that he had vowed to love me for all eternity, then bolted when my father was found guilty, made sense to them. Gran, Boone, and I were the only ones who hated him for walking out on me during the worst period of my life. Even my other best friend, Poppy, had a soft spot for my ex-boyfriend.

Recently, Noah had tried to convince me that I had incorrectly interpreted his actions at the time. He claimed he'd had a good reason for breaking off with me, and that he'd even tried to come back. But I still wasn't sure I believed him, and if I did believe him, I wasn't certain it mattered to me anymore.

True, until I met Jake, I had never felt the same passion toward any other man that I had felt for Noah. But how did I know those feelings weren't just a teenage crush? And did I really want to risk being hurt again in order to find out?

Which is exactly why I had been ducking Noah for the past several weeks. I liked to deal with most problems head-on, but my love life was another matter entirely.

"Dev?" Noah asked after a lengthy silence on my part. "Are you there?"

"Hi, Noah." I guess I still could have hung up, but I felt guilty for avoiding him this past month.

We had supposedly cleared the air between us when I helped him find out who had murdered his fiancée, and I knew he was probably confused by my behavior.

"Oh. Hi. I thought maybe I had gotten your answering machine again."

"Nope." I pulled out a chair from the kitchen table and sat down. "It's me."

"That's great." There was a hint of happy surprise in Noah's silky tenor. "I was afraid you'd be out. I never seem to catch you at home."

"Yeah." I concentrated on keeping my breathing even and sounding as casual as possible. "I'm pretty busy between the store and Birdie, and—" I broke off. I had almost said *seeing Jake*.

"I know what you mean. I really wish I could talk another doctor or two into joining my practice." Noah's tone was rueful. "But for some reason that I can't figure out, no one else seems to want to put in twelve-hour days and accept payment in livestock."

"Who paid you in chickens this time?" I asked, having heard through the grapevine about the hens that had gotten loose at his clinic. "Or do you have a cow grazing in your waiting room now?" It was common knowledge that Noah was too kindhearted to turn away patients in need, despite their inability to pay by cash, check, or credit card.

Farm families strapped for money had taken to

using the barter system around town. Just the other day, I'd been offered a couple of rabbits and half a dozen chicks in exchange for quilting fabric. I wasn't sure if I was supposed to have the animals for dinner or put them in Easter baskets, but neither alternative worked for me, and the woman and I had come to an alternative arrangement.

"The Browns," Noah answered, laughing, "but it was a piglet, so no harm, no *fowl* this time."

I snickered at his bad pun. "What in the world did you do with a pig?" I had forgotten how much I enjoyed Noah's dry sense of humor.

"I gave it to the women and children's shelter," Noah answered. "The kids are raising the piglet and the chickens, and they'll enter them in the county fair this spring. Then the animals will be processed to provide food for the shelter."

"That was really nice of you." My heart melted a little. "But how do you keep your clinic in the black when you do stuff like that?"

For years, I had tried to convince myself that Noah couldn't possibly be the wonderful man the townspeople all proclaimed he was. I had been sure that everyone was blinded to his true self by his profession, his good looks, and his family's position in Shadow Bend. However, since we had finally discussed the past and I'd heard his side of what had happened in high school, it was harder and harder for me to ignore what a good person he was.

"You know I'll never starve." I could hear the shrug in his voice. "A lot of people aren't as fortunate."

"Of course." How could I forget about his wealth, even for a minute?

We were silent for a couple of seconds, then Noah said, "Hey, I didn't call to discuss my cash flow."

"Oh?" I'd relaxed, but now I felt myself becoming anxious again.

"Yeah." Noah cleared his throat. "The thing is, I need a favor."

"Oh?" I repeated myself, tension thrumming through my shoulders.

"I have to attend this dance at the country club tonight." When I didn't respond, Noah hurried to explain. "It's a fund-raiser for the shelter, and I was on the committee. It would seem strange if I didn't show up."

"Sure."

"My cousin was going to go with me, but she bailed out at the last minute." He took a deep breath, then said in a rush, "So I was kind of hoping that you'd be free and could go with me."

"Why can't you go alone?" The last thing I needed was to appear at a dance with Noah. His mother was sure that I was the spawn of Satan—or at least a criminal—and my grandmother thought Noah was a coward for breaking up with me when my dad was convicted. Being seen in public with him would create a mess I wasn't sure I wanted to deal with.

"Since Joelle was killed and I'm unattached again, it's been a little awkward at social gatherings because . . ." He trailed off.

"Because now you're fair game and all the single women in town are after you again." I finished what he'd been too modest to say.

"Uh." Noah paused, then said, "Anyway, if you were with me that would solve a lot of problems."

"For you, maybe." I shook my head for emphasis even if he couldn't see it. "But think of the gossip, not to mention your mother's reaction."

"Not to mention your grandmother's, you mean," he chided me good-naturedly.

He had a point. Gran had spent her whole life in a small town that took family feuds seriously. So despite the fact that Noah's betrayal had occurred more than a decade ago, any mention of his name made Gran bristle like a porcupine. And I certainly didn't want to get in her way when she released her sharp spines at what she perceived as a threat.

When I didn't respond, he added, "And I don't care if Mom is unhappy. I've been living my own life for quite a while and there are a lot of things I do that she doesn't approve of. She certainly didn't like Joelle."

"Hmm." That was true, but what he didn't know

was that his mother, Nadine, had told me that she had been confident he would never marry Joelle. And, as it turned out, she'd been right—just for the wrong reason.

"Actually, as well as helping me out, this could be good for you, too."

"Why is that?" I asked.

"My college roommate will be at the dance and he's the owner of a huge Kansas City real estate firm. He's looking for a new company to make the gift baskets they give the people who buy one of their properties. Their current supplier's product has become too repetitive." Noah dangled the bait in front of me. "I mentioned how unique all your baskets are, and he was definitely interested."

My heart raced at the thought of making such a potentially lucrative connection. "How many baskets are we talking about?" I had put all the money I had into the dime store and needed the shop to succeed—for Birdie's sake as much as my own.

"Twenty or so a week," Noah enticed me. "More once real estate sales pick up again."

"Well . . ." Between Birdie's medical costs and the store's mortgage, I could definitely use that kind of cash. I made an enormous profit on the gift baskets, since I was selling my creativity more than the actual contents. "Gran would really be upset about our being together."

"Tell her you're using me," Noah cajoled.

"Let me think about it for a minute." I covered the mouthpiece of the receiver and played Jake's message one more time. Then I looked at my reflection in the glass-front cabinets and said into the phone, "It seems my Saturday night has just opened up. When are you picking me up?"

CHAPTER 4

Noah tossed the phone onto its base and pumped his fist in the air. *Yes!* He had a date with Dev. After several weeks of her failing to return his phone calls, mysteriously disappearing whenever he went into the dime store, and ignoring messages he left, she had finally said yes. Now he just had to figure out how to make her trust him again.

His wide smile faded a little when he recalled her parting words. Why was she suddenly free on a Saturday night? It sounded as if she'd had plans that fell through. He drew his brows together, contemplating the various possibilities. After a few seconds of pondering, he slowly grinned. Had that U.S. Marshal she'd been seeing stood her up? Or maybe they'd had a fight. Both of those scenarios worked for Noah, since either could provide just the opening he needed to woo Dev away from that hotshot Deputy Dawg.

Whistling, Noah strode from the desk to the sofa, flopped down, grabbed the remote, and turned on the TV. After a few minutes of channel surfing, he punched the OFF button. Nothing on the screen captured his interest.

As he looked around the room for something to do, it occurred to him that this was the only spot in his house that felt like home. When he'd bought the place two years ago, he'd allowed the decorator free rein. But after she'd finished and he'd written her a check for an obscene amount of money, he'd gradually added his own stuff to the den.

Why had he even hired an interior decorator? Oh, yeah. It had been simpler than fighting his mother. Noah had never liked discord, and except for his willingness as a physician to fight for his patients, he prided himself on being a laid-back kind of guy. Although considering Nadine's reaction to his engagement to Joelle, that decision certainly hadn't been that of a man who wanted to avoid conflict. Or had it?

Noah frowned. Maybe his girlfriend's desire for marriage had been more of an immediate stressor than Nadine's displeasure at the prospect. Joelle had certainly pressed for a commitment, stating her age—which he'd later learned was a lot older than she claimed—and her desire to have children. He'd fallen for her sad tale of growing up an only child, losing her parents when she was a teenager, and having no one in the world that she could call family. Too bad the whole story had been a lie.

Truth be told, he'd been drifting, doing what was expected of him, neither happy nor sad, sort of numb. He hadn't loved Joelle; he'd just settled for her. In fact, he'd thought he'd lost the ability to love. But the prospect of getting Dev back seemed to have jump-started his heart. Maybe she was what he'd needed all along.

Leaping to his feet, Noah strode down the hall and into the spare bedroom that the decorator had converted into a home gym. He wasn't picking up Dev for more than an hour—the dance didn't start until eight—and he refused to sit around and think about the poor decisions he'd made in the past. Tonight would be a new beginning.

He pushed the PLAY button on his CD player and the latest Black Eyed Peas album blared from the speakers. After stripping off his T-shirt, he pulled on fingerless leather gloves, lay down on the bench, and started his routine. He was up to two hundred pounds, and sweat poured off his face and body as the muscles in his arms strained to raise the heavy barbells again and again.

He'd always been more the intellectual than the athletic type, but when he'd enrolled in a weight-lifting class in college, he discovered that the monotonous activity was oddly soothing. He hadn't had time to work out in a couple of days, so it took him a while to get his rhythm, but once he did, his mind wandered.

Skittering away from the subject of Dev—not wanting to jinx the evening ahead—he thought about the strange phone call he'd received that afternoon from the Shadow Bend Savings and Guaranty Bank president, Max Robinson.

An Underwood had been on the bank's board of directors since the institute was founded, and when Nadine had stepped down last month, it had been understood that her son would replace her. Generally, the board met once a month and reviewed various issues ranging from managing risk to allocating resources to compliance with relevant legal statues. Most of this was routine.

Although the bank president prepared and presented reports to the board, Noah was fairly sure it was rare for Max to telephone an individual member. It wasn't as if he and Robinson were friends. And after Robinson had hung up, Noah still wasn't sure why he'd called.

What had the man said? Something about welcoming him to the board and hoping that he and Noah could work together as well as he and Mrs. Underwood had, and how much he admired Mrs. Underwood. He'd gone on and on about what a fine woman she was and how much she'd done for the community as a whole and the bank in particular.

Wait a minute. Noah stopped mid-lift. Could

Max Robinson have a crush on Nadine? Maybe the bank president had been testing the waters to see if Noah would object to him asking her out.

Completing his ascending thrust of the barbell, Noah considered his mother dating the bank president. Robinson was probably ten years younger than she was, not that a difference in age was a big deal. He seemed like a nice enough guy. The townspeople respected him, and he certainly was a hard worker. He appeared almost to live at the bank. So why not?

Noah finished up, wiped his face and neck with a towel, and rose from his prone position. He grabbed a bottle of Dasani from the mini fridge and downed half the contents in one gulp. As he drained the rest of the bottle, a thought occurred to him and he smiled. If his mother were dating someone, maybe she'd be too busy to poke her nose into Noah's life.

If things worked out with Dev, Noah definitely wanted his mother occupied with something besides her son's love life. This might be his only chance to show Dev that he was a different person from the boy she'd known in high school. The fact that he was no longer tied to his mother's apron strings was one of the big changes he'd made since then, and he wanted to prove it to Dev.

Turning off the music, Noah strolled to his bedroom and into the master bath. Lucky, the

Chihuahua he'd inherited from Joelle, was asleep in the sink, but he lifted his head and opened one eye when Noah turned on the shower. Sometimes Noah wondered if the little animal realized he was a dog and not a cat.

Once he was out of the shower and dried off, Noah shaved. He was so fair-haired he probably didn't need to worry about five o'clock shadow, but since he was hoping for a good-night kiss or two from Dev, he didn't want to take any chances.

After splashing on Amouage Dia Pour Homme, he walked into his bedroom and checked the clock on the nightstand. It was seven fifteen. He had half an hour before he had to pick up Dev. Plenty of time, even allowing for traffic, which was nonexistent in and around Shadow Bend.

Once he was dressed, he went to his dresser and pulled out the polished cherrywood box in which he kept his jewelry. Rummaging among the watches and tie clips, he found the cuff links that his father had given him on his twelfth birthday, only a few months before Montgomery Underwood had died. The sterling silver discs with his initials engraved in the center were by far the most inexpensive cuff links Noah owned, but they always brought him luck. And he had a feeling he would need all the good luck he could muster in order to get Dev back again.

CHAPTER 5

I stood at the back door, keeping a watchful eye on the driveway. Gran had not been at all pleased to hear that Jake had stood me up or that he was on his way back to St. Louis. Luckily I had never told her that his ex-wife was his supervisor and they'd be together nearly twenty-four/seven while working cases.

As it was, it had taken me a half hour to calm down Gran after telling her that Jake wasn't showing up for our date. So when I dropped the second bomb—that instead of going out with the man she hoped I'd marry I was now attending a dance with a guy she hated—her ballistic reaction was fairly predictable.

Birdie didn't buy Noah's claim that after breaking up with me, he had explained and apologized a few days later. She especially didn't accept his justification for ending our relationship in the first place. Which, according to Noah, was because if he didn't stop dating me, his mother, a member of the bank's board of directors, had threatened to have Gran charged with aiding and abetting my father's embezzlement scheme.

After a lot of fast-talking, I had almost convinced Birdie that exploiting Noah for his connections was the best revenge of all. Of course, the glass of Jack Daniel's Gran had consumed had probably helped more than any of my verbal tap-dancing. The second shot hadn't hurt either.

Still, I wasn't taking any chances, so as soon as Noah's headlights appeared, I yelled good-bye, raced out the door as fast as my high heels could take me, and hopped in his car almost before it came to a complete stop. He was still putting the Jaguar in park when I finished buckling my seatbelt.

He looked at me with a slightly bemused smile, and asked, "Escaping from Stalag 17?"

"Nope." I smoothed my trench coat and tucked my evening bag next to my side. "Just avoiding an encounter between you and Birdie."

"She didn't take the news of our date very well?" Noah made a three-point turn and headed back down the lane toward the county road.

"This is not a date," I quickly corrected him. I definitely wasn't ready to admit that I was out with my high school ex for any reason other than a professional one.

"Of course not," Noah teased, his gray eyes crinkling at the corners. "Just because we're both all dressed up and going to a dance doesn't make it a date." He lifted one eyebrow. "Right?"

"Don't go there," I warned. "If this is a social engagement, you can just turn around and take me home." I lifted an eyebrow and stared.

"It's strictly a business arrangement." Noah gestured surrender with his hands, then grabbed the steering wheel as the sports car veered over the yellow line. "I provide you with an introduction to a potential customer, and your presence makes my life easier."

"Fine." I relaxed. "As long as we're clear on that, I'm good."

The country club was only a few miles out of town, and as we drove, Noah entertained me with stories about medical school and his residency. I couldn't believe that he and a buddy had kidnapped a cadaver, dressed it as Santa, and left it sitting on a lawn chair in front of the university president's house. And what they did with a hand they had dissected . . . Well, let's just say it appeared that doctors had the same dark sense of humor as other high-stress professionals.

Ten minutes later, Noah made a right turn between two enormous brick columns and drove along the golf course. It was too dark to see much, but from the glow of the streetlights, I could tell that the grass was just starting to turn green and the local ducks and geese were making full use of the water traps.

Although I had driven by the entrance of the country club several times, I had never ventured past the gates. Still, I wasn't surprised to see that the clubhouse was an ultramodern design. People who had recently moved to Shadow Bend and commuted to jobs in Kansas City tended to favor contemporary architecture over traditional or historic. And they definitely appreciated flashy over stately.

I had to admit that even though I preferred vintage buildings, the angled entrance and mahogany double doors were impressive. And the overhead windows that appeared to hover unsupported over the steps took my breath away. I stood gazing upward, trying to figure out how the windows had been constructed, until Noah clasped my elbow and led me inside.

When we stepped into the foyer, an African American woman dressed in a stunning red silk suit greeted us. She introduced herself as Kiara Howard, the country club's event planner, and pointed out the coat check. Once we'd handed over our wraps to the attendant, Kiara directed us down the hall before turning to greet the next couple.

The ballroom reminded me of the inside of one of the Easter baskets I'd created. Pink, blue, and yellow stuffed bunnies standing guard over baskets brimming with goodies acted as center-pieces on the tables, and festive Easter bonnets dangling from satin ribbons were strung from the ceiling. Garlands of pastel spring flowers were wound around whitewashed tree trunks whose branches were festooned with golden eggs.

I was so busy admiring the decorations, I

missed the reaction to our entrance. When I felt Noah tense, I realized that several women were staring at me with blatant resentment in their eyes.

Oops! How dumb could I be? He had invited me to discourage the amorous advances of the women in attendance; I certainly should have realized that the ladies I was protecting him from wouldn't be happy to see me.

Noah took my hand and murmured in my ear. To the others, it might have looked as if he were whispering sweet nothings; in reality, he was asking if I wanted a drink. Which I did. A big one.

We made our way to the nearest of the two bars set up at opposite ends of the large room, and Noah got in line. As I waited for him to rejoin me with the martinis—a chocolate one for me and a traditional one for him—I looked around, hoping to see a few friendly faces.

Because of the Sinclair family's banishment from the Shadow Bend upper class, I didn't socialize with these people. But I recognized most of them, having either waited on them in my store or grown up with them. Several individuals nodded pleasantly, but no one made an effort to include me in their groups.

After so many years, I should have been used to such treatment, but it still stung a little. I wondered for a second if Birdie felt the same way, then realized that even before our family's fall from grace, she had never been one to hang out with the movers and shakers. That had been more my mother's choice than hers.

Just as I was questioning my decision to accompany Noah for the fiftieth time, Winnie and Zizi Todd marched up to me and enveloped me in a group hug. Mother and daughter were part of the Blood, Sweat, and Shears sewing group that met at my store on Wednesday nights. And although neither was the type you'd expect to see at a country club dance, both were passionate supporters of the women and children's shelter, the focus of tonight's fund-raiser.

Zizi was in her early twenties and attending graduate school to become a clinical social worker. She had a quirky sense of style and tonight she wore her carrot red hair in braids wrapped around her head. Her blue skirt, white blouse, and red vest made her look like the girl from the Swiss Miss hot chocolate package.

Zizi's mother Winnie was the original flower child, and her fashion sense hadn't changed since her teens. She had on a groovy patchwork maxi dress, and her long gray hair was a cascade of frizzy curls down her back. I thought the silver peace symbol hanging from a leather thong around her neck was just the right touch, but the sunflower painted on her cheek might have been a tad too much. Still, I loved that neither she nor her daughter ever bowed to the

Shadow Bend peer pressure to conform and blend in.

Winnie had left Shadow Bend to live in San Francisco during the mid-sixties and had returned, sans husband, in the late eighties to have her only child. Several of the townspeople had been vocal with their advice and opinion of a single woman Winnie's age having a baby. But she blithely ignored their condemnation, gave birth to a healthy infant, and continued to do her own thing. Clearly she had raised her daughter to value her independence, too.

Stepping back from the double hug, Winnie said, "I didn't expect to see you here." She swiveled her head. "Are you with someone?"

"Uh . . ."

Before I could answer, Zizi elbowed her mother, then gestured at Noah, who had finally reached the head of the drinks line. He waved and smiled back before turning his attention to the bartender.

"Dr. Underwood." Winnie nodded knowingly. "I thought you two might end up together again. Although I figured that hot U.S. Marshal you've been seeing might edge out the gallant doctor."

"Noah and I are just friends," I protested. "His date cancelled on him at the last minute." After a nanosecond, I quickly added, "And Jake and I are just . . ." I trailed off, not sure what Jake and I were, and if we ever would be anything now that he was back in St. Louis working with his ex.

Zizi poked her mother again. "There's no reason she can't have both guys. One's hot and one's sweet—just the right combo."

"So true." Winnie's voice was reminiscent. "That was what was so great about the whole free-love movement in the sixties. Living in Haight-Ashbury was like being in the middle of a gigantic Whitman's Sampler filled with men. You could try a different flavor every day. Heck, even every hour, if you had the stamina."

"Which is why you have no idea who my father is." Zizi snickered, but her robin's-egg-blue eyes were a little sad. "You don't think I believed the sperm-donor story of yours for a minute, did you?"

I had been silent while Winnie and her daughter went back and forth; it was hard to join a conversation with that duo. But seeing Zizi's expression, I decided it was time to change the subject. "So." I searched my mind for something to say. "Noah mentioned he's on the dance committee. Are you both on the committee, too?"

"I was." Zizi raised her hand. "Mom didn't think the dance was a good idea for a fund-raiser." She gestured around the elaborately decorated room. "She thought it cost too much to put on and we wouldn't make a profit."

"And I still do." Winnie shook her head and

*tsk*ed. "For most of the women, this is just an excuse to buy a new dress and show off."

"Which is why we added the auction," Noah said, joining us. "We know we'll only make a small amount on the dance tickets, but we should make quite a bit on the drinks and even more on the auction items."

"What do you have for us to bid on?" I asked, looking around for a table full of goodies.

"Mostly merchandise or services donated by local businesses," Noah explained.

"Why didn't anyone ask me for something from the dime store?"

"You never returned my call." Noah held my gaze. "Guess you didn't get my message."

"Sorry. My phone's been eating my voice mail lately," I lied.

"Right." Noah's expression was skeptical. "That must have been what happened."

I stared back at him, refusing to admit I'd been deleting his messages without even listening to them.

"Some people gave us stuff they didn't want," Zizi said, breaking the tense silence.

"You mean like their junk?" I didn't think this crowd would bid for used books, old exercise equipment, or last year's coat.

"No." Zizi giggled. "Mostly either new items that had been gifts they didn't like or antiques and collectibles they were tired of."

"I see." My ears perked up at the words *antiques* and *collectibles*. "Where are the auction items?" I glanced around again. "I'd love to check out the old stuff."

"Behind those folding doors." Noah tipped his head to our right. "We're keeping it all a surprise until we start the auction. Then we'll do a big reveal."

"Although you might be able to persuade the auctioneer to give you a sneak peek," Winnie said with an innocent look on her face.

"Oh?"

"Yeah," Zizi joined in, sliding a mischievous glance between Noah and me. "I bet the auctioneer could be bribed. Say, with a kiss."

"I'm sure that's not true." It didn't take a rocket scientist to catch Zizi's drift, and I glanced at Noah before adding, "Guess I'll just have to wait along with everybody else."

"In the meantime"—Noah's ears were red, but his voice was unruffled—"if you ladies will excuse us, I promised to introduce Dev to an old friend."

"Sure." Winnie smiled and waved us away. "We'll catch you later."

With a hand on my elbow, Noah steered me toward a short, rotund man with his arm around a tall, beautiful woman.

As we neared the couple, Noah said, "Oakley, it's great to see you."

"Thanks for sending me the tickets." Oakley clasped Noah's shoulder, then said, "This is Faith Nelson. Faith, my old college roommate, Noah Underwood."

Noah shook the brunette's hand, then turned to me and said to the couple, "This is Devereaux Sinclair. Dev, this is Oakley Panigrahi and Faith Nelson. Dev runs the basket business I told you about."

"It is very nice to meet you at last," Oakley said. "Noah has told me a great deal about you, and I've been wanting to discuss a proposition with you ever since he mentioned your company."

"Terrific." I wondered what else Noah had said about me and when he had said it.

"Why don't you two go tango while Ms. Sinclair and I have a little talk," Oakley said, pushing Faith toward Noah.

"I'd love to." I mentally rubbed my hands together, thinking of the money this meeting could add to my bottom line.

Noah dipped his head toward Oakley and me before taking the stunning brunette's hand.

I kept a smile pasted on my face as Noah murmured in Faith's ear while leading her onto the dance floor, but a part of me was not happy to see such a gorgeous woman in his arms. They made a striking pair, moving together in perfect harmony to the beat.

After a moment, I forced myself to focus and,

raising my voice, asked Oakley, "Would you like to sit in the lobby? The music in here makes it a little difficult to have a meaningful conversation."

Oakley agreed, and within half an hour, he outlined the type of gift baskets he required for his real estate clients. He explained that he handled high-end luxury properties and he wanted unique items customized to the tastes of his buyers. He was willing to pay top dollar to provide a memorable thank-you gift for his customers.

I assured him that I was the woman for the job, and he promised to send an e-mail with the particulars for the first twenty orders. He then wrote me a large check for the down payment—the rest would be paid on delivery—and we returned to the ballroom, where we found Noah and Faith seated at a side table, chatting.

Oakley took the chair next to Faith, but when I started to slip into the one beside Noah, he stopped me, stood up, and said, "Let's waltz."

For the next hour, we rarely left the floor. I had forgotten what a great dancer Noah was; he was even able to make someone like me, with two left feet, feel graceful. I had also forgotten, or more likely blocked from my mind, how much I enjoyed being in his arms.

Finally we both needed a rest. Once we claimed a vacant table, Noah fetched us two more martinis. Sipping our drinks, we chatted about the event and the people, but eventually we ran out of small talk.

As I toyed with the stem of my glass, Noah cleared his throat. "Dev, I—"

Before he could finish his sentence, Winnie rushed up to us and announced, "It's time to start the auction. I've noticed a few couples have already left."

"Okay." Noah sighed, then asked me, "How would you like to be Vanna White?"

"Huh?"

"You know, point to the item and look beautiful," Noah teased.

"Okay." I smiled. "I can handle at least one of those two assignments."

"I know you're not just a pretty face. I'm sure you can point, too."

Winnie chuckled, then hurried off to whip the bidders into a frenzy.

Noah stood and, taking my hand, escorted me toward the door that led to the room holding the auction items. He gave me an inventory of the objects up for bid and their donors, then asked me to read them off as he lined them up. We were halfway through the list when I noticed several pieces with the name Elise Whitmore next to them and a note saying that she preferred not to be identified as the contributor.

Her gifts included a set of antique golf clubs, a

couple of signed baseballs in little Plexiglas boxes, and a bottle of Château Lafite Rothschild Pauillac 1996, which I knew retailed for close to eleven hundred dollars. Apparently Elise was cleaning her house of more than just chocolate molds, and she didn't want anyone to know it.

Just as we were opening the folding doors to the ballroom, my phone rang. I would have ignored it, but it was Boone's ring tone—"Sue Me" from *Guys & Dolls*. Since it was nearly eleven and he should have been dining in a Kansas City restaurant, if he was calling me, it had to be an emergency.

I gestured to Noah that I would only be a minute and stepped through the rear exit into a hallway. After fishing the cell from my evening bag, I said, "Hello." I waited, and when there was no response, I asked, "Boone, are you there? Is everything okay?"

Amid static, I heard Boone's voice say, "I've just been arrested for murder."

"What?!"

"Come to the Shadow Bend Police Station right away."

"Who was killed? Boone, tell me what happened," I demanded, but the line was dead, and when I hit Redial, the call went immediately to his voice mail.

Damn! What in the world had Boone gotten himself into?

CHAPTER 6

Well, this was awkward. The animosity between Noah and Boone was legendary. It had started when Noah ran against Boone in the sixth-grade election for class president. There had been a brief hiatus in their hostilities during high school while Noah and I were dating. But the minute Noah and I were no longer a couple, the men's true feelings resurfaced. From that moment on, they hadn't bothered to conceal their contempt for each other.

People who have never lived in small towns have no idea how serious and lifelong a feud can be, but I knew. Which meant that asking Noah to abandon his auctioneer duties in order to drive me to the police station to help Boone wasn't a good idea. Noah would either agree, in which case he'd be present for Boone's humiliation, or he would refuse, in which case there'd be a major rip in our slowly mending relationship. I didn't like either scenario.

Adding to my dilemma, I was pretty sure Boone wouldn't want news of his arrest to get out. Although considering that Shadow Bend's grapevine grew as if some superfertilizer had been applied, I wasn't sure there was any way to keep it quiet. Still, I didn't want to be the source of the leak.

My only alternative was Poppy. Although she was Boone's friend and would want to help, her father was the chief of police and she didn't get along with him, so her presence might cause more of a problem than it solved. Unfortunately, I couldn't figure out another way to get from the country club to the police station without telling someone who might start the gossip mill grinding. At least Poppy wouldn't blab.

Praying that her less-than-reliable bartender had shown up and she could leave her bar, I punched her speed-dial number on my cell. She owned Gossip Central, the most popular watering hole in the county, and as soon as she answered, I could tell that, as usual, the place was crowded. Saturday nights were her busiest time. Without any pleasantries or chitchat, I immediately told her about Boone's call.

It took a while for her to hear me over the noise of the bar, and even longer for me to convince her that I had no more information. Finally she said she'd pick me up in fifteen minutes—an ETA I thought was optimistic, considering that Gossip Central and the country club were on opposite sides of Shadow Bend.

Now that my transportation was secured, I had to decide how to inform Noah that I was leaving and why. The why was hard enough to explain, though I was hoping a generic announcement that I had a personal emergency would be enough. The how was tougher.

While I had been talking to Boone and Poppy, Noah had concluded his speech, and the auction was in full swing. He was completely occupied taking bids and interacting with the potential buyers. I couldn't exactly march up to the podium and make an announcement.

Hmm. Maybe that was my out. If I wrote him a note, I could slip away without having to explain my predicament. No, that wouldn't work. What if he didn't get the note? Okay. I could leave him a message with someone I trusted to deliver it. From the glares I had been receiving all evening from the other single women, it was a fair bet that most of them would be happy to see my backside and even happier to allow Noah to think that I had abandoned him without an explanation.

That narrowed the field to Oakley, Winnie, or Zizi. I quickly ruled out Oakley. I definitely didn't want my brand-new client to see me as someone surrounded by crises. And Winnie tended to be a little scattered. However, while Zizi's appearance suggested she might be less than dependable, I knew that no one maintained a 4.0 average in grad school without being reliable.

Having made my choice and asked Zizi to tell Noah that I had to leave due to a personal emergency, I fended off her questions. Then I hurried to the lobby and retrieved my coat. I had at least five minutes before there was any possibility of Poppy's arrival, so I made a quick visit to the ladies' room for an insurance pee. As Birdie always said, go when you have the chance.

By the time I had finished in the bathroom and walked out of the country club lobby, Poppy's ginormous silver Hummer was idling by the curb. Since Poppy's preschool days, males had been misled by her froth of silvery blond ringlets, striking amethyst eyes, and delicate build. Despite her angelic appearance, she had always been a wild child. I felt a little sorry for the guys who were fooled by her ethereal beauty. There really should be truth in advertising where men and women are concerned.

Considering that Poppy's father was the chief of the Shadow Bend police force, the irony that Poppy was the town bad girl was not lost on me. Then again, maybe instead of an incongruity, it was a cliché. Wasn't the preacher's son often a troublemaker? It didn't take a psychologist to figure out why the offspring of an authority figure might behave badly.

As soon as I climbed into the H1, I grabbed the seatbelt. When Poppy was at the wheel, it was always a bumpy ride. Her philosophy was, "Drive it like you stole it." Thank goodness she'd quit taking that idea as literally as she had when she was a teenager. Stopping her from going on unauthorized joyrides in any car that caught her fancy had been one of the trials and tribulations of my adolescence.

My derrière had barely touched the seat when Poppy floored the accelerator and demanded, "Tell me again exactly what Boone said."

I finished buckling up, then repeated my brief conversation with him, ending with, "So I have no idea who the victim is or why he's been arrested or what he thinks we can do to help him."

"Obviously my father's behind this whole thing," Poppy snapped.

Her relationship with her dad had been shaky for years, but something had happened last Christmas to push it into open hostility. I had never found out exactly what had caused the final falling-out. I suspected the reason was the apparent one: Poppy's devil-may-care lifestyle was about as opposite as could be from the chief's paramilitary-type existence, and one of them finally did or said something the other couldn't tolerate.

"Dad's only harassing Boone because he's a friend of mine," Poppy added.

I made a noncommittal sound, hoping to soothe her anger without blatantly disagreeing with her. I was reasonably certain Chief Kincaid wouldn't be that unprofessional, but Poppy firmly believed that her father was the love child of Lizzy Borden and Vlad the Impaler. Nothing I said would change her mind.

As Poppy raced her Hummer toward town, I felt an overwhelming sense of déjà vu. A couple of months ago, Chief Kincaid had taken my grandmother into custody over an episode that had been blown all out of proportion, and I had been summoned to her rescue. Eventually Gran had been released to me and the event forgotten. I could only hope that this incident would end as well.

When Poppy barely missed hitting a man in a gray hoodie and black jeans walking along the side of the road, I gasped. The guy leapt off the pavement and into the grass, shaking his fist.

Poppy grinned and waved as she sped by. Then she asked me, "Do you know the two kinds of pedestrians?"

"No."

"The quick and the dead."

I shook my head but couldn't stop a little giggle from escaping. Poppy was one of a kind. We'd been friends forever, and I'd stopped trying to change her a long time ago. Now I only attempted to intervene if arrest was imminent.

We arrived at the police station much faster than I would have thought possible. Due to the PD's location between the hardware store and the dry cleaners on Shadow Bend's main street, daytime parking was often a problem. But since it was long past normal business hours, all five spaces were free. Poppy wheeled into the one nearest the entrance, squealing her tires as she jerked to a motion sickness–inducing stop.

Relieved as I was that we had arrived safely, and anxious as I was to make sure Boone was all right, I still dreaded going inside. The police station's square cinder-block building, newly installed front window bars, and overall depressing air reminded me of a mini prison. Which was a problem for me on several levels, the most important one being that during my one and only visit to the penitentiary where my father currently resided, I had developed a sort of jailhouse phobia. I tended to hyperventilate at the thought of incarceration. Sadly, fainting rarely helped matters or left a good impression.

However, when Poppy slammed out of the Hummer and headed for the entrance at a jog, I knew I had to get inside before she did, or she might end up in the cell next to Boone's. So I took a deep breath and raced past her. My stomach churned as I pushed open the door. Why on earth did the cops think Boone was a murderer?

Although the lobby was empty when we entered, I could hear loud voices coming from the top of the short flight of concrete stairs that led to the rest of the station. Poppy tried to elbow her way in front of me, but since she had a Tinker Bell–like build and my figure was more along the lines of a full-bodied Wonder Woman, she didn't succeed.

As I stepped into the reception area, I saw that the entire Shadow Bend police force had been called in. All four of the full-time and the two part-time officers were milling behind the counter, seemingly unsure what to do, yet apparently unwilling to sit idly by. The woman manning the desk behind the bulletproof glass seemed ready to shoot them all.

Fortunately there was no sign of Eldridge Kincaid. He was probably in his office or maybe in the interrogation room. Either way, it was best to keep Poppy and her father apart for as long as possible. The two of them were like matches and gasoline—and I wasn't fireproof.

I approached the dispatcher, and with my mouth inches from the small speaker in the bulletproof glass, said, "May I speak to Boone St. Onge?"

She looked me up and down and I pulled my trench coat closed, trying to conceal my strapless bodice and short skirt. Without answering me, she turned and yelled, "Can St. Onge have visitors?"

The officers behind her froze, suddenly intent on staring at the ceiling or their shoes. Apparently no one was prepared or able to make that decision. Were they scared of Chief Kincaid or had they never been asked that type of question before?

Finally the sergeant must have realized he was the one in charge, and after straightening his shoulders, he said, "He's with the chief."

"He's probably water-boarding a confession from Boone," Poppy said as she joined me at the counter. Before I could comment, she commanded, "Tell my dad to release him this instant."

I stared at her. Did she really think she could issue an order like that and expect instant compliance? No. Probably not. Knowing her, I suspected she just felt the need to make her position clear.

To my surprise, one of the cops—I was guessing a rookie—disappeared down the hall, presumably to deliver Poppy's demand. As we waited for Chief Kincaid's response, I tried to overhear the conversations going on among the officers, but I couldn't make out individual words. They seemed excited and maybe a little scared. I speculated that this might be the first real murder case the Shadow Bend police had ever had to handle.

My bet was that they were mostly used to dealing with drunk driving, domestic violence, and the occasional cow tipping. Outright homicide was almost unheard of in our small community. Would that be a positive or a negative for Boone in his situation?

I leaned close to Poppy and whispered, "I understand that Boone's a lawyer himself, but why do you think he called us instead of an attorney?"

"No clue." She shrugged. "I doubt knowing

how to draw up an airtight will or get the best divorce settlement will help him defend himself from a murder charge." She scowled and added, "Even a trumped-up one."

"Do you know any criminal-defense lawyers?" I asked, thinking if we weren't allowed to see Boone, that might be our only option.

"There's this guy that comes to the bar once in a while." Poppy bit her lip. "I think he said he was a defense attorney." She twitched her shoulder. "But they all lie about stuff like that, so he could very well work in a local factory or spend his days asking, 'Do you want fries with that?'"

"Great."

Poppy didn't seem to want to talk, and I certainly didn't have anything to say, so I stared at the second hand on the big round wall clock as it ticked from line to line and number to number. While I watched, I tried unsuccessfully to think of something to do for Boone.

Twelve hundred ticks later, Chief Kincaid marched into the reception area and said, "What do you two girls think you're doing here?"

The chief's highly starched khaki uniform looked as if it had been ironed five seconds ago, and his gray buzz cut stood at attention. He scrutinized my party clothes—I'd had to take off my coat, since it was so hot in the station—then inspected his daughter's outfit.

Poppy was dressed to entice—her usual style when she tended bar. His gaze flicked from her stiletto-heeled boots to her body-hugging leather pants, then stopped at her spaghetti-strapped black lace camisole that exposed tantalizing glimpses of porcelain skin. His mouth tightened and a glimmer of unbearable sadness crossed his steel-blue eyes. A nanosecond later, he had himself back under control and his face was once again expressionless.

Poppy crossed her arms, a slight smile playing around her lips. Clearly she had seen her father's momentary weakness and intended to take full advantage of it. I braced myself for the explosion.

Leaning close to her dad, Poppy hissed, "We are here to free Boone."

The chief didn't respond.

Poppy narrowed her eyes. "You probably think you've been embarrassed by my behavior before," she said in a conversational tone, "but if you don't release Boone to us this instant, you ain't seen nothing yet."

Unfazed, Chief Kincaid raised a brow. "Is that so?" He stepped aside so we could see one of the part-time officers lead a handcuffed Boone past us and toward the jail cells on the other side of the building. "I doubt there's anything left you could do that you haven't already done to dishonor our family name."

Boone tried to call out something to us, but

Poppy's howl drowned out his words. She screamed an obscenity—one I had given up using—and lunged at her father. Without thinking, I grabbed her by the back of her top. Thankfully the material was stretchy and didn't tear, because I was fairly sure she wasn't wearing a bra.

She turned on me, snarling, but I wrapped my arms around her middle and dragged her backward. I fought to keep Poppy restrained and finally plopped her into a chair and sat on her. She might be small, but so is a Tasmanian devil. And female wolverines weigh only twenty pounds. Besides, Poppy had plenty of practice breaking up bar fights, not to mention the years of resentment she had built up against her father. Even as I squashed her, she continued to struggle, attempting to get at her dad.

Chief Kincaid watched us battle. He was silent and unmoving until Poppy exhausted herself; then he said, "Get her out of my station."

While Poppy and I had scuffled, the officer escorting Boone had halted, apparently mesmerized, or maybe turned on, by the girl fight. Finally he must have realized the chief might notice his lack of discipline, because he jerked Boone by the handcuffs, trying to make it seem as if his prisoner was the one who was at fault.

When Boone didn't walk fast enough, the creep ordered, "Move it."

Boone staggered and said, "Please. Just one second. Let me talk to Dev."

The part-timer ignored Boone and yanked him toward the doorway.

Since Poppy seemed subdued, I got up and, using my most authoritative voice—the one I had used on indecisive investors—I called out, "Wait!"

The cop stopped abruptly, causing Boone to stumble and fall to his knees. The officer ignored the downed man and instead looked uncertainly between the chief and me.

Before Chief Kincaid could react, I hurried up to him and tugged him out of earshot. I was a little surprised he allowed me to move him, and I wasn't sure what I would say until the words left my mouth. "Sir, I know you don't have any reason to do me a favor." I stopped and corrected myself. "Actually, you do, since I was the one who kept Poppy out of numerous jams when we were teenagers, and you know it."

His brows rose into his hairline, but he didn't deny my claim.

"If you could just give me five minutes with Boone," I pleaded, "I really think it would help the whole situation enormously."

"How?" Chief Kincaid huffed. "Unless I missed something, you haven't attended law school, and I doubt he needs financial advice or a gift basket."

"True." I stalled, trying to think of a reason he might go for.

The chief started to return to the group, who was staring at us. Miraculously, Poppy was still seated.

"How about this." I improvised. Luckily I was used to thinking fast on my feet. "You put us in the interrogation room where you can hear everything he says to me." I trusted Boone was smart enough to realize that Big Brother was monitoring us and would not incriminate himself. And, just to be safe, that would be the first thing I said to him. "Maybe you'll find out something."

The chief paused but didn't bother to look back at me. "Not good enough." He took a step, then asked, "What else do you have for me?"

"If you don't let me talk to Boone, I'm afraid Poppy will do something stupid." I hated saying that about my friend, but she was irrational where her father was concerned. "And I know you don't want her getting hurt, even if you aren't willing to admit it."

At that, he turned around, concern softening his normally severe gaze, and stepped back toward me. "And you think if I let you talk to St. Onge, it will stop Poppy from doing something foolish?"

"Yes." I crossed my fingers, praying that I was right. "I do."

"Why?"

"Uh." *Shoot!* I'd been hoping he wouldn't ask that. "Because I'll make sure Poppy understands that you allowed me to talk to Boone even though you didn't have to. She'll see that you compromised, not for me or for Boone but for her. Because you love her."

"Fine." He puckered his lips as if he had taken a gulp of sour milk. "You can have five minutes, and don't forget we're recording you."

"Of course." I shook his hand. "Thank you."

He smiled and my stomach clenched. I sure hoped I hadn't just made a deal with the devil.

CHAPTER 7

As I waited for Boone in the interrogation room, I examined my surroundings. Shadow Bend might be a small town, but Chief Kincaid hadn't skimped when it came to the police station remodel. The space contained only a narrow metal table and two chairs, but one entire wall was glass—obviously, a two-way mirror—and cameras and speakers were placed liberally at intervals near the ceiling.

The chief had written a grant to get the money for the modernization. We all knew that the city council would never have approved the funding, since it was common knowledge that Chief Kincaid thought the present mayor, Geoffrey

Eggers, was a complete idiot, and the feeling was mutual. So His Honor and the chief were by no stretch of the imagination on cooperative enough terms for the financing to have come from the town's coffers.

I glanced at my watch. What was taking so long? Had Chief Kincaid changed his mind? Was Boone being locked in a cell this very minute? *Damn!* Thinking about him being locked in made me remember my phobia, and I started to breathe faster. Immediately, I felt lightheaded. What had I been thinking when I agreed to be shut into a space the size of a walk-in closet? Could I get through this without fainting? If they didn't hurry, my five minutes with Boone would be spent with him trying to get me up off the floor.

Just before I started screaming to be released, the door banged opened. A moment later, Boone was shoved across the threshold, where he stood as if in a daze. Instantly, the door was slammed closed and I heard the bolt slide home. It took all my willpower not to run over, pound on the metal, and beg to be let out.

The sound of the lock must have penetrated Boone's fog, because he lurched across the interrogation room, tripping over his own feet as he nearly fell into the chair. Once seated, he sat slumped forward as if his head was too heavy for his neck to support. This was not the confident, debonair Boone I had known all my life. What in hell had the cops done to him?

"Boone." I reached out to touch him but drew back. Chief Kincaid had agreed not to attach his handcuffs to the bolt in the middle of the table-top if we promised to keep the table between us at all times. "Are you okay? What took you so long to get here?"

"I'm physically fine, but emotionally, not so much." Boone's hazel eyes were haunted. "The cretins insisted on another body search before they allowed me in here to speak to you. What in heaven's name did they think I could have possibly gotten my hands on, not to mention concealed, since the last time they patted me down?"

"I hear that a seasoned criminal such as yourself can do wicked things with a paperclip and a rubber band," I offered in a feeble attempt at humor.

"What? Make a slingshot?" Boone rubbed his temples. "Fat lot of good that would do against the cops' Berettas and Tasers."

"Was the officer who searched you at least cute?" I tried once more to get the old Boone back—the fighter who wouldn't take this lying down.

"No. They chose the ugliest one." Boone straightened his spine. "That alone will increase the lawsuit I'm filing against the Shadow Bend

Police Department by ten thousand dollars."

"At least." I smiled my encouragement, then said, "You know they're recording everything and that we only have five minutes, right?"

"Right." His usually tanned face was a sallow yellow, and even his ultrawhite teeth seemed less bright. "First, I didn't do it."

"Of course not. I never thought for a minute that you had," I assured him, then said, "Let's start with the victim. Who was murdered and where?"

"Elise Whitmore, in the living room of her house." He started to say more, but his voice thickened and he choked to a stop.

Shit! It took me less than half a second to realize that she was the woman who had sold me the chocolate molds.

"Was she the one you were escorting to the gallery opening?" I forced myself to sound calm, but I didn't like coincidences.

"Yes." Boone shoved his fingers through his tawny gold hair.

Knowing how much he hated having his hair messed up, I winced. Then again, his customarily perfectly styled coif was already standing on end, and I suspected that for once his hair was the least of his worries. As was the fact that his six-hundred-dollar DKNY suit was torn at the shoulder.

"How did you know her?" I asked, wondering if

Boone had sent her to me to sell the antique molds or maybe just mentioned my interest.

"I was representing her in her divorce proceedings, and she asked me if I would accompany her to the opening." Boone toyed with a loose button on his shirt. "Since I was free that evening and it sounded interesting, I agreed."

"Are those the only reasons?" I probed. Boone tended to be a bit impulsive.

"She was afraid she might run into her husband there and didn't want to face him alone," Boone admitted. "She said he might be violent."

"That's great!" I nearly shouted. "He's much more likely to have killed her than you. What possible reason do the cops have to think you did it?"

"Well . . ." Boone concentrated on his shoes, trying to rub a scuff out with his thumb. "You see . . ." He was clearly hiding something.

"Was this a date?" I asked. Although Boone was my best friend and I'd known him all my life, I still wasn't sure which team he batted for. He'd taken out women, but somehow he never seemed all that interested in them. Then again, he'd never seemed all that interested in men, either. "Were you involved with her?"

"Absolutely not." He shook his head vehemently. "It's unethical for an attorney to date a client." He swallowed hard. "But that is why the cops think I murdered her." He grimaced. "Their theory is that we had an intimate relationship, but then had a fight that resulted in Elise threatening to report me to the bar association, so I killed her."

"Okay, that's motive." I checked the time. We had only two minutes left.

"And since I was the one to find her body, I obviously had means."

"Tell me about that." I could guess, but wanted to make sure.

"I arrived at ten p.m. and rang the bell. When she didn't answer, I tried phoning, but both her cell and landline went to voice mail, so I was worried. She has—I mean, had—asthma. I was concerned that she might have had an attack and not gotten to her inhaler in time." Boone wrinkled his brow. "The house was dark and I was trying to decide what to do—whether to dial nine-one-one or not—when I noticed that the front door wasn't quite latched, so I went inside to check on her."

"And?"

"And I found her lying in front of the breakfront." Boone wiped a tear from his eye. "She was barefoot and wearing a robe that had fallen open. She didn't have anything on underneath, and at first I thought she had been looking for her inhaler and passed out, since I knew she kept her spares in the drawer of that cabinet. But when I knelt down next to her, I noticed the blood on the floor and saw that there was a bullet hole in the middle of her forehead."

"Did you call the police immediately?" I asked, afraid I already knew the answer. "I mean, as soon as you saw the bullet wound."

"First I checked to see if she was still alive," Boone answered.

"So you touched her?" I said almost to myself. That wouldn't be good.

"Just her neck," Boone explained. "I was looking for a pulse."

"Was the gun there?" I latched on to the one thing I thought might clear him, since his fingerprints wouldn't be on it.

"No."

"What do the cops think you did with the weapon?" I asked, figuring they had to have some theory or we wouldn't be sitting here.

"According to them, I hid it somewhere before I called nine-one-one."

"Great." I checked my watch. We were running out of time, so I asked the most important question I could think of. "Why did you want to talk to me? Shouldn't you have requested a lawyer?"

Before Boone could answer, the door to the interrogation room swung open. Chief Kincaid marched in and stood behind Boone.

"Your five minutes are up," he said to me as he put his hand on Boone's arm and pulled him to his feet. "Time to go, St. Onge."

As Boone was being led away, he said in a rush,

"Dev, you solved Joelle's murder; I need you to figure out who killed Elise."

I ran after him, but an officer blocked the hallway, so I shouted, "Should I call a lawyer or your folks?"

"My attorney, Tryg Pryce, is on his way from Chicago. Get in touch with him," Boone yelled back. "But if you could tell my parents before they hear it from someone else, I'd appreciate it."

Damn! Boone's folks hadn't spoken to each other in twenty-five years. Even though they were still married and lived in the same house, they communicated only through notes. Talking to them was never easy, and conveying this kind of news would be really tough.

Boone had disappeared into the jail wing of the police station, so there was nothing left for me to do except find Poppy and leave. *Hey.* I brightened. So far, I'd done all the heavy lifting. It was Poppy's turn. She could break the news to the St. Onges.

Poppy didn't believe me when I said that her father had let me talk to Boone because he loved her. She did agree it had been a concession on his part, so she promised not to do something outrageous just to embarrass him. At least, she promised once I emphasized how much her behavior could hurt Boone.

She also weaseled out of telling the St. Onges.

Poppy argued that it was nearly one a.m. so they'd be asleep, and waking them up when they couldn't do anything to help Boone would be cruel. Instead, she talked me into meeting her at their house at eight the next morning. We both agreed that even if they weren't early risers, we couldn't wait any longer than that, or else one of the town gossips would get to them first.

Before crawling into bed, I set my alarm for six a.m. There was no way I was facing Boone's folks on an empty stomach—or without a shower and some makeup. Four hours later, when the radio announcer's chipper voice woke me from an uneasy sleep, I reconsidered my need for food and tried to convince myself that untamed curls and under-eye circles were currently in fashion.

After a couple hits on the snooze button, I finally dragged myself out of bed and into the bathroom, where I hoped hot water and expensive concealer would compensate for lack of sleep. Thirty-five minutes later, not entirely convinced that either had been successful, I put on a pair of khakis and a black silk sweater. Then, bracing myself for Gran's cross-examination, I headed in to breakfast.

As I entered the kitchen and said good morning, Gran turned from the stove and waved a spatula in my direction. "What are you doing up so early on a Sunday? Don't tell me my prayers have been answered and you're finally going to church with me." She shook her head. "No. That can't be it. I haven't seen any signs of the apocalypse or the Second Coming."

Instead of responding, I studied Gran's latest outfit—a dress straight out of the 1950s. It was a Wedgwood-blue wool crepe with a narrow skirt and a boat neckline. Completing her outfit were navy leather Cuban-heeled pumps and a cloche. Because she was on her way to eight o'clock Mass and didn't want to splatter her outfit while cooking, she also had on a red-and-white-checkered bib apron.

Finally I said, "Sorry, no church today." I hadn't been to services in twelve years. I figured if God had forsaken my family, then I wasn't visiting him. "I'm still waiting for a sign that He wants me back."

"So why are you up?" Gran squinted at me. "Not to mention wearing something other than jeans." She put her hand to her chest. "And, sweet Jesus, you have on uh . . ." She pointed to her face.

"Makeup," I supplied. The doctor had said it was best to provide the word she couldn't recall rather than let her become stressed trying to come up with it. What I couldn't understand, and the gerontologist hadn't been able to explain, was how she could come up with a less-used word like *apocalypse* but not an everyday word like *makeup*.

"Right." She nodded. "You have on makeup for the second day in a row."

As I explained about Boone, I kept a wary eye on Gran's cat, Banshee. He was in his usual mealtime spot, perched on top of the fridge. He liked to skulk in the shadows just below the cupboard, then launch himself onto my head as I walked by and dig his claws into my scalp. Gran claimed that it was his way of showing affection, but Banshee and I both knew he hated my guts.

While Gran added bacon to the pan and poured more pancake batter on the griddle, she said, "Eldridge Kincaid's slinky has always been a little kinked, but for him to think that that sweet boy had anything to do with killing that woman is outlandish."

"Definitely." I poured myself a cup of coffee, added skim milk and fake sugar, then sat down at the table. "Chief Kincaid must have lost it."

"And the reason he thinks Boone killed her is really ridiculous."

"Oh." I took a sip from my mug. "Really? I read somewhere that a love affair gone bad is among the top ten causes for murder."

"Maybe so." Gran slid a steaming plate of pancakes and bacon in front of me. "But Boone wouldn't be having an affair with that woman."

"And how do you know that?" I asked. Considering that he was my best friend and I wasn't sure which sex he preferred, I wondered if

Gran knew something I didn't. Or was she jumping to conclusions?

"Because he wouldn't be that unprofessional." Gran put her own dish on the table and joined me. "Boone has wanted to be a lawyer since he was in diapers. That boy would never risk being, uh . . ."

"Disbarred?"

"Right."

I nodded my agreement, then poured syrup over my pancakes and inhaled the rich maple scent. Before taking my first bite, I said, "I hope the attorney Boone hired from Chicago made it here, and Mr. Pryce can at least get him released on bail. Although I bet if he can, he'll have to wait until Monday when the courts open, which isn't good. Boone won't handle being in jail very well. You should have seen how beaten-down he looked last night."

"I can imagine." Gran picked up a slice of bacon and examined it. "He always hated getting dirty." She crunched the crispy strip. "And he purely cannot abide having his hair messed up."

Since neither of us could think of anything more to say on the matter of Boone's arrest, Gran asked me about my evening with Noah. I assured her that I had gotten what I wanted—a new business contact and big fat order. She seemed really happy that I'd had to leave Noah early, even if it meant my friend was in trouble.

As Gran gathered up our dirty plates and took

them to the sink, she said, "I just hope you won't be fooled by Noah's charm."

"Of course not." I deposited the butter and syrup inside the refrigerator door. I crossed my fingers. "I'm only interested in Noah as a friend."

"Right." Gran's tone was skeptical. "And I have an arch in St. Louis I can sell you."

"It's the truth," I protested, backing out of the room so I could stop lying to my grandmother. "I just want to bury the hatchet and be pals again."

"In that case"—she nodded to the table where I had laid my cell—"you better not answer your phone."

I glanced down. Noah's name was glowing in the center of the little window and my cell was vibrating. As per Chief Kincaid's rules, I had turned off the ringer when I was in the police station the night before and had never turned the sound back on.

Stepping toward the table, I said, "I'll take this in my room."

Gran frowned. "Don't answer it. Maybe he'll go away."

"I need to thank him for introducing me to his friend." It was a good thing she didn't know that my heart was beating faster and a little zing was buzzing up my spine at the memory of our dancing together.

"Leave the phone there and step away." Gran made a grab for the cell.

Snatching up the tiny rectangle just before her fingers closed around it, I scooted backward and hurried out of the kitchen, saying over my shoulder, "Just this one time."

CHAPTER 8

Noah had slept poorly, tossing and turning and trying to find a comfortable spot. Which should have been a damn sight easier to do, considering the Tempur-Pedic mattress and ridiculously expensive sheets the decorator had insisted he needed in order to get a good night's rest. Too bad the woman hadn't factored in the thoughts of Dev that had kept him awake. He'd alternated between staring at the ceiling and watching the numbers change on his bedside clock. By six a.m. he was already dressed in his workout clothes and lifting weights. At this rate, he'd be muscle-bound by summer.

According to the radio announcer, today would be bright and shiny—a promise that springtime was around the corner. The cold, rain, and snow they'd been having during all of March made people think nicer weather would never arrive. During the last few weeks, the Underwood clinic had been filled with patients fighting colds, flu, and pneumonia.

Not that the below-average temperatures

caused these illnesses, but Noah believed that the seasonal depression that so many Shadow Benders were feeling was negatively affecting their health. Maybe the improved forecast would lift everyone's spirits. The medication and care that he provided could do only so much; the rest depended on the person's attitude, lifestyle, and emotional state.

The good weather forecast had momentarily improved Noah's mood, but as he worked out, he returned to brooding about Dev's actions the night before. One minute she was laughing and joking with him, and the next minute she was gone. He felt as if he'd been sucker-punched.

Having Dev in his arms on the dance floor had been incredible. During their long years apart, he'd forgotten how soft she was, and when her curves pressed against him, it had made him want to find the nearest bedroom. He'd envisioned stripping off her pretty dress, arranging her gorgeous hair around her shoulders, and making love to her all night long. The last thing he wanted to do was stop dancing, but he knew he had to release her and put some distance between them before he lost all control.

Then, later, when they were lining up the items for the auction, it had seemed like old times. It had made him think back to all the high school events they'd planned and put on together—the play rehearsals, pep rallies, and homecomings that had marked their time as a couple.

So why had Dev run away? What kind of emergency could she have had? It couldn't be a medical one. As soon as he'd received her message, Noah had called the hospital. And with the nearest urgent-care clinic sixty miles away, the county emergency room was the only choice the locals had for after-hours illnesses and accidents.

The ER clerk had told Noah that there hadn't been any sign of Birdie Sinclair, Boone St. Onge, or Poppy Kincaid. And Noah knew Dev had no other family or close friends in town. At a loss for what else could have happened, he had tried to phone her, but, as usual, the call went to her voice mail.

At the sound of her recorded message, a weight had settled on his chest. Was she avoiding him again? Maybe as soon as she'd gotten the basket order from Oakley, she had called someone to pick her up. Had she really just been using him?

With a sinking feeling, Noah had decided that was it. She'd gotten the business contact she wanted and disappeared. He couldn't blame her. It wasn't as if she'd pretended she was going out with him for any other reason. Still, it hurt.

The dance had been nearly over when he'd learned she'd left, and Noah had been able to leave soon afterward. Zizi and Winnie had given him sympathetic looks as he said his good-byes, but no one else seemed to notice that he'd been dumped. No one, that is, except the redhead who'd begged for a lift home. She'd claimed that her date was drunk and she was afraid to get in a car with him.

There was no way to turn down her request without being a jerk. Too bad the woman had thrown a fit when Noah dropped her off and refused to go inside with her. Her cursing would have made a rapper blush.

It had been tough enough listening to the woman's mindless chatter on the ten-minute trip from the country club to her house without dealing with her comments about his manhood—or lack thereof. Especially when all he could think about was Dev.

It had been even tougher ignoring the voice inside his head that insisted he drive to Dev's house, pound on the door until she opened it, and demand to know why she'd taken off without an explanation. He wanted to tell her how much he still cared for her. How much he'd missed her the past thirteen years. And how much he wanted them to try again.

Intellectually, he knew it was better to cool off before he spoke to Dev, so he could maintain his image as the imperturbable physician. But in his heart, he was tempted to do something so out of character that she'd have to take notice. In the end, he'd chickened out. Years of acting like the responsible and unemotional town doctor had been too much to overcome.

Even as Noah had made the decision not to confront Dev, he'd berated himself for being such a wuss. If he didn't show her that he'd changed, he would never get her back. Since he'd broken up with her in high school, relationships had never worked for him.

One reason for their failure was his detachment. In the past, he hadn't cared when the women he dated called him cold and distant. But he knew that the only way to win Dev's heart was to show the emotion he tended to keep hidden. The big question was, could he do it?

On the drive home, Noah had nearly managed to convince himself that he had done the right thing in waiting to contact Dev until the next day. That is, until he'd noticed her scarf stuck between the passenger seat and the console. As he'd picked it up, he'd caught a whiff of her perfume. It was the same one she'd used in high school, Chanel's Cristalle. Its crisp yet sweet scent brought his desire for her rushing back.

When Noah had slammed through his front door a few minutes later, Lucky had been waiting for him in the foyer. But Noah's body language must have scared the little dog, because instead of his usual barking and tail-wagging greeting, the Chihuahua had cocked his head, then almost sighed and silently led Noah into the bedroom.

Now, while Noah finished up his last set of lifts and headed to the kitchen for breakfast, Lucky followed him. The dog had already had his morning constitutional, but sat patiently waiting for Noah to dish out his canned food and fill his water bowl.

Once Noah had fed Lucky, started the coffeemaker, and turned on the radio, he grabbed the box of Cocoa Puffs from his cupboard. As a child, his mother had never allowed sugary cereals in their house, and Noah's loathing for dry, nutritional twigs and flakes hadn't abated in the years he'd been on his own. This was his secret indulgence and he wasn't giving it up any time soon.

While he ate, Noah flipped through the Sunday paper. The local news would be on in ten minutes. He opened the comics section, but as he tried to find humor in the cartoon strips, the radio played Freddy Fender singing about some woman making him blue, and Noah crumpled up the funnies and threw them across the room.

Lucky, thinking it was a game, ran over to the corner, fetched the paper ball, and laid it at Noah's feet. When his master didn't immediately respond, the Chihuahua nudged the ball closer and whimpered.

Glancing at the little dog, Noah patted his head and said absently, "Good boy."

Lucky quivered with happiness.

"Hey, if you weren't fixed and you wanted to get a girl dog to like you, what would you do?"

The Chihuahua barked.

"So you think I should talk to her." Noah took a drink from his mug. "But what if she refuses to talk to me? In fact, what if she runs away?"

Lucky moved closer to Noah, leaned against his leg, and barked again.

"I should be persistent?" Noah reached down and scratched the dog behind his ears, then straightened and took another thoughtful sip of coffee.

The Chihuahua's expression was mournful, and he leapt up on Noah's lap.

"I shouldn't let her avoid me." Noah quirked his mouth. "I figured as much."

The dog exhaled noisily.

"But if she doesn't want to see me, maybe I should honor her wishes." Noah's tone was stubborn. "After all, I've showed her I'm interested. If she's not, maybe I should just back off and leave her alone."

Lucky yipped, jumped to the floor, and sat facing away from Noah.

"Okay." Noah thought back to the good parts of the previous evening. "You're right. I should try at least once more. She probably still doesn't trust me, considering the way things ended last time."

Noah rose from his seat, took a Frosty Paws

from the freezer, and flipped the treat to Lucky. While the Chihuahua devoured the doggie ice cream, Noah put his cereal bowl and mug in the dishwasher.

As he was closing the appliance door, the local news came on the radio and the announcer said, "Last night, Shadow Bend resident Elise Whitmore was found dead in her home. Police Chief Eldridge Kincaid stated that it's believed foul play was involved and a suspect is in custody."

Noah froze in shock. Elise had been a patient of his. Had she interrupted a burglar? She'd mentioned that she was getting a divorce and her husband wasn't taking the situation well. Could her soon-to-be ex have killed her?

Before Noah could speculate further, the newscaster continued. "Although Chief Kincaid refused to reveal the suspect's name, an inside source claims that local attorney Boone St. Onge found Ms. Whitmore's body and has been detained, pending further investigation."

"Well, damn!" Noah hit the counter, startling Lucky, who ran from the room.

That was why Dev had left so abruptly last night. St. Onge must have called her down to the police station, which also explained why she hadn't answered her phone. Chief Kincaid was notorious for his rule that all personal cells be silenced inside the PD.

Dev was fully aware that Noah and St. Onge had never been friends. She was probably afraid that Noah wouldn't be sympathetic. But was she right? Noah didn't like St. Onge, but he couldn't imagine him killing anyone. And if he had, he was too smooth an operator to get caught.

Noah smiled, snatched up the kitchen phone, and punched in Dev's number.

CHAPTER 9

Clutching my cell, I escaped into my bedroom before answering Noah's call. I closed the door just as Gran's curious face appeared on the other side of the threshold. Figuring she would have her ear pressed to the keyhole, I moved to the other side of the room before I pushed the On button and said, "Hello."

"Good morning, Dev." Noah's voice was smoother than a really good chocolate milkshake—and probably just as bad for me.

It was a little unnerving when he didn't say anything more—Noah wasn't generally the strong, silent type—so I hastily said, "How are you? Did you . . ." I trailed off, fairly certain that he was angry with me for deserting him last night. But had he called me just to give me the cold shoulder? No. Come to think about it, I knew what he wanted. Too bad it was a word that didn't come easily to me. "Uh. I suppose I owe you an apology."

"Five minutes ago, I would have said yes." Noah's tone was light. "But now that I've heard the local newscast, I completely understand."

"Thank you." I hadn't been expecting that. For a moment, I savored the fact that Noah wasn't upset with me. "That's really nice of you."

"You're welcome. So—"

"Wait a minute," I interrupted him as the full implication of what he'd just said hit me. "What exactly did you hear on the news?"

"That St. Onge is in custody for the murder of Elise Whitmore."

"Damn it all to hell!" Poppy and I had blown it. We should have woken up Boone's parents last night after all. "They said that on the radio? That he's been arrested? But Chief Kincaid assured me that they weren't releasing his name."

"The chief stated that a suspect had been apprehended and was being held for questioning," Noah corrected. "The announcer said that the information came from an anonymous tip from an inside source."

"Thank goodness!" I leaned against the wall and sank to the floor, relieved that at least it hadn't been Chief Kincaid who'd blabbed. "Poppy would have never forgiven her dad if he was the one who leaked the info."

"Yeah." Noah's tone was rueful. "It seems that a lot of us have parent issues."

"I hadn't thought about it, but you're right." Pausing, I made a mental list. I put myself as number one, then Poppy and Noah. Boone got along with both his folks, but the fact that they didn't speak to each other was tough on him.

Did Jake get along with his mom and dad? He hadn't mentioned them, and I kind of guessed that if he had a good relationship with his parents, he would have. Plus, he'd spent every summer and holiday with his great-uncle rather than with his folks. That had to mean something.

If I weren't afraid Gran would get the wrong impression, I'd have her ask Tony. But I didn't dare show that much interest in Jake, or Birdie might book the church hall for our wedding reception.

"Anyway," Noah said, interrupting my musing, "I called to see if there's anything I can do for St. Onge."

"Really?" Why was Noah offering to help someone he disliked?

"Yes." Noah paused, then said, "I know he and I don't see eye to eye on a lot of things, but he's one of your best friends. And he stuck by you when a lot of people didn't."

Noah's unspoken words *like me* hung in the air between us—a wall I needed to tear down if I ever wanted to find out whether our adult selves had the same passion for each other as our teenage selves. But the memory of him telling me he couldn't be with me anymore because my dad was a criminal overwhelmed me. I tried to banish it by replacing that image with a picture of him apologizing a few days later.

Too bad I had to make up that scene. Because even though Noah had assured me it had happened, I had no recollection of it. It's truly amazing that two people could experience the same events and totally disagree on what had happened. Then again, maybe not. Reality isn't always what it's cracked up to be.

"Well, it's really sweet of you to offer to help, but I have no idea what to do." I summarized what I knew, which wasn't much, then asked, "Any ideas?"

"It's tricky because you basically have to prove a negative."

"Exactly," I agreed, surprised. I had forgotten how often Noah and I could almost read each other's minds. "How do we substantiate Boone's claim that he wasn't having an affair with Elise?"

"Well, I always thought maybe St. Onge wasn't interested in women, so . . ." Noah trailed off. "Is that an option that could be pursued?"

"Probably not." I took a moment to gather my thoughts. "First, because I don't know if that's the case. And second, because if he hasn't confided in me or Poppy after all these years, and considering all the stuff about ourselves that we've told him, then it's not a subject he's willing to discuss."

"Why?" Noah asked. "In this day and age no one cares anymore."

"Oh, please." I blew a raspberry into the phone. "If no one cares, why is gay marriage such a big deal? Why is there still gay bashing? Why can't gay men donate blood?"

"I see your point," Noah conceded.

"Anyway, the real problem for Boone would probably be that Shadow Bend has only one foot—no, make that one toe—in the twenty-first century, and only part of the time at that. If he lived in a big city, whether he's gay or straight wouldn't be such an issue."

"Right. You and I both love this town, but it's not without its flaws," Noah commented. "But don't you think if it would save him from prison, St. Onge could deal with the fallout?"

"*If* it were true and *if* it would really help him. Maybe." I tapped my chin. "But we're not sure that either of the above assumptions is accurate."

"In that case, I think you should contact St. Onge's attorney and find out what he or she has in mind for a defense." Noah's tone was clinical. "Do you know if the lawyer is in town?"

"Boone said he's coming from Chicago, which means he's probably staying at either the Cattlemen's Motel or the B and B." I stood up.

"And he's number two on my list. First, Poppy and I have to go see Mr. and Mrs. St. Onge and tell them their son is in jail. Unless, of course, they already know."

"Good luck with that." Noah's voice was rueful. "Afterward, if I were you, I'd try the B and B first," Noah advised. "The Cattlemen's is an acquired taste."

"Definitely." I slipped on my shoes. "A city boy might not appreciate the antler chandeliers or the cowhide bedspreads and rugs."

Noah chuckled. "While you and Poppy are busy with the St. Onges, I could ask a few people on the shelter fund-raising committee about Elise Whitmore. Since she donated some expensive items for the auction, maybe one of the committee members is a friend of hers."

"That would be great." I was touched by Noah's suggestion. He really did want to help. "She's not a customer of mine, so I don't know anything about her."

Which was technically true. She hadn't bought anything from me, and I'd decided there was no good reason to mention that I had purchased the antique molds from her—and there were several excellent reasons to keep quiet about my acquisition and possession of them. The list included that the molds might not have been Elise's to sell, I could get into trouble for having bought items that might technically be considered stolen, and, topping the charts, I didn't want to have any association with another murder victim.

"So how about we meet for lunch at the new Chinese restaurant and compare notes?" Noah suggested. "You should be done by noon or so."

"Okay." I wasn't sure I was ready to spend more time with Noah, but for Boone, I'd risk it. Besides, Poppy would be with me. "I'll call you when we're through with the parents and the lawyer. Poppy and I have been wanting to try that place for a couple of months now."

"Good." Noah's voice held a shade of disappointment, then it brightened. "It'll be nice to have the three of us working together again."

"Yeah." I was about to say good-bye when I thought of a question. "Was Elise your patient?" People in Shadow Bend either doctored with Noah or had to drive to one of the neighboring towns for medical services.

"Sorry. I can't answer that." Noah's tone was absolute. "Confidentiality."

"But she's dead."

"The obligation of secrecy doesn't cease to exist after a patient is deceased."

"Oh." That was interesting. I had no idea that the dead had rights. "Well, I better get going. Thanks for not being mad about me leaving last night, and for helping with Boone's case. Bye."

• • •

It was five after eight when I pulled my Z4 into the St. Onges' driveway. They lived in a large tri-level that had been cutting-edge contemporary when it had been built in the mid-1970s. Now it reminded me of the house from *The Brady Bunch*; Gran liked to watch the show's reruns on the TV Land channel.

Poppy was parked by the curb when I arrived. She climbed out of her Hummer as soon as I turned off my engine and was waiting for me when I stepped onto the sidewalk.

"You're late." She put her hands on her hips and tapped the toe of her black suede ankle boot. "Did you hear the local news this morning?"

"No, but I heard about it."

I hadn't mentioned that I'd been with Noah when I'd asked Poppy to pick me up the night before, and she'd been too obsessed with her father's arrest of Boone to ask what I'd been doing at the country club all dressed up. I wasn't sure how she'd react to me seeing Noah, and right now wasn't the time to go into it.

"Cross your fingers that Boone's folks didn't have the radio on," Poppy instructed.

I nodded, then asked, "Do you have a plan on how to tell them?"

"Since we're flying blind here"—Poppy turned on her heel and headed toward the entrance, still talking—"we'll have to wing it."

I followed her, and as she rang the bell and waited, I said, "But you will be the one to break the news, right?" She tended to wiggle out of things she didn't want to do, leaving me holding the bag.

Instead of answering me, she commented, "Maybe they're not home."

"You wish."

"I'm out of here if someone doesn't appear in ten seconds." Poppy pressed the button again, crossed her arms, and stepped back.

"Give them a couple of minutes." I blocked her from ringing a third time. "They could still be asleep, and this is a big house."

"I want to get this over with," Poppy grumbled, trying to reach around me.

Before she succeeded, the door swung open and Mrs. St. Onge said, "Dev, Poppy, what are you doing here so early?" She was dressed in a terry cloth robe and slippers, and her short brown hair was flat on one side. There was a crease in her cheek and mascara smudges beneath her eyes.

"May we come in, Mrs. St. Onge?" I asked, moving over the threshold. I sure didn't want to have this conversation on the front steps.

"How many times have I told you girls to call me Janice?" she said, a worried look on her face as she stepped aside so we could enter.

"Sorry, Janice." Even approaching thirty years old, I found it hard to call the parents of my childhood friends by their first names.

"What's this all about?" Janice asked as she led us around an open staircase that swept past a tall stonework wall and into the kitchen.

I glanced at Poppy, who refused to meet my eyes. After a long, awkward moment, I realized that Poppy would not take the lead despite her promises, so I said, "Is Mr. St. Onge home? We'd like to talk to you both together. Poppy could run and get him for you."

Janice must have finally fully woken up and put the pieces together, because she sank into a chair and in a tear-clogged voice she said, "Oh, my God! Something's happened to Boone. Was he in an accident? Is he okay? Tell me he's not dead."

"He's not dead and he wasn't in an accident," I assured her. "But we really do need Mr. St. Onge to be here when we explain what happened."

Janice took a quivering breath, then nearly gave me a heart attack when she screamed at the top of her lungs, "Steven, come here!"

Afterward, she seemed surprised at herself. And since this might have been the first time in twenty-five years that she had spoken to her husband, I, too, was a little shocked.

A half second later, Steven St. Onge rushed up from the basement. He was a tall, spare man dressed in loose slacks, a white shirt, and a cardigan. His thinning hair was combed neatly and he held a pipe. He looked as if he were trying out for the role of Mr. Rogers.

As he burst into the kitchen from the basement doorway, he demanded, "Janice, what's wrong? Are you hurt?" When he finally noticed Poppy and me, he asked, "What are you two girls doing here?"

Once again, I waited for Poppy to speak, and once again, she remained silent. Shooting her a venomous look, I said, "Boone asked us to come and tell you in person that he's being held by the police."

"Oh, my God!" Janice grabbed my hand. "What do they think my baby did?"

Steven had seated himself next to his wife and was patting her shoulder.

I turned slightly so I could address both of them. "They suspect him of killing Elise Whitmore. Last night when he went to pick her up to escort her to an art gallery opening, he found her dead."

"Are they sure she didn't die from natural causes?" Janice asked.

"Yes. There's no way this wasn't murder." I eased my fingers from her death grip. "There was a bullet wound in her forehead."

"Then she must have committed suicide," Janice said in a pleading tone.

"I'm so sorry." I looked at Poppy again, but she had her back to me, apparently fascinated by the olive-green refrigerator. "Since the gun was missing, Elise couldn't have killed herself."

Steven finally spoke. "Boone can't handle jail. It will destroy him."

"I know." Searching for something comforting to say, I added, "We're hoping his attorney can arrange bail." Honesty forced me to continue. "But that probably won't be until Monday morning."

"Oh." Steven stared into space, and Janice slumped in her seat.

While I waited for the St. Onges to process what I'd said, and unable to bear the devastated looks on their faces, I glanced around the kitchen. Spotting a coffeemaker on the counter, I jumped up and asked, "Okay if I make a pot?"

They nodded their consent, and I went to work. It wasn't hard to find the coffee beans in the freezer, and everything else was arranged on a tray next to the sink. Poppy, whose mute button had apparently gotten stuck in the On position, took the mugs from me and brought them to the stricken couple. She then filled the creamer, picked up the sugar bowl, and took them over to the St. Onges. Finally she poured herself a cup and joined Boone's folks at the table.

I followed with my own caffeine reinforcement in hand and slipped into the last of the four chairs. After we'd all added what we wanted of the cream and sugar and taken a few sips, I asked, "Did either of you know Elise Whitmore? Had Boone ever mentioned her?"

Steven shook his head, but Janice said, "Boone

told me how sorry he felt for her, and how fond of her he was."

"Anything else?"

"I can't remember exactly what he said, but I do recall thinking that maybe he'd found the girl for him." Janice's voice grew animated. "And that we might finally get some grandchildren to spoil. All my friends have grandchildren and it's so hard to hear them—"

"Oh, my God!" Poppy screamed, interrupting Janice's babbling. She turned on the startled woman and ordered, "You *cannot* tell that to anyone else. That information could mean a life sentence for Boone."

CHAPTER 10

How in God's green earth could you say that to her?" I demanded as soon as Poppy and I were out the St. Onges' front door and a few feet down the sidewalk. "Who blurts out to a mother that her words could send her only son to the slammer for the rest of his life?"

Every so often, I had to marvel over Poppy's lack of sensitivity. She looked like a woodland sprite and acted like a lumberjack. Not that I was the most tactful person, but at least I made an effort not to make people cry—unless they really deserved it.

"Hey, I was just trying to help." Poppy stopped moving and shoved her hands into the pockets of her skinny jeans. "Someone had to tell her to keep her mouth shut, or she might gossip Boone right into a lethal injection." She stared back at me, daring me to disagree with her.

I shook my head and kept walking. She was right, but there had to be a kinder way to have informed Janice of that danger. It had taken us nearly an hour to calm her down, and then Steven had insisted I repeat verbatim everything his son had said to me the night before. Once Boone's dad was satisfied he'd wrung every last word from me, Steven had asked us to wait while he called the police station and begged the dispatcher to let him speak to his son.

Despite the dispatcher's negative answer, Janice and Steven decided to go to the police station and plead their case to someone higher up. Although it was Sunday, it was a safe bet that Chief Kincaid would be on duty. Murder changed everything.

When Janice went to get dressed, I finally convinced Steven to allow Poppy and me to leave. He gripped both our hands at the door, and it was sad to see how much he'd aged in the short time since our arrival.

With both Boone and his parents in mind, I returned to where Poppy was standing and said, "We need to find Boone's lawyer and see what we can do to help."

Poppy nodded, and as we walked toward our vehicles, she said, "At least that conversation shouldn't be an emotional train wreck the way this one was."

"We can only hope."

"Do you have his cell number?"

"No." I grabbed Poppy's arm and tugged her toward my Z4. I'd had my fill of riding with her in the short distance from the country club to the police station last night. "Let's take my car and check the B and B for him."

"But I want to drive." Poppy dragged her feet.

"No way. I'm not going to press my luck again so soon."

"You were happy to have me pick you up last night." She slid into the BMW's passenger seat. "Which reminds me, why didn't you have who-ever took you to the dance give you a lift?"

As I drove the short distance across town to the Ksiazak Bed and Breakfast, I told Poppy about Jake breaking our date and my evening with Noah. I outlined my reason for going and stated that it had been a business arrangement, then added that Noah had offered to help us investigate Elise's murder in order to clear Boone.

Confident that I had fully explained the situation, I turned and said to Poppy, "So, isn't it great that Noah and I are friends again?"

"Since you're back with Noah, can I have

Jake?" Poppy, like many people, heard only what she wanted to hear and filled in the rest.

In my head, I patiently repeated what I had just said, clarifying that Noah and I didn't have a romantic relationship and that the elusive U.S. Marshal had moved back to St. Louis. Regrettably, what came out of my mouth was, "Keep your paws off Jake."

Poppy's eyes widened in surprise, but she wasn't half as shocked as I was by my response. *Where in the world did that come from?*

We were both silent for the next couple of minutes, and it was a relief when I pulled the car into the driveway. The B & B was a huge Italianate-style house—a Victorian design that had been popular in the mid-1800s. I loved the cupola in the center of the nearly flat roof, and its ornamental brackets and wraparound porch suggested a renaissance villa.

Poppy got out of the Z4 and, apparently recovered from my less-than-characteristic possessiveness over a man, bounced up the sidewalk. She was already at the door before I had exited the car.

When I joined her, she said, "If this guy is here, will he even talk to us?"

"I'm hoping he's spoken to Boone, and Boone told him to cooperate with us."

We stepped inside the large foyer and I spotted the reception desk nestled inside the curve of a beautiful wooden staircase. Veronica Ksiazak was busy typing on a laptop. As soon as she noticed us, she closed the computer and slipped it out of sight.

"Dev, Poppy. What a nice surprise." She smiled and came around the desk. "Welcome. I don't think you've ever been to my place before."

"Hi, Ronni." Poppy hugged her. "I've been meaning to stop by."

Poppy and I knew Veronica from Chamber of Commerce meetings, where the town's women business owners had banded together to get our voices heard. Ronni and I had found that we had a lot in common. Although I was a native Shadow Bender and Ronni had moved here a couple of years ago, her story was much like mine. She'd gotten tired of working in the city, bought the B & B, and, with a thankful sigh, settled into the simpler life.

"This is gorgeous." Poppy gestured around the space. "I'm glad I finally got to see it."

"Thanks." Ronni beamed. "It's taken a lot of money and a ton of work, but I nearly have her back to the grand lady she used to be."

"Hi, Ronni," I said, interrupting before she and Poppy got lost in a discussion of architecture. I loved old houses as much as they did, but this wasn't the time. "We're here to see if you have a guest by the name of Tryg Pryce. We need to talk to him."

"Yes, he's here." She *tsk*ed. "He e-mailed me around midnight requesting a room. He's just lucky I'm an insomniac and that my laptop is Velcroed to my side, or he would have been stuck on the porch until I came down to start breakfast at six."

"What time did he arrive?" Poppy asked as she ran a finger over the intricately carved mahogany of the newel post's finial cap.

Ronni stepped back to the desk and glanced down at the ledger. "Two a.m."

"How in the world did he get here so fast?" I turned to Poppy. "Doesn't it take over eight hours to drive from Chicago to KC?"

"At least."

"There can't be any flights that late at night." I tilted my head, trying to remember the airline schedules from when I was a frequent business traveler. "The last one is around nine p.m."

"Which would be a problem, unless you fly yourself." Ronni's blue-gray eyes twinkled. "He's a pilot and owns his own plane."

"Wow." Poppy perked up. "So he's rich." She moved closer to Ronni and lowered her voice. "Did you notice if he had on a wedding ring?"

"His finger was bare," Ronni confided. "So I sniffed him, and he passed the test."

"What?" I asked, puzzled.

"If he smells like fabric softener, he's probably married," Ronni explained. "That's how married women mark their territory. Men can take off a ring, but it's hard to get that April-fresh scent out of their clothes."

"Really?" I snickered. "That's your litmus test?"

"That, and I asked if Mrs. Pryce would be joining him." Ronni wrinkled her nose.

"And?" Poppy urged.

"He said the only Mrs. Pryce was his mother."

"What's he look like?" Poppy asked. "Tell me he's not a complete troll."

"He's hot." Ronni grinned. "Think of a cross between Josh Duhamel and Mark Wahlberg."

"Zowie!" Poppy squealed. "Is there any chance in hell that he's straight?"

"Ladies." Once again, I had to interrupt them. "Poppy, I know how few cute guys there are in Shadow Bend, but let's focus on why we're here." She looked at me with a blank expression, so I added, "To help Boone."

"Oops." Poppy sobered. "Sorry. The whole situation is so outrageous, I keep forgetting about it." She looked apologetic. "I must be blocking it out of my mind. I need to work on not doing that."

Ronni had been listening intently while Poppy and I went back and forth. Now she tapped her chin and said, "Well, that explains a lot." She bit her lip, a thoughtful expression on her pretty face. "Tryg was very mysterious about why he was in town, but he must be Boone's lawyer. I heard on the news this morning that Boone had been arrested for murdering Elise Whitmore."

"Unfortunately, you're right," I confirmed. "Is Mr. Pryce here?"

"Yep." Ronni nodded. "He just got back. He was gone for a couple of hours. I bet he was at the police station, conferring with his client."

Before I could respond, I heard a masculine laugh above my head; then a pleasant baritone floated down the staircase. "Boone told me confidentiality is impossible to maintain in this town, but I think less than nine hours has to be a record."

We all looked up and then watched as a handsome man in his early thirties descended the steps. I could see why Ronni had compared Tryg Pryce to the two sexy actors she'd named. His dark good looks did remind me of Mark Wahlberg, and his widow's peak definitely brought to mind Josh Duhamel's often commented-on hairstyle.

I briefly wondered if under his expensive suit Tryg's body had the same chiseled perfection as Wahlberg in his legendary Calvin Klein under-wear ad. But then I mentally slapped myself and focused.

Edging past me, Poppy met him at the bottom of the stairs and said, "I'm one of Boone's best friends, Poppy Kincaid." She tossed her silvery blond ringlets. "I own the hottest nightspot in these parts, Gossip Central. You'll have to come by for a drink while you're in town."

Apparently, Poppy had already forgotten her resolution to concentrate on Boone's problems, so I nudged her aside, stuck out my hand, and said, "I'm Devereaux Sinclair, and you must be Boone's attorney. When you talked to him, did he mention he asked Poppy and me to help figure out who really killed Elise Whitmore?"

"Yes, he did. He indicated you had solved another murder not long ago." He looked over at Ronni, who was avidly listening to our exchange, and asked, "Is there somewhere private where Devereaux, Poppy, and I can speak?" He smiled at her. "I don't want to cause even more gossip by taking these beautiful women up to my room."

It was all I could do not to snort at his blatant flattery. Yes, Poppy was gorgeous, but I was more . . . unique. Granted, my aquamarine eyes were striking and my hair was an appealing cinnamon gold color—which is why I shouldn't wear it scraped into a ponytail as often as I did— but beauty was out of my reach. Especially since I was curvier than was currently in fashion. On a good day, I could do attractive, and if I really put a lot of effort into my looks, I could occasionally achieve pretty.

While I had been thinking about my appearance, Ronni had shown us to a small parlor. When she lingered, Tryg smoothly escorted her to the threshold, thanked her for her hospitality, and slid the doors closed behind her.

Poppy and I seated ourselves on a pair of Louis XV armchairs arranged in the middle of the room on an Oriental rug. Tryg took the matching cream damask settee. We faced one another over an ornate coffee table comprised of six gold cherubs perched on top of a marble base holding up a glass top.

Once we were settled, Tryg pulled a small leather notepad and a slim gold pen from his inside jacket pocket. He flipped the pad open and said, "Tell me everything you know about Elise Whitmore."

"Well," Poppy said, "she lives in town, but she doesn't hang out at Gossip Central, so I really don't have the scoop on her."

"How about you, Devereaux?" Tryg trained his deep green eyes on me.

"She's in the process of getting a divorce. She was afraid of her husband. And she liked unusual art." I paused, trying to think of anything else I'd heard about her, then remembered. "And she donated some fairly expensive things to a charity auction."

"Oh." Tryg perked up. "What kind of items?"

"A set of antique golf clubs, a couple of signed baseballs, and a bottle of pricey wine." As I recited the list, it dawned on me what they all had in common. "Those were probably her husband's belongings."

"Which might be why she's afraid of him," Poppy commented. "He's probably mad as hell that she's getting rid of his stuff like that." She crossed her legs. "The real question is, what is she so pissed at him about?"

"I have no idea what her story is." I usually didn't tap into the Shadow Bend rumor mill unless there was a subject in which I was particularly interested. And since I hadn't known Elise, conversations about her wouldn't have snagged my attention.

Poppy asked Tryg, "Did Boone say why the Whitmores were splitting up?"

"He's bound by lawyer-client confidentiality," Tryg answered, "but I bet that's something you two can find out." He smiled. "I generally hire a private investigator for murder cases, but Boone assures me that in a small town like Shadow Bend, you women will be more successful in getting the low-down than a PI would."

"That's probably true about any personal stuff," I agreed. "Actually, another friend of ours is asking his crowd about Elise right now, so we should have some information by the end of the day."

I didn't mention Noah's name to Tryg, since I thought I should be the one to tell Boone that his nemesis was helping us. It would be hard for

Boone to trust Noah. Heck, it was hard for me to trust him.

"I'll keep my ears open at my store, and Poppy can monitor what's said at the bar," I added, leaving out the fact that Poppy had strategically placed concealed listening devices all over Gossip Central.

She liked to know what was being said, though she never talked about anything she heard with anyone, except very occasionally to Boone and me. It was purely about a need for her to hold all the power due to her father's iron-fisted control over her during her childhood.

"I'm sure that will be useful." Tryg made a note to himself, then was silent as he tapped his pen against the memo pad.

After a few moments of watching him, I said, "I have some questions for you."

"Shoot."

"Since your law practice is in Illinois, can you represent Boone here in Missouri?"

"Yes. I passed the bar in both states." Tryg arched a brow. "I attended Washington University in St. Louis, which is where I met Boone. He was a first-year student when I was in my third year."

"Oh." I nodded. "That's good." I should have realized that Boone wouldn't have called him if he couldn't practice in our state. "Do we know the time of death?" I figured that would be kind of important if we were looking for suspects without alibis.

"The medical examiner says she was killed somewhere between eight and eleven p.m.," Tryg answered. "He couldn't be more precise than that."

"Sure." I nodded. "I understand it's hard to pinpoint TOD." All those crime shows that I watched with Gran were coming in handy. "One more question: Do you believe that Boone didn't do it?" I thought Tryg would do a better job if he was convinced Boone wasn't guilty.

"That's not important." Tryg tilted his head. "We lawyers say that all our clients are innocent until proven penniless."

I gave a polite laugh, but I didn't like his answer. I would definitely need to chat with Boone about his choice of attorney.

"What else should we do?" Poppy asked. "I could do a Mata Hari on one of my father's guys and get the inside scoop on what the cops know."

I could tell from Tryg's expression that he was considering her offer, so I vehemently shook my head at him. All we needed was to tick off Chief Kincaid. It would be bad for Boone and probably worse for Poppy. Not to mention the poor officer she chose to seduce, suck dry of information, and discard.

"We'll keep that option in reserve," Tryg said to Poppy, then winked at me. "I can legally get most of the facts that the police possess, so why don't you two concentrate on finding out everything you can about Elise and her husband, Colin Whitmore? Especially any enemies they may have."

"His enemies, too?" Poppy asked. "But she's the one who was killed."

"Husbands and wives are often collateral damage for each other," Tryg explained, leaning back. "Which is why I sure wish Boone had taken my advice about not handling divorces. I told him there's always one that comes back to bite you in the butt."

From Tryg's expression, I could tell that he was speaking from personal experience. What was the story behind that?

CHAPTER 11

Poppy and I left the B & B at a little past noon, and as soon as we got into the car, I phoned Noah to update him. After hearing me out, he reported that he had already gathered some interesting material about the Whitmores' divorce, but he wanted to check out one more fact before he met us.

Although I assured him there was no rush, he told me he'd be at the restaurant in twenty minutes. As I pulled into the street, I relayed to

Poppy what Noah had said and headed into town.

Poppy's excited chatter about Tryg, "the hot lawyer," droned from the passenger seat while I drove us to the Golden Dragon. I absentmindedly responded to her comments as I thought about seeing Noah again. He said he understood why I had left the dance the night before, but the teenage Noah had tended to hold behavior like that against me. That younger Noah had been hurt and angry if I chose to spend time with my friends instead of him. Had he really changed? Or was the adult Noah just better at hiding his feelings? And why did I care so much whether he had?

Not wanting Poppy to notice my preoccupation and question me about it, I forced myself to focus on her remarks about Tryg. I could tell that she was already half in lust with him, and, like most men, he'd definitely appreciated her charms. However, I had a feeling he wasn't the typical guy that she could beguile, then throw away. He seemed more the type to use than be used.

Reminding myself that Poppy could take care of herself, and would neither appreciate nor heed my warning about Tryg, I turned in at the restaurant's entrance. *Shoot!* The parking lot was packed. Was everyone in town eating here? It took all my concentration and Poppy's cunning to find an empty spot, but finally she pointed out a set of backup lights one row over.

I cut off a black Escalade that was trying for the same space, then whipped my BMW into a slot that had just been vacated by an old blue pickup truck. The Cadillac's owner wasn't happy with the outcome, but Poppy and I ignored his shouting and fist shaking and strolled toward the restaurant without acknowledging his bad behavior.

A year or so ago, after the Methodists put up a new church near the highway, they sold their old building to the current owners. I was eager to see how the interior had been renovated from a place of worship to an eatery. Apparently, so was everyone else in Shadow Bend, since the line for a table extended all the way out to the sidewalk.

Surprisingly it didn't take long for Poppy and me to make it inside the door. The smells of ginger, soy sauce, and other exotic aromas greeted us as soon as we stepped over the threshold. Ten minutes later, we were giving the hostess the number of our party.

As usual, Noah had impeccable timing and showed up just as we were being seated. He greeted Poppy with a hug, but I moved casually out of his reach. He frowned, then the corners of his eyes crinkled and he took a step toward me, but the hostess, a stunning Asian woman in her early twenties, glided between us.

She smoothed her gorgeous red silk cheongsam over her slim hips and said in a melodic soprano,

"Dr. Underwood, I didn't know you were the one joining these ladies, or I would have put them at your customary table." She laid a delicate hand on his arm. "If you can wait a teeny tiny bit, I can move you and your party there."

The restaurant had been open for only six weeks and Noah already had a regular table? I arched my brow at him and he shrugged. Shaking my head, I once again realized that Noah had it all—money, good looks, social position. And that didn't even take into account that he was the town's beloved doctor.

Noah patted the hostesses' fingers. "I wouldn't want to inconvenience anyone, but if the back booth is available, that would be great."

"It's no trouble at all, Doctor," she assured him. "Follow me."

As we trailed her, Noah murmured into my ear, "I thought it would be better if we had some privacy, and the reason I like this table is that it's a little apart from the others and behind a screen."

"That's perfect." I tried to keep the resentment out of my voice. "You're right. It's best if we aren't overheard." It wasn't his fault that folks fawned over him or that his father hadn't disgraced his family name. And, to be fair, I hadn't ever seen him either ask for or abuse the privileges that people showered on him.

Once Noah's admirer had cleaned off the table, handed us menus, and reluctantly departed, the question of who would sit where arose. I quickly slid onto the bench on one side of the booth and dragged Poppy in after me. She rolled her eyes but didn't comment. When the three of us were settled, we flipped open the large red leather folders.

As with many Chinese restaurants, the menus were multipage. My mouth watered as I perused the many choices. It had been ages since I'd had Asian food—probably since I quit my job and bought the dime store—and I could hardly wait.

Given that Noah was a regular at the restaurant, I asked him, "What do you recommend?" I was happy to try almost anything.

"Kung pao chicken is my favorite, but the moo shu pork is a close second. I love the plum sauce." He grinned. "I could order one and you could order the other and we could go halfsies."

"That sounds good to me," I said, then looked at Poppy, whose face was still buried in the menu. "Unless you want to go thirdsies. Two entrées are probably enough for the three of us."

"Nope. I'm having ma po tofu." She flipped closed the laminated pages and crossed her arms as if daring us to disagree. "And I'm not sharing. If there are leftovers, they're going home with me."

"How about an order of pot stickers?" I asked, admiring my friend's unabashed appreciation of food and that she never seemed to worry about her weight. Of course, she never seemed to gain any ounce, either, which might explain her indifference to the calories. "Would you be willing to share that?"

"Okay." She nodded grudgingly. "But I want hot and sour soup, too."

"Sold." After we conveyed our orders to the server and poured the tea she brought us, I said to Noah, "So, tell us what you found out about Elise. Why were she and her husband getting a divorce?"

"It took quite a few phone calls, but I finally found someone Elise had confided in." Noah leaned back and stretched an arm across the back of the booth. "I was surprised there wasn't any buzz around town, especially once I heard the story."

"Who did Elise tell?" I asked, curious as to whom she had trusted.

"Vaughn Yager," Noah answered. "He was only willing to tell me about it after I assured him we needed to know in order to catch Elise's killer."

"That was very loyal of him," Poppy commented.

Vaughn had been a classmate of mine. His father had been the school custodian, and, like me, he'd been a victim of the other kids' rejection and teasing. These days he was a different person. After making a fortune playing professional poker, he'd had his nose straightened and gotten a chin implant, then come back to town, bought a factory that was in bankruptcy, and turned it around. Now he was a successful, sought-after bachelor—a regular pillar of the community.

"How did Elise become friendly with Vaughn?" I asked. "Was she originally from Shadow Bend?"

"No. She moved here with her husband." Noah consulted an index card he'd pulled from his pocket. "Elise and Vaughn met when the ad agency she worked for did a campaign for his factory."

"You know the definition of *advertising,* don't you?" Poppy asked, then answered before either of us could respond. "It's the science of freezing human intelligence long enough to get money from otherwise smart people."

"Very funny." I shook my head. Poppy had a really twisted sense of humor. "So, Vaughn and Elise were friends. Was he the reason her marriage was ending?"

"No, they just both liked to play bridge." Noah tapped the index card on the tabletop. "Elise's husband didn't play and she needed a partner. Vaughn's pa—"

Poppy interrupted, "Forget the background stuff and get to the good part: the cause of the divorce."

"Elise caught her husband at a motel with their twenty-two-year-old pet sitter," Noah answered. His expression was difficult to read.

"The Cattlemen's?" Poppy clarified, and when Noah nodded, she *tsk*ed. "How much of a moron is Colin Whitmore? If you're going to screw the help, at least go to the hotel in the next town to do it."

"How did she catch him?" I asked, not well versed in tracking down cheating husbands or boyfriends. Although now that Jake was marshaling with his ex-wife, that might be a talent I should cultivate. That is, if he was still my boyfriend. A little detail that was currently unclear.

"Lindsey Ingram, one of Elise's coworkers, saw Colin's car in the Cattlemen's Motel when he should have been at work," Noah explained.

"How did Lindsey know it was Colin's?" Poppy asked, then answered herself. "He's got a vanity plate, doesn't he? What does it say?"

"CMP WZD," Noah answered. "He's the bank's computer wizard. He started out there fourteen years ago as an intern and has stayed ever since. My mother mentioned that his boss says that Colin's fingers are a blur when he's at the keyboard. And that it's truly miraculous what he can do with a PC."

"Interesting," I mused, then felt a flash of sadness. Elise's husband must have been there when my father worked at the bank. It could be awkward if I needed to talk to Colin. Would he see me as Dev Sinclair, successful business owner, or as Dev Sinclair, daughter of Kern Sinclair, embezzler and drunk driver?

Poppy must have known what I was thinking, because she squeezed my hand and changed the subject. "Does Lindsey live in town, too?"

"I'm not sure." Noah paused while our soup was served; then when the waitress left, he continued. "The ad agency they both work for is in Kansas City, so she might live there. She was dropping off something for Elise, who was home sick that day with the flu."

"What did Elise do when her colleague told her about Colin being at the motel during working hours?" I asked as I dipped my spoon into the rich soup.

"She went to the motel, and when she caught Whitmore with his pants down, she Maced him and spray-painted a giant red A on the pet sitter's bare chest." Noah didn't quite succeed in keeping his lips from turning up. "I can't imagine how the poor woman got the paint off."

"How did Elise find out what room they were in, let alone get the door open?" I asked.

"I bet she bribed the clerk for the number and the key," Poppy guessed.

"Right you are," Noah confirmed. "Once I got the scoop from Vaughn about Elise catching her husband with another woman, I remembered that my receptionist's cousin works the daytime shift at the Cattlemen's and I went over to see him. It took a little persuasion, but—"

"So who was this pet sitter?" Poppy interrupted

121

again. "I'm thinking she might have held a grudge about having her boobs shellacked."

Noah leaned forward and lowered his voice. "Willow Macpherson, but no one, not even Vaughn, seems to know it was her." He paused as the server put the platter of pot stickers on the table.

Once the waitress was gone, Poppy squealed, "You've got to be kidding me."

"Nope," Noah affirmed. "I have to admit, it surprised me, too."

"Willow Macpherson," I repeated. "Where have I heard that name before?" It definitely sounded familiar. I put a dumpling on my plate, used my fork to break it in half, then chewed thoughtfully. Was she one of my basket customers, or had someone mentioned her to me at the store?

Before I could dredge up the elusive memory, Poppy poked my shoulder and said around a mouthful of pot sticker, "Come on. Think. Her picture was on the front page of the newspaper a month or so ago. 'Local girl makes good.' There was a huge headline and a two-page story about her."

Now I remembered. "The young woman who got the big New York book deal."

Poppy nodded.

"She graduated from college last summer, and when she couldn't find a writing job, she started a blog that went viral," I confirmed, then looked from Poppy to Noah, still puzzled as to why it was such a major to-do that she'd been caught committing adultery.

"Do you know what her blog and upcoming book are about?" Poppy asked.

"Not offhand." I had only skimmed the newspaper article about her, and I hadn't listened very closely to the customers' talk at the dime store. I did recall that my high school helper, Hannah Freeman, had been extremely excited about the topic. The only thing I could think of was Willow's occupation, so I guessed, "Pets?"

"Nope," Noah answered, as he helped himself to a pot sticker. "Chastity."

"Cher's daughter? I mean, son?" I corrected myself. "Willow was blogging about being transgendered?" No, that couldn't be it. As much as I would like to think that my fellow Shadow Benders would embrace diversity, I knew they wouldn't have considered Willow changing sexes and publishing a book about it as a local girl making good.

"Not Chaz Bono," Poppy sneered. "The other kind of chastity. Abstention from all sexual intercourse."

"Seriously?" I held back a giggle. "She blogged about purity and was . . ."

"Screwing a married man," Poppy ended my sentence. "Yep, and that's why it's such a huge deal. Who's going to want to read a book about purity written by a woman who was found in a motel boinking her brains out?" Poppy paused, then said, "I wonder if Elise took pictures. Maybe that was what her murderer was after. Without photographs, Willow has plausible deniability, since it doesn't sound as if Elise blabbed all over town."

"That's a very good question." I dug through my purse until I found a pen, then made a note on the back of an old post office receipt. "Also, with Elise out of the way, Colin and Willow could get married, and that would certainly mitigate the whole situation if the story did get out. Willow could still claim she'd only had sex with one man, and that guy was now her husband. And it could be that she felt that Colin being a widower rather than a divorcé might somehow make the whole affair less tawdry."

"Maybe, but except for the three of us, it looks like only the motel clerk and the Whitmores knew that the woman Elise left her husband over was Willow," Noah interjected. "So if she's the killer, her motive was most likely to keep Elise quiet, not to marry Colin."

"So, if the motel clerk didn't tell anyone when it happened, why did he suddenly decide to blab to you?" Poppy challenged Noah.

When he didn't answer right away, I prodded, "Why *didn't* the clerk tell anyone about Willow? And, more to the point, why *did* he tell you?"

"It seems that originally Willow had snuck into the motel," Noah explained. "So the clerk didn't know who was with Colin. But after Elise branded Willow with the paint, Willow ran out a back door stark naked, just as the clerk was taking a cigarette break by the Dumpster. When Willow realized that the clerk recognized her, she begged him for his T-shirt and his silence. She promised he could guest blog for her sometime if he kept her secret, and she would even acknowledge him in her book as someone who had helped her with it."

"But?" Poppy urged.

"But the guy decided that cash in the hand trumped possible fame in the future," Noah admitted. "You'd be surprised what a few crisp hundred-dollar bills will buy you." He shrugged. "Actually, they probably don't have to be all that crisp to work."

"Boone will pay you back," I promised, thinking again how sweet Noah was being for helping out someone who wasn't even a friend of his. "Thank you so much for everything you've done for us today."

"Don't worry about it." Noah shrugged off my thanks. "I meant it when I said I don't think Boone is guilty, and I'd never want to see someone else in your life go to prison for a crime he didn't commit."

I felt tears well up at Noah's words. I never

knew he thought my father was innocent. He had more faith in my dad than I did. In what other ways had I misjudged Noah?

"Did you find out anything else about Elise or her husband?" Poppy asked, breaking the silence that had lengthened as Noah and I stared at each other. "Did either of them have any enemies?"

"Not that anyone mentioned." Noah pushed away his empty appetizer plate. "I did hear that she changed the locks on the house and got rid of all of her husband's things." Noah wiped his lips on his napkin. "Whitmore told anyone who would listen that she was selling or giving away stuff that had been in his family for years and was irreplaceable. He also said that he was going to sue whoever bought his belongings for receiving stolen property."

Yikes! If the chocolate molds Elise had sold me were Colin's, I had to figure out a way to get them back to him without admitting that I'd ever had them. I so didn't want to be named in a lawsuit. Too bad that would mean I had flushed eight hundred dollars down the toilet.

"So Colin could have broken in to the house in order to try to grab some of his heirlooms before Elise had a chance to dispose of them, and when she discovered him, he killed her," Poppy suggested. Then she pointed at me with her chopsticks and ordered, "Add him to your list."

While I wrote Colin's name after Willow's, the

waitress brought three heaping dishes containing our main courses. We spooned the food onto our plates, and once Noah convinced us that he didn't have any more information about Elise, Colin, or Willow, we turned the conversation to reminiscing about the good times we'd had together in high school.

Half an hour later, Poppy pushed away her empty dish and said, "I need a potty break."

As soon as she left, Noah stood up, walked to my side of the table, and slid in next to me. Before I could react, he pressed his hard thigh to mine, and I had a sudden desire to crawl into his lap. Regaining my senses, I moved over and plopped my purse between us. His lips twitched and his expression said that I had won that round, but he was far from defeated.

He handed me my scarf and said, "You left this in my car last night."

"Thanks. I didn't even miss it." I tucked the silky rectangle in my pocket.

"You're welcome." Casually, he plucked a morsel of chicken from my dish, and before popping it into his mouth asked, "Was the lawyer able to get Boone released on bail?"

"No." I shook my head. "Tryg said that when someone is arrested, they can be held for twenty-four hours without a case being filed against them. And the twenty-four hours doesn't start until the actual arrest is made, not when the person was first taken into custody." I made a face. "Unfortunately, Boone wasn't formally arrested until right before Poppy and I saw him being led to a jail cell last night. Which means that he can be held until one a.m. Monday morning before they have to give him a chance at bail."

"How does the whole bail thing work?" Noah asked. "Is there a preset amount depending on the crime you're charged with, or does it have more to do with how likely you are to flee the country?"

"Tryg said that Boone has to go to court for an arraignment hearing," I reported. "It's entirely up to the judge whether bail is granted, and if it is granted, how much it costs."

"So, Boone has two chances of getting out of jail," Noah said.

"Yes." I ticked them off on my fingers. "One, bail is set and in an amount he can afford." I felt my throat close with either hope or fear.

Noah handed me my glass and urged softly, "Have a drink of water."

"Thanks." I took a sip, then continued. "Or two, which is our best hope, that since there's no real evidence against Boone except his presence at the scene of the crime, the prosecutor will choose not to file. Instead he or she will decide to wait for the police to investigate further before bringing charges against him, and Boone won't have to go through an arraignment or face a judge."

"That's what will happen," Poppy declared, as she returned and took a seat on the opposite bench. "Once someone other than my father looks over the police report and sees the lack of evidence, they'll see how stupid it was for the cops to have arrested Boone in the first place."

"That would be great," Noah said, but he shot me a look that conveyed he wasn't convinced of Poppy's optimistic scenario.

"Yes, it would be," I agreed. But, like Noah, I wasn't nearly as certain as Poppy was about a positive outcome, and I fully intended to continue trying to find someone, or several someones, to offer up as an alternative suspect. Right now, Elise's soon-to-be ex-husband and his mistress were at the top of my list.

CHAPTER 12

I woke up Monday morning with a nagging question going round and round in my head. If Willow Macpherson had been the Whitmore's pet sitter, what had happened to that pet after Elise's murder? No one had mentioned an animal. Not that I would have expected Chief Kincaid or Boone to be talking about the dead woman's cat or dog.

Still, if it had run away in all the excitement, was anyone even aware it was missing? From what Noah had reported yesterday, I doubted that Colin had gotten custody of the pet. Heck, it sounded as if he barely got custody of his own underwear.

Reassuring myself that even if the cat or dog wasn't with him, Colin had probably rescued his pet after the police were finished processing the scene, I tried to put the thought out of my head. But the picture of some helpless animal locked, starving, in the house or wandering the neighborhood haunted me through breakfast and as I drove to work.

The dime store didn't open until noon on Mondays, but I used the morning to fill gift basket orders. I especially liked the privacy when I was designing one of my more erotic creations. Today I had dual baskets to make for a couple getting married next Saturday. One was for the bachelor party and the other for the bachelorette bash. I had challenged myself to find items for both baskets that the pair could use together.

Each basket would also include my trademark: the perfect book for both the occasion and the person receiving the gift. Since the matron of honor and best man had told me that the bride and groom were enthusiastic amateur chefs, I selected *The New InterCourses: An Aphrodisiac Cookbook* for him and *Fork Me, Spoon Me: The*

Sensual Cookbook for her. Nestling his volume on a black velvet bathrobe and hers on a red satin nightie, I stepped back to admire my work. The baskets needed something more.

Scanning the potential items, I fingered each possibility. Finally I selected a box of chocolate-covered strawberries, a lacy apron, and high heels for her basket, and a can of whipped cream, a pair of silk boxers, and a chef's hat for his. As I was deciding which one should get the edible body paint and which should get the lickable massage oil, my phone rang and I dove to answer it.

I was relieved to see Boone's name on the little screen. I'd been waiting all morning to hear if he was out of jail, and with each passing minute I had felt less and less hopeful that he'd been freed.

"The prosecutor didn't press charges." Boone's weary voice came out of the tiny speaker.

"That's wonderful." I sank into the chair behind the old kitchen table I used as a workbench. "So, you were released at one a.m.? Why didn't you text me right away? I've been worried."

"Sorry." Boone's tone was resigned. "The police had a lot of 'trouble' finding my paper-work. Tryg had to threaten them with a lawsuit in order to get them to actually let me go." He sighed. "I think Chief Kincaid had told his officers to keep me on ice while he tried to persuade the prosecutor to change her mind."

"I wonder why he's so convinced you're the

murderer." I didn't believe Poppy's claim that it was all about her father's crusade to punish her by destroying her friends. "Is there anything you haven't told me about you and Elise or the situation?"

"Listen. Let's get together and talk about it all tonight," Boone said, ignoring my question. "We still need to find out who killed Elise, because I'm sure the cops aren't through with me. But right now, I need a shower, some decent food, and sleep."

"The dime store closes at six and Gossip Central is dark on Mondays, so how about Poppy and I come to your house around seven?"

"Perfect." Boone yawned. "Do me a favor and get in touch with Tryg at the B and B. He should be there to hear everything, too."

"He's staying in town?" I was surprised that a high-priced attorney would stick around when there wasn't currently any case against his client. "I thought he'd be heading back to Chicago."

"He's still here." Boone yawned again. "He said he'd hang out for a while. Either he thinks the prosecutor will file soon or he has the hots for Poppy." Boone snickered feebly. "Probably both."

"Okay, I'll call Poppy and Tryg, and we'll all see you tonight at seven." Since I needed to explain to Boone about Noah's assistance but wanted to do it face-to-face, I added, "I might ask one other person to come, since he's helping, too."

"Sure," Boone agreed. "Bring Jake along and pick up a couple of pizzas while you're at it. I've got plenty of beer and wine."

Boone hung up before I could correct him, which no doubt saved me a lot of dancing around the truth. While I finished up the erotic baskets and put together one of the baskets that Oakley had ordered—his list of requirements had been waiting for me when I checked my e-mail that morning—I planned the evening ahead.

It was clear that I had to get to Boone's house before anyone else so I could explain the Jake/Noah situation to him in private. That would take at least fifteen minutes, so Poppy and Tryg couldn't arrive until quarter after. And Noah definitely had to be the last one in the door, so I'd tell him seven thirty.

Having figured out the sequence of entrances, I texted all the people involved and gave them their times. Thank goodness Poppy had thought to ask Tryg for his phone number before we left the B & B yesterday. Once that was accomplished, I did paperwork until it was time to flip on the neon OPEN sign, unlock the front door, and greet Hannah, my part-time clerk.

Hannah Freeman was a senior at the local high school. She worked for me four mornings and one afternoon a week as part of her vocational ed program. I admired that she was her own person and didn't even know the meaning of *peer pressure.*

Here in Shadow Bend, most of the teens tended toward either the preppy or jeans-and-T-shirt look, but Hannah's style was unique. I called it Hello Kitty chic.

Today she had on hot pink spandex leggings featuring the Hello Kitty face peeking out of a faux pocket on the left thigh and a long black top sporting a trompe l'oeil necklace complete with Hello Kitty charms.

On her head Hannah wore a black knit hat with a white feline face emblazoned on the front. It also had pink ears on the top and braided yarn ending in tassels that dangled down either side of the girl's cheeks.

After a few seconds of trying to figure it out on my own, I pointed to the cap and asked, "Where did you get that and what do you call it?"

"It's a critter hat." Hannah reached to take it off. "Do you want to try it on?"

"Maybe later."

"Whatever." Hannah shrugged.

She and I turned on all the lights, and the place began to fill with the first customers of the day. The hours after lunch and before school let out were usually slow. Often I didn't see a single shopper from one to three, which is why during the rest of the week Hannah worked mornings.

But on Mondays, because the store had been closed for the past forty-four hours, there was always a crowd.

The excited voices created a cheerful hubbub that wasn't muted by any acoustical tile or cork matting. Instead the sound of people socializing echoed off the old tin ceiling and hardwood floors. When I bought the place, I also purchased the adjoining building and knocked out the shared wall, which had doubled the interior space, but I had tried to keep the character of the original variety store intact.

Hannah and I worked steadily, helping customers find items, cleaning up messes created when people rummaged through our carefully arranged stacks of merchandise, and, my favorite, ringing up purchases on the old brass cash register. Its distinctive *ding* always made me smile.

At quarter to two, the dozen or so members of the Knittie Gritties, a knitting club that met at my shop, started to trickle in. I gladly provided them with the space, and—as with the other craft groups that met at the dime store—I gratefully reaped the benefit of their purchases. In addition to buying the materials for their projects from me, they also bought refreshments and any other bits and pieces that caught their eye.

I welcomed the participants, then walked them to the crafting alcove. Generally, I didn't hang around during the club's meeting, but today I was hoping to hear some gossip about Elise Whitmore and her murder, so I stayed.

For the scrapbookers, quilters, and sewers, I set up long worktables, but when the knitters, crocheters, and needlepointers held their meetings, I hauled out the comfy chairs and ottomans.

When the group had first started meeting at my store, I'd been surprised by the participants, figuring it would be mostly little old ladies. But the ages ranged from early twenties to nearly ninety, and there was even one man. Interesting how often we're wrong when we try to pigeonhole people.

I greeted Irene Johnson as she plopped into the seat next to me. She was a new addition to the group, and this was only her second time attending. Irene kept house for several individuals in town, and Noah had mentioned that he was now one of her clients, as well.

She was a tall, solidly built woman, and it was clear from her stoic air and calloused hands that she worked hard to support herself. Cleaning up after other people wasn't an easy way to make a living, and I sympathized. After buying my store, I finally understood the saying "Nickeled-and-dimed to death." If it wasn't one expense, it was always another.

Irene and I chatted for a few minutes; then I asked her, "Did you hear that Elise Whitmore was murdered over the weekend?"

"Sure." Irene rummaged in her knitting bag. "It was all over the news."

"Did you know her?" I kept my voice low, but the others were busy getting their materials ready and not paying any attention to us.

"No." Irene shook her head. "She didn't do much business in town. She even used some fancy cleaning service from the city rather than one of us locals."

"How silly." It seemed to be a common practice of the Shadow Benders who worked in Kansas City to spend all their money in KC, even when they could get the same items or services cheaper and/or better locally.

Excusing myself, I got up and wandered over to Vivian Yager, the founder of the Knittie Gritties and the owner of Curl Up and Dye. I particularly wanted to talk to her because not only was her beauty shop a hotbed of gossip, but she was also Vaughn Yager's aunt. She had raised him after his mother passed away, and I figured if he'd confided in anyone about Elise's marital problems, it would be her.

Vivian embodied all that was great about a small town. She had a sparkling personality and a heartfelt smile. She'd grown her little group of knitters from three or four to more than twelve, and welcomed the new additions as if they were old friends.

I leaned one hip against the wall near her chair

and said, "How's Vaughn doing? I understand he and Elise Whitmore were good friends."

"He's devastated." Vivian didn't question how I knew about her nephew and the dead woman. This was a small town. Eventually everyone knew everything.

"Did you hear that the police released Boone St. Onge?" It had dawned on me that Vivian was a good person to spread the news about my friend's innocence. "Turns out the prosecutor declined to press charges against him."

"No, I hadn't heard." Vivian ran her finger over the embroidered daisy pattern on her knitting bag. "But I'm not surprised. Boone's too sweet a guy to do something like that. The cops probably just wanted a quick answer and didn't care if they got the right person."

"The whole situation is so awful." I pasted a shocked expression on my face. "I can't believe we've had a murder like that in Shadow Bend."

"It is downright scary." Vivian clanked shut the round metal handles of her bag. "To think that someone is breaking into people's houses and killing them. I guess I'd better start locking my door."

"Absolutely," I agreed. "Is it true that Elise was getting a divorce?"

"Yeah." Vivian tsked. "Her husband, like so many other men, just couldn't keep it in his pants." She arched a brow at me. "Speaking of men, how's that hunky U.S. Marshal of yours?"

"He's doing great. He's returned to duty," I answered noncommittally.

"In St. Louis?"

"Uh-huh." I nodded, then brought the subject back to the murder. "Do you know who Elise's husband was messing around with?"

"Nope. Elise refused to tell Vaughn who she was." Vivian slipped the point protectors off her needles.

"I wonder why," I murmured. "So Vaughn never knew the name of Colin's lady friend?"

"Right." Vivian gave me a strange look. "That's what I just said."

"Sorry. My mind must have wandered."

"No problem." Vivian patted my hand.

After checking that she had everything she needed for her group, I returned to the front of the store. The after-school crowd would be in soon, and I had to make sure the soda fountain was fully stocked and ready for the onslaught. I'd found out the hard way that making hungry teenagers wait for food was never a good thing.

While Hannah and I made sundaes and milk shakes and doled out candy, I kept an eye on the front door. Luckily, except for the kids and the knitters, there were no other customers, so both my clerk and I could concentrate on feeding the adolescent masses.

Just as we got done serving the last of the

teenagers, the Knittie Gritties took a fifteen-minute break. For five dollars each, I provided coffee, tea, and a selection of cookies and pastries. Payment was on the honor system—the group members deposited their money in an old cigar box—so after putting out the cups, plates, utensils, napkins, and goodies, I went over to the front register. I sat on a stool with my laptop on the smooth marble counter and surfed various online rare-book sites, looking for titles I could use for current and future basket orders.

When the Knittie Gritties finished their treats, they strolled past where I was sitting as they headed back to their corner. Generally, I blocked out their chatter because most of the conversation between members was about their projects, their children or grandchildren, and the weather—an always fascinating topic in rural Missouri. But today I listened in, and as the last pair drifted by, I was rewarded.

"What do you think about that murder over the weekend?" the youngest member of the club asked Addison Campbell, the only male Knittie Grittie. "Do you think we should be scared that some serial killer is running around town, or is it someone she knew?"

Addie, as he was known, owned and operated the Shadow Bend Pawn Shop and Jewelry, which was a fertile field for the local grapevine, so he usually had the lowdown.

"My money's on her husband." Addie laid a giant paw on the tiny brunette's arm. "I heard the lawyer was released and nothing is missing, so in my book that leaves Computer Boy as the prime suspect."

Addie was a huge man with multiple tattoos. Rumor had it that he had ink in places most men couldn't stand a single needle prick. I admit it: When he'd first joined the club, my preconceptions had reared their ugly heads. I had been shocked that a guy had signed up, especially one with tats, earrings, and a shaved head. That he'd arrived on his Harley had really startled me.

But Addie had explained that his anger management coach had suggested the hobby and that working with the needles and various fibers soothed him. Now as I approached him, I had to smile at the T-shirt he was wearing. Against a gray background was a picture of two green skeins of yarn and the words REAL MEN HAVE BALLS.

The young woman nodded, then said, "But why would Colin kill her?"

By this time, the twosome was nearly out of earshot, and I quickly rounded the counter and followed them back to the craft alcove. I ducked behind shelves and displays as I went, and then hid next to a rack of scrapbooking accessories once they reached their destination.

"He might have been banging everything in

skirts," Addie said, his voice disapproving, "but Elise was really screwing him royal in the divorce."

"How's that?" the brunette asked as she settled back in her seat.

"Not only did she sell all his possessions; she emptied their joint accounts, canceled their mutual credit cards, and then tried to get him fired." Addie grunted as he dropped into the chair.

"But eventually Colin would get his share." The woman picked up her needles. "When I went through my divorce, my husband tried to take everything but the judge ordered him to give me my cut."

"Maybe he didn't want to wait." Addie concentrated on executing an intricate stitch, then added, "Or maybe for some reason he couldn't wait."

Hmm. I narrowed my eyes. Addie had a good point. Had Elise's husband needed something she was keeping from him so badly that he had to kill her to get it?

CHAPTER 13

It was almost closing time before I had a chance to check my text messages. Poppy and Tryg had confirmed that they'd be at the meeting at Boone's that night, but Noah hadn't replied. It was a shame there wasn't an app that allowed me to tell if my text had been read. Then I would know if he was just too busy to check his phone or if he didn't want to come but was too much of a wuss to tell me no.

Granted, it would be an awkward situation for both men, and I sympathized. However, if Noah truly wanted to be back in my life, he and Boone would need to bury the hatchet. I just hoped it wouldn't be in each other's skulls—or in mine, for that matter.

As I locked up the front entrance, shut off the lights throughout the store, and walked from the storage room's exit into the tiny parking lot behind the building, I contemplated my next move. Should I let the matter drop? Noah had already told Poppy and me all he knew. Maybe he didn't truly need to be present tonight.

No. Noah had to pull up his big boy boxers and show me that he had truly reformed. When we dated in high school, I was always the one who gave in and tried to be the way he wanted me to be. But I was no longer that girl, and now it was his turn to do the changing.

Having settled that matter in my mind, I needed to figure out what to do about Noah's non-response. I had forty-five minutes to do that, pick up the pizza, and get to Boone's place. At least I didn't have to run back to the house to check on Gran, because she and her friend Frieda were on a senior bus trip.

A couple of times a month, the Shadow Bend Savings and Guaranty Bank organized an excursion for the golden-oldies crowd. One of the bank employees arranged for the group to attend a play or go shopping or—as in this trip—travel to one of the gambling boats. They weren't due back until nine, so there was plenty of time before I had to get home.

After some thought, I decided to phone Noah rather than text him again. That way, if he answered, I'd know, and I wouldn't have to guess whether or not he saw my message. I wasn't sure what hours his medical clinic was open, so it was possible he was still working. Because I was reluctant to deal with his staff—who knew how they felt about me after all the years Noah and I had been on the outs?—I tried his cell first.

He picked up on the first ring. "Dev, I was just going to call you."

"Oh." Why did his voice cause my heartbeat to accelerate? A friend, which is all he was, shouldn't have that effect on me. "Then you saw my text?"

"I only read it a few seconds ago," Noah said. "My last patient walked out the door at six fifteen and I don't carry my phone while I'm in the examination room. I figure if anyone wants me, they'll call the clinic."

"Right. Good to know." I stalled, unsure what to say next. Why did this feel so uncomfortable?

Was it because I really wanted Noah to come to the meeting? Would that prove to me he had really changed?

"Anyway," Noah said, interrupting my thoughts, "I'm free this evening, and if it's all right with St. Onge, I'd be happy to join you guys."

"Great." Now all I had to do was clear the way with Boone. "I know he'll want to thank you for all your help." I crossed my fingers that Boone would be in a reasonable mood and see things my way.

"Yeah, well." Noah's tone indicated he was unconvinced. "So, I'll see you at seven thirty."

"Yep," I agreed, then added, "There'll be food, so don't worry about dinner."

"Sounds good," Noah said. "Can I bring anything? How about I get something for dessert? That new place that opened up next to the tearoom is supposed to have terrific pies."

"Perfect." I sure wished he would quit being so doggoned nice. This new Noah was making it very hard to resist falling for him again.

After we hung up, I stopped at the local pizza joint and picked up the two unbaked pizzas I had ordered earlier. I'd asked for them uncooked so that once everyone arrived at Boone's we could pop them in the oven and wouldn't have to worry about them getting cold before we were all present and ready to eat.

With the pizzas safely ensconced on the

passenger seat, I drove to Boone's. He lived in the old-money part of town, in a neighborhood full of stately hundred-year or older residences. This was where Noah had grown up and where his mother—the Medusa of Shadow Bend—still lived. Because Mr. and Mrs. St. Onge had made it clear to Boone's grandmother that they preferred their contemporary home, she had left Boone her Prairie-style house.

Boone loved the place and had lavished it with his cash and attention. And although he had kept the original structure intact, he had enlarged and remodeled the master bathroom, converted one of the four upstairs bedrooms into a walk-in closet, and added a detached garage out back.

If anyone questioned his decision, Boone always replied that vintage was wonderful, but there was no need to go overboard in the quest for authenticity. After all, he liked reading Jane Austen, but he had no desire to live in England's Regency period, when people bathed only once a week and there was no deodorant.

I parked in Boone's empty driveway. I was never comfortable when I was forced to leave my Z4 on the street, vulnerable to all the idiot drivers just waiting to sideswipe it. I had minimal auto insurance and a sky-high deductible, which meant I'd never be able to afford to have the car repaired if it got dented. And call me shallow, but it would kill me to drive around in a beat-up vehicle.

I frowned as I got out of my BMW and glanced at the house. The grouping of multipane windows that was the focal point of the second floor was typically lit up, but tonight it was dark. Not a good sign. Boone claimed the windows were the one distinctive touch on what otherwise would have been a rather characterless façade, and he always made sure they were illuminated.

It took several rings of the bell before Boone opened the front door. He greeted me without his usual exuberance, silently let me into the foyer, and hung my jacket in the coat closet. Then, finally, the old Boone emerged; he inspected me from head to foot—I was wearing my customary store uniform: jeans and a red sweatshirt with DEVEREAUX'S DIME STORE embroidered across the chest—and *tsk*ed. "Girl, where is your sense of style?"

I narrowed my eyes in mock outrage and retorted, "I must have left it in my other purse."

Instead of his usual snappy comeback, Boone shook his head, took the pizza boxes from the small table where I had placed them, and led me into the kitchen. I followed, biting my thumbnail. Boone reminded me of a deflated balloon, and I wasn't sure how to pump him back up.

"How are your parents doing?" It was lame, but it was the only thing I could think of to say.

"Better, now that I'm out of jail."

"Are they still talking to each other?"

"So far."

As Boone placed the cartons in the refrigerator, he glanced at the wall clock and said, "I wonder where everyone else is. Tryg is always punctual."

"Actually, I needed to talk to you alone, so I asked Tryg and Poppy to come at seven fifteen." I pulled out a wooden slat-back chair from the matching square-leg table and sat down. "Have a seat."

"Is Jake coming then, too?" Boone joined me. His forehead was wrinkled questioningly, but his voice was flattened by dejection.

"No." I took a deep breath. This was so hard. Knowing how much Boone disliked Noah, I felt as if I was kicking a puppy that already had a sore paw. "Jake is in St. Louis. Saturday he left me a message that he was cleared for duty and had to report in right away because they had an urgent case they wanted him on."

"Oh." Boone scrubbed his face with his fists—clearly, he was still exhausted—but then a tiny spark appeared in his eyes and he asked, "Then who helped you yesterday?"

"Noah Underwood." I put my hand over Boone's and watched as a variety of emotions chased across his face. "He's changed, Boone."

"No. He hasn't." Boone shook off my fingers. "He was always willing to do whatever it took to make himself look good in your eyes."

"Except stand up to his mother," I murmured almost involuntarily.

"Exactly. When push came to shove, Dr. Dreadful let you down." Boone got up and poured us each a glass of merlot.

"That was more than a decade ago." I could hear the pleading in my voice and didn't like it. "He explained what happened back then, and I've decided to give him a chance to prove he's the guy he claims to be."

"If that's what floats your boat." Boone handed me the wine and sat back down. "I guess I shouldn't say anything. After all, it's your tacky little cruise ship."

"Thanks for understanding." I let the sarcasm drip from my words. "Be nice."

"I'm not trying to be difficult." Boone's expression was stubborn.

"You don't have to." I snickered. "It just comes naturally."

"Well, I don't trust him." Boone crossed his legs.

"Whether you trust Noah or not, he's the one who found out all the information about the Whitmores yesterday," I pointed out.

"I'm sure I already know everything he discovered." Boone pursed his mouth in a pout.

"Fine." I hated arguing with Boone, mostly because as a lawyer he was so much better at it than I was. "I don't want to go over the whole thing until the others arrive, but do you know the name of the woman Colin Whitmore was boinking when Elise caught him?"

"No . . ." Boone drew out the word. "Elise said she was saving that as an ace in the hole if Colin gave us any trouble with the divorce settlement." Boone frowned. "She said that keeping the little slut's identity a secret was extremely important to her cheating husband."

"Well, Noah found out who the woman was." I explained how he had obtained the information and ended with, "And it looks as if this Willow Macpherson had an excellent motive for murdering Elise. It certainly was as good, if not better than, the one the police think you have. So learning her identity was an important discovery."

"All right, I can see how that could be useful." Boone wavered. "And it was good of Dr. Dull to pitch in and use his connections for me."

"So, it's okay if he comes tonight?" I pounced at the opening Boone had given me. "And you'll be civil and not call him names?"

"Fine." Boone's lips turned up. "But this is a temporary truce. Don't expect Dr. Dreary and me to become BFFs anytime soon."

"Fine," I agreed. "I gave up asking for miracles a long time ago."

When Poppy and Tryg showed up a few minutes later, it was no surprise that they arrived together. Judging from the secret glances, sly remarks, and little touches they exchanged, I was fairly certain that they were on their way to becoming an item. Boone, on the other hand, seemed taken aback, and I wondered why. Poppy nearly always inspired men to lust, and Tryg was exactly her type—rich and successful.

While the newly hatched couple took off their coats and Boone hung them in the closet, I nipped into the kitchen and turned on the oven. Once it was preheating, I met the trio in the library. This was my favorite room in Boone's house. Its large windows were framed in whiskey-colored draperies that pooled on the shiny hardwood floor. An oak table holding a crystal vase full of fresh lilies and tulips was positioned behind a nutmeg leather sofa, and an assortment of brass lamps was scattered throughout the space.

Tryg and Poppy shared the couch, and Boone sat on a matching club chair to their right. I sank into the identical seat on the other side of them and checked my watch. Noah was due any minute, a fact I should mention to Poppy so she didn't blurt out something awkward when he walked in. Not that she would deliberately try to make him feel uncomfortable, since she was one of his fans, but because she was one of the few people close to me who would be happy to see Noah and me resume our former relation-ship.

Before I could speak, Boone wrinkled his nose and said, "Poppy, I suppose you're aware that Dr. Do-Good is joining us this evening."

She opened her mouth, glanced at me, then closed it and nodded. "Sure."

"And she thinks it's a good idea," I said, shooting her a grateful look, then turning to Boone and admonishing, "You promised to stop calling him names."

"Which I will." Boone adjusted the creases in his khakis—even depressed, he managed to be immaculately dressed and groomed. "To his face." He smiled sardonically. "Unless, of course, you love him so much you can't bear to hear a word against him."

I started to protest, but the doorbell rang and Boone jumped to his feet. I debated following him out to the hallway, then decided it might be a good idea to let the two men have a couple of minutes alone to sort out past grievances and readjust their attitudes.

While Poppy and Tryg cooed at each other, I focused on the muffled conversation going on in the foyer, but I couldn't hear a single word. The voices faded, and I could tell the men were walking toward the kitchen—probably to put away the dessert Noah had brought.

A few seconds later, Boone ushered Noah into the library. Instantly, Noah's smoky gray eyes locked onto mine, and I felt a sizzle that started in my chest and traveled due south, where it burst into flame.

Boone frowned at me. Had he read my mind or a more embarrassing part of my body? His mouth tightened; then, after he introduced Noah to Tryg, he asked, "What can I get everyone to drink?"

"A martini straight up," Poppy and Tryg answered in unison.

"Wine for me," Noah said, stepping over to the brimming bookcases built into three of the four walls and running his fingers across the spines. "Whatever is open is fine."

Boone and I retreated to the kitchen, where I put the pizza in the oven and set the timer for twenty minutes. Then, while Boone made the martinis, I poured Noah a glass of merlot and topped off Boone's glass, as well as my own. When I brought the wine to Noah in the library, I discovered that he had taken the desk chair from the corner and placed it next to where I had been sitting.

Noticing that Poppy and Tryg were preoccupied with each other, I leaned close and whispered to Noah, "Thanks so much for coming tonight. It's very sweet of you to give up your free time. There are probably a million places you'd rather be than here making nice with Boone."

"Maybe." Noah's silky voice filled my ear and his warm breath feathered my cheek. "But there's no one I'd rather spend an evening with than you." He took my hand, his thumb caressing my palm, and I felt goose bumps form on my arms.

"Uh." Why was I having trouble breathing? Instead of the flippant reply that I had intended to make, I croaked, "Me, too."

Okay. Where had that come from? I had to get my mind on Boone's problems and remember that Noah wasn't anything more than a friend. Luckily, before I could make any other awkward remarks, Boone came in with the martinis and we got down to business.

Poppy took a sip of her drink and asked, "How should we do this?"

Tryg sat forward. "Let me summarize what the police have, and we'll go from there." He took a notepad from the breast pocket of his polo shirt and read, "The authorities arrived within five minutes of Boone's nine-one-one call. He was immediately escorted from the living room and placed in a squad car. After the house was searched and no one was found, the EMTs examined the victim. The coroner was summoned, and she pronounced Elise dead."

"What did they find at the scene?" Boone asked, sitting back in his chair. "No one would tell me anything. I only know that they didn't find the weapon, because they kept asking me where I had hidden it."

"The back door had been jimmied and the house had been ransacked," Tryg answered. "The police believe the killer was searching for something that Elise had hidden, because containers were opened and flung aside. In fact, a can of varnish was spilled on the kitchen floor. The crime techs are checking it for evidence."

"Did you go in the kitchen, Boone?" I asked.

"No."

"Good." I smiled at him, then asked Tryg, "Was Colin Whitmore able to say if anything had been stolen?"

"No." Tryg shook his head. "He claimed he couldn't tell."

"Because Elise had been getting rid of his stuff," I speculated, then added, "but the pawn shop owner says he heard that nothing was missing."

"He's probably basing that info on the fact that he's the local fence and no one has tried to sell him anything," Poppy guessed.

"Interesting." Tryg shrugged. "Unfortunately, since I was only able to get a copy of Boone's arrest report and nothing else, I can't say if the police suspect that or not."

"Well, the fact that her husband was furious with Elise for getting rid of his belongings is something that we need to make sure the cops know about," Poppy informed Tryg. Then she asked him, "Is Colin even a suspect?"

"That's hard to say." Tryg sighed. "They don't seem to have taken a hard look at him. Then again, I haven't seen any paperwork other than Boone's arrest report. And, of course, none of the officers is sharing information with their prime suspect's lawyer."

"So, that's it?" Boone whined. "That's all you were able to find out? What have you all been doing while I was rotting in jail?"

"Boone . . ." Tryg raised a brow at his client. "We talked about your attitude not helping matters."

"You may call it bitching," Boone snapped. "I call it motivational speaking."

"Boone was never one to suffer in silence," Poppy told Tryg.

"Why should I?" Boone screwed up his face. "I'd much rather moan, whimper, and complain."

While I was happy to see Boone acting more like his snarky self, I thought it was time we all focused back on the case, so I said, "As I mentioned earlier, Noah learned quite a bit about the Whitmores."

"Right." Tryg nodded. "Let's turn the floor over to Dr. Underwood and let him tell us what he found out."

"Call me Noah." Noah smiled at the attorney. "I like to leave all that doctor stuff at the clinic." When Tryg nodded, Noah turned to Boone and filled him in. After he finished up, he asked Poppy and me, "Did I leave anything out?"

"Nope." Poppy took another sip of her martini. "Not that I can think of."

"That about covers it," I agreed. "But I did hear an interesting tidbit today from the one of the knitters at my store. It seems that not only did Elise cripple Colin financially; she was also trying to get him fired."

"No shit?" Poppy bounced on her seat. "How could she do that?"

"I have no idea." I took a swallow of wine. "I've been wondering that same thing myself."

"So how do we find out?" Boone asked. "That could be important."

"Since Colin works at the Shadow Bend Savings and Guaranty Bank and I'm on the board, maybe I should go talk to Max Robinson," Noah offered. "As bank president and Colin's boss, he was probably the person Elise contacted if she was trying to have her husband sacked."

"That would be great." Poppy beamed at Noah, then turned to me with a mischievous grin. "I bet Dev would love to go with you."

"Of course." I narrowed my eyes at Poppy, but she had already looked away.

"Meanwhile, Tryg and I can keep digging around to see what the police are doing," Poppy proposed. "I'm sure I can convince someone at the PD to spill the beans."

"That's probably not a good idea," I cautioned. "You don't want to do anything to upset your dad. That would only make things worse for Boone."

"Right," Poppy mumbled noncommittally.

"Hey, I almost forgot." I turned to Boone. "Since Elise found her husband in bed with the pet sitter, I take it the Whitmores have a cat or dog."

"Yes." Boone's expression was puzzled. "She had a Russian Blue named Tsar."

"Do you know where the cat is now?" I asked. "Did the police take it or give it to Colin?"

"I have no idea." Boone shrugged. "I don't recall seeing him that night at all." He wrinkled his forehead. "Which is odd, because Tsar was usually glued to Elise's side."

I bit my lip. "Then we need to find out what happened to him."

While everyone was murmuring in agreement, the timer beeped and we all trouped into the kitchen for pizza. As we ate, the conversation turned to other subjects, and Noah joined in. Observing him, I could see why he was so beloved by his patients. His self-deprecating humor and ability to empathize made it seem as if every word a person uttered to him was important.

Even Boone appeared to be seeing Noah in a new light, and he joked about doctors and lawyers being natural enemies. Poppy had always liked Noah, and she treated him like an adored older brother. Then when Tryg and Noah discovered a mutual love for travel, they bonded, discussing at length their various excursions and comparing hotels and restaurants in exotic locales.

We had just polished off the last bites of the luscious pies that Noah had brought when the phone rang. Boone excused himself to take the call in the library. He returned a few minutes later, his smile gone and a defeated look back on his face.

"Who was it?" Poppy and I asked at the same time.

"Chief Kincaid," Boone said. "He requested that I come into the police department first thing in the morning to answer some more questions." He sighed. "He said they have new information that they'd like me to help them understand."

"Do they want you as Elise's attorney or as a suspect?" I asked.

"He didn't say. He just asked me to come in." Boone glanced at Tryg. "I guess it was a good thing you stuck around."

"I presumed the matter wouldn't be closed until they caught the real killer, so I figured they'd want to talk to you again." Tryg's expression was unperturbed, but I detected a flicker in his eyes that might have been worry. "What time should I pick you up tomorrow?"

"Quarter to eight." Boone's tone was morose. "I have a feeling that if we're late, I'll be taking another trip in the back of a squad car."

I glanced at Poppy and mentally asked her to stay the night with Boone. Someone needed to watch over him, and she knew I didn't like to leave Gran alone overnight.

She immediately picked up on my message and said, "Oh, I almost forgot. I need to sack out here tonight, Boone. My apartment is being painted and the fumes are awful."

"Sure," Boone muttered, clearly distracted. "You know you're always welcome. Tryg prefers to stay at the B and B, because if the cops decide to search my house, he doesn't want them seeing his notes. He knows my guest room is available if he changes his mind."

After the phone call from the police, no one had much left to talk about, and I finally said, "I should be getting home to Gran."

Once we helped Boone clean up the kitchen, Tryg, Noah, and I left. Tryg's rental was parked on the street so we parted at the front door, but Noah followed me. His Jaguar was behind my BMW, and as I walked over to my car, he opened the door for me.

We stood there silently until Noah cleared his throat and said, "It was really nice being with you and your friends tonight."

"It was really nice having you with us." I blushed at how lame that sounded.

"I think Boone is okay with me being around," Noah commented.

"He did seem fine." I backed up until my butt was pressed against the inside of the car.

Noah closed the gap, brushed a stray curl behind my ear, and asked, "Do you know what I

160

was most disappointed about when you left the dance early Saturday night?"

"No."

"This." He covered my lips with his.

I meant to give him a light peck, but it quickly turned into much more. He kissed me until my worry about Boone disappeared, then continued until I melted into him. I wound my arms around his neck, hanging on as if I would fall to the ground if I let go.

His hands slid down my hips, cupping my derrière and pulling me against him. The feel of his mouth, the warmth of his body, and the touch of his hands left me unable to talk myself into pulling away. My eyes drifted shut and I gave myself over to the sensations.

When Noah finally lifted his mouth from mine, he ran his thumb across my bottom lip. I had never seen him look so passionate. His pearl gray eyes had turned into chips of ebony, and his gaze was locked onto mine. Drawing a ragged breath, he started to say something, then stopped and instead leaned his forehead against mine.

He stroked the back of my neck with his fingers, cleared his throat, and said hoarsely, "I'll call you tomorrow."

"Great." I forced myself to step away from him. "About going to talk to the bank president?"

"That, too." Noah touched my cheek. "And, yes, the kiss was great. But it can be even better.

Just give me a chance and I promise not to screw things up this time."

Since I didn't have an answer, I got in my car.

As Noah closed the door, he whispered, "Sleep tight."

CHAPTER 14

Noah backed his Jag out of the driveway and drove off. In his rearview mirror, he watched Dev's rear lights disappearing in the opposite direction. If only instead of going their separate ways, she was in the passenger's seat beside him. Better yet, still in his arms.

Intellectually, Noah knew he shouldn't have kissed her. Both the timing and the public setting were bad ideas. What if one of St. Onge's neighbors happened to be out walking his or her dog or taking out his or her trash? All Noah needed was for someone to see him making out with Dev and report back to his mother.

If, for a second, Noah thought that he would be the one Nadine would target with her wrath, he wouldn't have cared less if the whole world knew that he and Dev were together. But he was certain his mother would direct her venom at Dev, and that was a problem he needed to solve before word got back to Nadine.

Since his mother was currently on a cruise in

the middle of the Caribbean, Noah hadn't worried about being seen with Dev at the dance. Nadine didn't check e-mail and had planned to turn off her cell phone. But once she was back in Shadow Bend, having a long talk with her was high on his to-do list. He intended to convince his mother that the consequences of her upsetting Dev in any way would be his immediate and total withdrawal from Nadine's life.

It had taken every ounce of willpower Noah possessed to step back and let Dev go, but until the situation with his mother was resolved, he had no other choice. His appearance at the dance with Dev might raise a few eyebrows, but Nadine's cronies would wait until she got home to tell her about it. However, if one of his mother's pals caught him necking with Dev, she'd hijack a rowboat, track down Nadine's ship, and row across the Atlantic Ocean to tell her about that.

His mother would be home Sunday, so waiting until he'd spoken with Nadine before taking the next step with Dev shouldn't be a problem. Of course, if that were the case, why had he kissed her? And why was he allowing her to affect him so strongly?

In most instances, Noah was a man who thought before he acted. He preferred to analyze the circumstances, assess the alternatives, and then find the perfect action to take. He had thought long and hard about what he would do if Dev ever gave him the opportunity to reenter her life.

The plan had been to take baby steps—first regain her trust, then her friendship, and only then try for her love. But now that he had the chance, it seemed he couldn't control himself around her.

At lunch on Sunday, he hadn't been able to stop from moving to sit beside her. Even though it had been painfully clear she wanted him to keep his distance, he'd felt compelled to get closer—to feel the heat radiating from her body and to touch her hand.

When he was around Dev, his resolve flew out the window. How had he gone from trying to win her friendship to kissing her silly in St. Onge's driveway? What had happened to his strategy to take things slowly and not scare her off? He had never been someone who was ruled by his desires, and he didn't like the sensation. Was he losing his mind?

When he had seen Dev's text that afternoon asking him to St. Onge's, Noah had felt a surge of triumph. She was allowing him into her life and into her friends' lives, as well. He had seen the invitation as a sign of real progress in their relationship.

Noah had made some telephone calls earlier in the day and learned that Jake Del Vecchio had left town and gone back to work as a U.S. Marshal.

With him out of the picture, Noah had just the opening he needed. This was the perfect time to win Dev back.

But he had to rein in his passion. If he scared her off, he might never get another opportunity. He had to play it smart. No more kissing her, no more caressing her, and no more fantasizing about her naked beneath him. *Shit!* Where had that thought come from? Noah whacked his forehead with his palm. Maybe he really was going crazy.

A rational man wouldn't have a burning wish to turn his car around and follow Dev home. A reasonable man wouldn't still be in love with a woman he hadn't been with in more than thirteen years. And a sane man would be able to stop thinking about laying that women down in the middle of his king-size bed, freeing her hair from its ponytail, and burying his face in the cinnamon gold strands. Since when did he have a thing for women's hair?

Noah pounded the steering wheel and reminded himself that for their relationship to work, he had to reestablish her faith in him. He had to stop acting like some lust-driven teenage boy and behave like the analytical man he'd always been.

Despite everything he'd just told himself, when Noah pulled into his garage and switched off the Jaguar's engine, instead of getting out of the car, he closed his eyes and savored the memory of Dev's response to his kisses. The thought of the soft whimper of need she'd uttered when she'd curled her arms around him sent a jolt traveling straight to his groin.

Something deep in his chest awakened. It had first stirred when he stared down into Dev's beautiful blue-green eyes, but now his heart clenched with a longing that he'd never experienced for any other woman. And he knew he had to do everything in his power to win Dev and keep her in his arms and in his life.

The feeling nearly short-circuited his brain. Not good. As a doctor, he knew that acting impetuously could cost people their lives, and personally, the concept of his heart ruling his head scared him to death. So why was he suddenly so out of control?

Noah scrubbed his face with his fists. He couldn't allow his feelings for Dev to override his common sense. When they met to talk to the bank president, Noah would treat Dev the same way he did the rest of his women friends. With warmth and affection and nothing more. And if that didn't work, he wasn't sure what he'd do.

A dusting of snow clung to the blacktop as Noah drove to work the next day. That morning the TV meteorologist had promised that the temperature would reach the mid-fifties, and the negligible accumulation would melt before noon. Noah certainly hoped so. The grueling winter and delayed spring had been hard on everyone. And since he and his staff were the ones who had to deal with the illnesses that it brought, the weather had been especially rough on them.

Noah had always wanted to be a small-town doctor. He'd attended the combined BA and MD program at the University of Missouri School of Medicine, which had allowed him to graduate in six years. Afterward, he'd done a three-year residency in family medicine, then returned to Shadow Bend and opened the Underwood Clinic. It would celebrate its fourth birthday in September.

One of the many things Noah loved about his job was the five-minute commute. After parking out back in the employee lot, he let himself in the private entrance. It was seven fifty when he entered the building, and as he walked to his office, he could hear the voices of his head nurse, Eunice Vogel, and her daughter, Madison, the clinic's receptionist, coming from the waiting room.

Although he didn't hear his physician assistant, Yale Gordon, speaking, Noah knew the PA had been on duty since six, dealing with the urgent-care walk-in patients. Yale and Noah alternated covering that early-morning shift.

Before alerting his staff that he'd arrived,

Noah switched on his computer, typed in his password, and opened up Elise Whitmore's file. With his new knowledge of her personal situation, he wanted to determine if there were any signs that she'd been a battered spouse. He was relieved to discover that he'd never treated her for any kind of injury that would indicate she'd been abused.

Next, Noah checked the list of the day's appointments. He liked to take a few minutes to prepare himself before answering questions or dealing with problems. For the most part, he treated acute illnesses and managed chronic medical problems. Anything more serious was referred to a specialist, and emergencies were transported by ambulance to the county hospital.

Today's agenda looked fairly typical, starting with Mayor Geoffrey Eggers's bimonthly blood pressure check and weigh-in. Eggers had exceptionally low blood pressure that hadn't responded well to changes in diet, increased fluid intake, or decreased consumption of caffeine. Noah suspected that the mayor's low weight and refusal to exercise contributed to his condition, but the man seemed incapable of putting on any pounds.

After signing out of the scheduling program, Noah put on his white lab coat and left his office. At the main desk, he greeted Madison, who smiled at him from her perch behind the check-in counter. She was in her early twenties and wore a pale-pink smock. Blond curls framed her heart-shaped face, and a tiny silver locket dangled from a chain around her neck.

Noah nodded to the full waiting room and asked, "What's going on?" Generally there were three patients scheduled per hour—one each for Noah and the PA, and one being prepped by the nurse.

Madison grimaced. "Most of them came in about an hour ago. Apparently, there was too much chlorine in the high school pool, and the six a.m. senior water aerobics class had a bad reaction."

"How's Yale doing?" Noah asked, studying the dozen or so people waiting to be seen. Several were scratching their arms and legs; others were coughing, sneezing, and rubbing their eyes.

"He's been with one woman for quite a while." Madison's baby-blue eyes were clouded with worry. "She was wheezing and she complained of chest tightness and shortness of breath."

"I'll go see if Yale needs any help with her." Noah did a quick head count, then mentally scanned the schedule he'd just looked at. "In the meantime, please see how many of this morning's patients are coming in for routine monitoring. Then try to contact them and postpone their appointments to another day."

"Gotcha." Madison reached for the phone.

"Mom's already got the mayor in exam one. Do you want me to ask if he can come back?"

"No." Noah was tempted, but it would take less time to see him than to deal with Geoffrey's petulance if he felt he wasn't being given his mayoral due. "I'll take care of him as soon as I check with Yale."

The PA assured Noah that the woman's allergic asthma reaction had responded well to the medication and inhaler she'd been given. He also informed Noah that he'd triaged the others and determined they were suffering from either contact dermatitis or allergic rhinitis—both of which were uncomfortable but not life threatening.

Promising to help deal with the remaining chlorine victims as soon as he'd finished with the mayor, Noah hurried to where Geoffrey was waiting.

He was seated on the examination table, but he got off when Noah walked into the room. "I've been waiting here for fifteen minutes, Doctor." The mayor scowled. "And I don't appreciate the implication that my time isn't as valuable as yours."

At well over six-foot-six and weighting in at a mere one hundred and seventy pounds, Geoffrey looked like a paper doll wearing an expensive suit.

"I apologize, Geoffrey." Noah stepped around the tall, gangly man, typed his password into the computer, and peered at the screen. "As you may have noticed when you came in, there was an emergency."

"That's not my problem." The mayor sat back down, slouching and ducking his head, then muttered, "No one looked as if they were dying."

"I see you've gained a pound since I saw you last," Noah noted, ignoring Geoffrey's whining. He scanned the readings that his nurse had typed into the mayor's chart. "But your BP is still only sixty-two over forty. Have you been doing the exercises I suggested?"

"When I have time." Knitting his scraggly eyebrows together over his beaklike nose, the mayor shook his head and looked self-righteous. "A city like Shadow Bend doesn't run itself, you know."

"How are you feeling otherwise?" Noah asked. "Any dizziness, fainting, lightheadedness, nausea, or blurred vision?"

"No."

"Lack of concentration, fatigue, depression, or rapid breathing?"

"Well . . ." Geoffrey smoothed the sides of his black pompadour. "I'm pretty damned depressed that our town has had its first murder since I took office. Elise Whitmore ruined my perfect record."

"I'm sure she wouldn't be happy about it, either," Noah commented with a straight face. "That's if she were still alive."

171

"And Kincaid's incompetence will end up costing the town a bundle if he doesn't start looking at someone other than Boone St. Onge as a suspect."

"Oh." Noah rested a hip against the small counter that held the computer. "Why is that?"

"St. Onge is a member of one of the founding families of Shadow Bend. After the scandal Kern Sinclair caused, we can't afford another pillar of the community suspected of a crime."

"Of course not." Noah pretended to agree with the mayor in order to keep him talking.

"Not to mention, St. Onge is a lawyer, so he'll sue our asses off if he's not found guilty." Geoffrey shook his head. "And I heard the prosecutor didn't feel there was enough evidence to even charge him."

"Anything else?" Noah's posture remained relaxed and his tone casual.

"I know for a fact there are several other people with much better motives than St. Onge to kill that woman." Geoffrey pursed his thick, rubbery lips, then blew them out. "Her husband, for instance. Ninety-nine times out of a hundred, the spouse is the killer."

"That's interesting." Noah's tone was encouraging. "But you said several other people. Who else do you think had it in for Elise?"

"Whitmore's mistress." Geoffrey glanced around the tiny room as if he expected the paparazzi to be hiding behind a chair, then lowered his voice. "Did you hear who he was banging?"

"No," Noah lied.

"Me, either." Geoffrey's expression was remorseful. "But whoever it was probably thought if she killed the old ball and chain, Whitmore would marry her." He *tsk*ed. "They all want that piece of paper so they can lead you around with a ring through your nose."

"Really?" Noah glanced at his watch. As much as he wanted to help St. Onge, he had to wrap this up and start dispensing antihistamines and corticosteroids to the chlorine sufferers in his waiting room. "Are there any other people who wanted to see Elise dead?"

"Let me think." The mayor screwed up his face and tapped his jutting chin with a bony finger. "Well, there's Lindsey Ingram. She's the woman from the advertising agency Elise worked at. She and Elise were both up for the same promotion, so Lindsey had a good reason to want her competition out of the picture."

"How do you know that?" Noah was astounded by the amount of gossip the mayor had at his fingertips. It must have taken an enormous amount of time to gather all the bits of information. Maybe he considered jumping to conclusions his way of exercising.

"They both pitched a promotional campaign for the town to me." Geoffrey got up and moved toward the door. "And that meeting was a real catfight."

"What on earth does the town need PR for?" Noah asked.

"To increase tourism." The mayor looked as if he expected to be praised for his wonderful idea. "There's a lot of money in the travel industry."

"You've got to be kidding me."

"Not at all." Geoffrey's stance oozed contempt, and he looked down his nose at Noah. "Although I understand that not everyone is as forward-thinking as I am. Which is why when I was approached to become mayor, I agreed to sacrifice my career and take the position. I knew that I could lead Shadow Bend to greatness."

Noah let go the matter of spending town money to attract sightseers, and Geoffrey's so-called sacrifice, and zeroed in on the key issue. "Even if Elise and Lindsey were competing for the same job, that doesn't mean Lindsey was willing to kill over it."

"Wrong!" Geoffrey jabbed a finger in Noah's face. "Lindsey said to me, and I quote, 'I'll do whatever it takes to get that promotion. I'll lie, steal, and sell my firstborn if that's what I need to do.'" The mayor smirked. "Now, tell me. Doesn't that sound like someone who is willing to commit murder to get what she wants?"

CHAPTER 15

According to the note Gran had left on my bed the previous night, she'd won big playing the penny slots on her casino bus trip—eighty-eight dollars and fifty-three cents, to be precise. Plus she'd scored a free buffet and a frozen ham, which explained why I could hear her whistling as she cooked breakfast.

I was relieved that she was in a good mood. Yesterday, before she left on her outing, she'd held me hostage on the phone for half an hour while she lectured me about Noah's shortcomings and Jake's virtues. She didn't normally interfere with my life, but on this matter she'd pretty much decided that Noah had single-handedly started the Iraq war and Jake should receive the Medal of Freedom.

Therefore, my first problem of the day was to sidetrack her before she asked me if Noah had been with me at Boone's last night. I'd mentioned my plans to see him, but not why or who else would be there. I also didn't want her to question me about the Jake situation. She wouldn't be happy with either of my answers, and I had too much on my mind to come up with lies that she'd accept.

Because of that, I kept up a steady stream of

chatter as I entered the kitchen and poured myself a cup of intelligence from the coffee machine. Unfortunately, I eventually had to take a breather in order to gulp down a much-needed hit of caffeine, and Gran pounced.

"I should make you get your own breakfast," she threatened as she placed three sausage links on my dish. "I told you that going to that dance with Noah Underwood on Saturday was a bad idea." I opened my mouth to protest, but she cut me off. "And when were you going to tell me you had lunch with him on Sunday?"

"Never," I muttered too low for her to hear. "Does never work for you?"

"What?" She peered at me suspiciously, and when I didn't respond said, "I hope you're happy." She turned and grabbed a pan from the stove; then as she spooned scrambled eggs on to my plate she grumbled, "It's all over town that you're dating Noah Underwood again."

"I'm sure that's not true." I knew my being seen with Noah would cause some gossip, but I'd hoped it wouldn't get out quite so widely or quite so soon.

"It was the talk of the senior bus trip. I told everyone that going to the uh . . ."

"Fund-raiser," I supplied.

"Right, you going to the fund-raiser with him was strictly business." Gran grudgingly plopped a slice of toast next to my eggs. "But when they brought up your lunch with him the next day, what could I say?"

"Did they mention it wasn't just Noah and me? Poppy was there, too, and she and I sat together."

Gran ignored my excuse. "What will Jake think when Tony tells him that the minute he leaves town, you're seeing someone else?"

I had to bite my tongue to stop from reminding Gran that Jake had stood me up and hadn't contacted me since his message on Saturday. And that he was probably spending a lot more time with his ex-wife than I was with Noah. Only the fact that I hadn't told Birdie that Jake worked with Meg, and that I didn't want to discuss his continuing lack of communication, kept me from mounting a defense.

Gran took my silence as a victory, and she ordered, "You need to make it clear that you aren't involved with Noah before it's too late."

I thought about what had happened in Boone's driveway last night and was afraid that train might have already left the station. What had I been thinking to let Noah kiss me that way?

Birdie sat down to her own breakfast and continued. "You need to tell everyone who comes into the store today how you can't wait for Jake to get back to town and that he calls you twice a day."

"So you want me to lie?" *Shoot!* That had slipped out of my mouth before I could stop it.

Note to self: Drink a lot more coffee before having early-morning conversations about my love life with Gran.

She paused, narrowed her eyes, and swallowed the bite of sausage she'd just taken, then said, "To which part of that statement are you referring?"

Uh-oh. When Gran started using agonizingly proper grammar, I was in trouble. "Uh, well, Jake doesn't call me twice a day."

"Okay . . ." She drew out the word. "You can leave that bit out."

Phew! I really needed to change the subject before she tried to pin me down any more, so I asked, "Who was the bank president when Dad worked there?" I didn't exactly like this topic any better, but I wanted to know if Max Robinson had been in charge when my father was accused of embezzlement. If I had some idea whether he would hold my dad's actions against me, I could be better prepared when I spoke to him.

"Our esteemed mayor." Gran raised a feathery white brow. "Why?"

I explained about Elise trying to get her husband fired, then added, "So Boone wants me to talk to the current president, Mr. Robinson, and see how she was attempting to accomplish that feat." I left out the part about Noah coming with me.

"Max was the branch manager back then." Gran

nibbled on her toast. "He really lucked out when your father was wrongfully arrested."

"Why is that?"

"Since Kern was vice president, he would have been next in line for president when Geoffrey Eggers decided to resign and run for mayor." She took a sip of her coffee. "As it turned out, when the bank's owner demanded the board hire someone local, Max was the only one left for the top position." She put down her cup. "Considering that Max's father was a drunk and never held a job for more than a month or two, Max has done all right for himself."

"I'm glad someone profited from our family's misfortunes." Suddenly, I lost my appetite. I stood, took my half-full plate to the counter, and scraped the remaining food into the compost bin under the sink. "The town sure hasn't benefited from Eggers as mayor, and the Sinclair name took a nosedive with Dad's conviction."

Leaving my grandmother nodding her agreement, I went to finish dressing and headed for work. On Tuesdays, both the Scrapbooking Scalawags and the Quilting Queens met at the store, and I needed to pick up goodies from the bakery for their breaks.

The sprinkling of snow we'd gotten overnight was already melting as I turned onto the street that marked the perimeter of the village square. This place was the heart of Shadow Bend. It always reminded me of why I loved my town, and the bandstand was my favorite part. The eight white cast-iron columns framed my memories of summer concerts, and the decorative arches that linked the pillars made me remember gazing up through their intricately carved curves, seeing the never-ending blue sky, and realizing that the world really was a place of boundless possibilities.

As I did six out of seven days a week, I cruised the four blocks leading to my store. For some reason a sense of peace settled over me as I passed the familiar landmarks. The first on my route was the Shadow Bend Savings and Guaranty Bank's Greek revival building, then the newspaper's unadorned cinderblock structure, Little's Tea Room in the Queen Anne, and the movie theater with its limestone façade and Art Deco entrance.

Last was the bakery, and since there was a parking spot right in front, I pulled to the curb. At eight thirty in the morning, there were only a few people on the sidewalks, but I could see through the bakeshop window that the place was packed.

Shadow Bend had a deeply divided population. The locals, mostly farmers, ranchers, and factory workers, had lived in or around the town all their lives. The transplants were mostly people who had relocated to the area either to raise their families in a wholesome atmosphere or to build

McMansions on the cheap land that was available.

Almost all of the newcomers were willing to face a long, arduous commute into the city to fulfill their dreams. Problems arose when the move-ins felt the town should adjust to them rather than vice versa. Honking your horn at a slow-moving tractor or attempting to take over the PTA in order to stop the school children from saying the Pledge of Allegiance were just a couple of ways in which the Johnny-come-latelies had alienated themselves from the natives.

Then there was the man who had called city hall and requested the DEER CROSSING sign near his house be removed. He told the road commissioner that too many deer were being hit by cars so he didn't think it was a good place for the animals to be crossing. The locals had gotten a good laugh over that guy.

Because I had worked in Kansas City for many years but always lived in Shadow Bend, my goal was to make my store a spot where both sets of people could feel comfortable. Unlike the upscale health club that catered mostly to the newcomers or the bakery where the townies hung out, I was determined to offer a place where the two factions could find some common ground and perhaps build some bridges.

The craft groups that I hosted were a start. The members included both natives and transplants.

Another of my triumphs was the kids who hung around after school. Early on, I had made it known that if I saw any evidence of cliques, discrimination, or bullying, everyone would be kicked out, not just the guilty parties. And since there was no other place in town that allowed the teens to gather, they self-monitored in order to keep their welcome with me.

As I pushed open the bakery's door, the enticing aromas of cinnamon, brown sugar, and yeast drew me inside. The half-dozen tables were filled with regulars. The white-collar crowd—real estate agents, insurance representatives, and the like—were reading newspapers or networking as they finished up their morning coffee and pastries. The others, mostly senior citizens, were chitchatting over donuts. One of the latter groups called me over, and an elderly man whom I knew but whose name I couldn't remember said, "What's the scoop with Boone St. Onge?"

"Uh." While I was relieved that they didn't ask about Noah and me, I didn't want to discuss Boone's situation, either. Then again, maybe they could tell me more about Elise and Colin.

A sweet-looking old lady who reminded me of Aunt Bee from *The Andy Griffith Show* tugged at my sweatshirt sleeve. "Is it true that he killed that woman because he wasn't able to get it up?"

"No!" I yelped. Where had that come from? "Boone didn't kill her, not for any reason," I quickly corrected her. "He had a strictly professional relationship with the victim."

"Then what was he doing in her house at eleven o'clock at night?" asked Mrs. Gordon, the mother of Noah's physician assistant.

"As a favor to Mrs. Whitmore, he was escorting her to a late-night event in the city." I paused to think over my next statement—would it help or hurt Boone? Deciding it could be useful to spin the story in a positive direction, I added, "Off the record, she was afraid of her husband, so she wanted her attorney present." There. I had given them another suspect, and by telling them that something was confidential, it guaranteed that the info would spread faster than caramel poured on top of a hot pecan roll.

"Colin Whitmore does have a temper," the first man commented.

"Really?" I was itching to take notes but knew that wasn't the approved protocol when participating in a round of Shadow Bend gossip. Like any other game, there were rules that had to be followed. "How do you know that?"

"I was in the bank once when Whitmore was screaming at one of the tellers about something the poor woman had done to make the computer break down."

"Ah." This was good intel, but I had to get to the store soon, so I needed to wrap things up. Still, I couldn't resist asking one more question.

"I didn't know Mrs. Whitmore. Was she a nice person?"

"She didn't do much business in town. People like that frost my buns." Aunt Bee's look-alike *tsk*ed. "And she did create quite a scene when she caught her husband at the motel with his dick out."

The mouth on that sweet little old lady continued to amaze me, but I certainly shared her outrage at people who refused to buy locally. Smiling, I said, "It's sure true that my dime store would be in real trouble without its loyal customers." I discreetly checked my watch. Quarter to nine. "Who was the girl Colin was with?" Let's see how much of a secret Willow's identity really was.

The group looked at one another, but no one seemed to know. Mrs. Gordon threw her hands up. "I don't recall ever hearing who she was."

"Well, I've got to get going and open up the store," I said, backing away. "It was good talking to you all. Please let all your friends and neighbors know that Boone is innocent."

After I picked up my bakery order—an assortment of Mexican hot chocolate cupcakes, peanut butter cup cookies, and browned-butter whole wheat muffins—I quickly drove to the store and started setting up for the day. The crafters began to arrive at the same time Hannah reported for work. I assigned her to the register and drafted a couple of the quilters and scrap-bookers to move tables and chairs from the storeroom. Generally, I liked to have everything ready, but I couldn't afford to hire more help.

Regardless of how strapped for cash I was, I never regretted buying the business. Not only did it give me the chance to spend more time with my grandmother, but I'd been able to save the place from becoming another cookie-cutter drugstore. When the Thornbee twins, age ninety-one, had decided to sell the five-and-dime, their only other offer had come from a pharmacy chain.

The twins' grandfather had built the dime store when Shadow Bend was no more than a stage-coach stop, and, lucky for me, the thought of the business being turned into a Rite Aid or CVS had dismayed them. Which was why they'd chosen to take my much-lower bid.

Every day when I walked into my shop, I said a silent thank-you to those women. As far back as I could remember, I had always loved this store. When I was six, my father had taken me here to pick out my Brownie uniform and all the accessories. Gran always let me come with her to the store whenever she went in to buy a sack full of her favorite sassafras candy sticks. And the day I turned thirteen, my mother allowed me to buy my very first grown-up book—a Harlequin romance—from the shop's spinner rack.

What with the two craft groups and the regular

customers, the morning's business was brisk. Predictably, it tapered off right about eleven forty-five. Fifteen minutes later, the store had completely emptied out and Hannah left to attend her afternoon classes.

Once I was alone, I checked my messages. Poppy had texted that Boone was in a fairly good mood when he went to the PD, and Boone himself had left a voice mail saying that the cops had mostly repeated their questions about his relationship with Elise and her divorce, then let him go. That wasn't the best scenario, but at least the police hadn't rearrested him.

I had just started working on the Stehliks' bon voyage basket when the sleigh bells above the entrance jingled and a young man carrying a large thermal cooler bag strode inside. He was in his early twenties and dressed in city chic—skinny jeans, black leather jacket with the hood up, and canvas sneakers.

He stopped just over the threshold and looked around; then, spotting me at my worktable, he jogged over and asked, "Are you Dev Sinclair?"

"Yes, I am." I ran the guy's face through my mental Rolodex but came up blank. He wasn't one of my regular customers and I didn't recall seeing him around town, either. "Can I help you with something?"

"I have a delivery for you." He plopped the carrier on the counter.

"But I didn't order anything." I peered suspiciously at the bag.

He took a notebook from his back pants pocket and flipped through it. "Well, it says right here that this stuff goes to Dev Sinclair at Devereaux's Dime Store on the main street in Shadow Bend."

"But—"

"Oh, yeah. I forgot that I picked this up on my way over here." He cut off my protest, then said, "Here," as he thrust an envelope into my hand.

I removed the pale-blue cardboard rectangle, saw the familiar handwriting, and my heart skipped a beat. The note read:

Dev,

There's been an emergency and the clinic is swamped with patients that need immediate treatment. I won't be able to call you until early evening, or maybe later. I'm sorry, but we'll have to postpone visiting Max Robinson until tomorrow.

I remembered that you like sushi, so I ordered an assortment for your lunch.

Noah

P.S. The delivery guy's been tipped already.

Touched by Noah's thoughtfulness, I stood unmoving for a few seconds until I noticed the delivery guy tapping his foot. Aware that there were no sushi restaurants within a thirty-mile radius of Shadow Bend, I gave him a ten-dollar bill, then sent him on his way. Once he was gone, I examined the three black plastic containers on the counter. Through the clear lids, I could see beautiful creations that were truly works of art.

There were avocado, spicy tuna, salmon, and shrimp tempura rolls, as well as kappa maki, unagi, and maguro. It was considerably more food than I could eat in one sitting, and I found myself wishing that Noah were there to share it with me. I'd had my first taste of the exotic treat years ago when he'd taken me to a sushi restaurant in the city. It had opened my eyes to the world outside our small town, an event I'd never forgotten.

Thinking about that date made me check to see where Noah had ordered the food. When I saw that it was the same place where we'd eaten as teenagers, I had to swallow the lump in my throat.

Having this lunch delivered from Kansas City had been expensive, but money didn't mean very much to Noah. What really moved me was that he had remembered what we had shared and that maybe the experience meant as much to him as it did to me.

CHAPTER 16

For a split second I considered putting the sushi containers back in their bag and going over to the clinic to share the meal with Noah, but a couple of things stopped me. One, I would have to close the store, which I did only in an emergency. Two, and more important, what if I was reading too much into the gesture?

Having been thwarted by my insecurities, I texted Poppy and asked her to join me for lunch. I knew she'd enjoy the treat. And since she was one of the few people I trusted completely, I decided it was time to tell her everything and get her opinion on the Noah situation.

Ten minutes later, Poppy and I were sitting at my worktable, eating slices of kappa maki and drinking the pot of tea I'd brewed while I waited for her arrival. As we scarfed down the cucumber roll, I revealed all the stuff I'd been keeping from her—Jake working with his ex, Noah wanting to be back in my life as more than a friend, my ambivalence over the newly rekindled feelings I had for him, and my confusion about his feelings for me.

Poppy nodded and chewed until I ran out of angst. When it was clear I had no more to add, she said, "Are you nuts? Of course Noah is still in love with you. He never stopped. You were the one mad at him, remember?"

I shrugged. That wasn't exactly how I recalled the situation, but I didn't want to argue.

"The real question is whether you're in love with him." Using her chopsticks to lift a piece of sushi from the plastic container, Poppy paused with the slice near her lips. "Or are you just pissed off at Jake?"

"I—I'm not . . ." I stuttered to a halt. Trust Poppy to cut to the heart of the matter.

"Of course you are," she chided, then popped the morsel into her mouth.

I was silent as she chewed. She was right. I was a tad upset over Jake's behavior—if a tad equaled the amount of water in the Mississippi River.

Swallowing, she asked, "But is it your heart or your pride that's wounded because Jake stood you up and hasn't called?"

"I don't know." My shoulders slumped. "And I hate not knowing."

"Sure you do." Poppy arched a brow. "You're almost as much a control freak as I am." She grinned. "I'm surprised you don't bug the dime store like I do the bar. Especially the craft corner. It must kill you not to know what they're all saying back there."

"*Moi?*" I teased, then sighed. "My real problem is that I vowed never to let my emotions get the best of me ever again." I grimaced. "Love has not exactly worked out for me in the past."

"Yeah," Poppy commiserated. "It's always sucked for me, too."

"So why do we even try to find someone to be with?" I knew not to mention her ex. Poppy never talked about her divorce or the man she referred to as Sir Jerkalot. "We should just take a vow of chastity. I mean, clearly it's hopeless."

"The drive is biological." Poppy selected a slice of unagi but paused before eating it. "Look at Willow Macpherson. She risked a huge book deal in order to boink Colin Whitmore."

I picked up a piece of spicy tuna roll. "Talk about making bad choices." I *tsk*ed. "Willow's has to be right up there with the Stupid Idea Award winners from the past—like Arnold Schwarzenegger and his love child or that congressman who was caught posting pictures of his hot dog on Twitter."

"Exactly."

"So why are you hooking up with Tryg?" I asked. "You know that's got to end badly."

"He whispered my favorite words when we were at the mall."

"And they were?" I had no idea what she meant, just that it wasn't a marriage proposal.

"He said, 'I'll buy it for you.' "

I laughed and shook my head.

"Hey, all men are animals." Poppy snickered.

"Some just make better pets. Which is exactly why I get what I want from a guy and then make sure I'm the first to say good-bye." She frowned. "That way, at least they're the ones who get hurt—not me."

"That means I should forget both Noah and Jake." I pointed to the box of erotic-basket supplies stashed below the table. "These things can take care of any biological urges, and, unlike a man, they do it without the risk of a broken heart or various diseases."

"And I thought I was unromantic." Poppy chugged the last of her tea.

"Like so many things that get too much hype, romance is highly overrated." I stood and started to clear away the debris from our meal.

"Sort of like Steve Jobs being so wonderful." Poppy snorted.

"Right." I nodded. "And the Prius being the best car that was ever invented."

"Did you hear about the survey that claims that the first thing a man notices about a woman is her eyes?"

"No." I made a face. "But I did hear that the first thing about a man that a woman notices is that he's a liar."

"So true." Poppy sighed. "If love were really blind, sexy lingerie wouldn't be half as popular as it is."

Having agreed that true love was a fairy tale

perpetuated by Hallmark, Harlequin, and sappy movies, we turned our conversation to Boone's precarious situation. However, there wasn't much new to add. The biggest lead we had was Elise trying to get Colin fired, and I promised to call Poppy as soon as Noah and I talked to the bank president.

Poppy and I finished cleaning up our trash from lunch and I waved good-bye. Once she left, I assembled the items I would need for my next project. In addition to the Stehliks' bon voyage order, I had two other gift baskets to complete before the afternoon rush started. Between the baskets, then, later, the customers, I worked steadily until closing time at six.

After locking the door, I finally had a chance to check my cell, but Noah hadn't called, so I headed home. During the short drive, my thoughts darted back and forth between the murder and my love life.

While I was putting together a birthday-bash basket, I'd remembered the pies that Noah had brought to Boone's the night before. One of them had been French silk, my favorite. Had he remembered that I liked it, or had his choice been a coincidence? *Hell!* For all I knew, French silk had been the pie shop's flavor of the day.

When I walked into the house, I could hear Birdie talking on the phone in the kitchen. "No. I don't think he's contacted Dev since he left."

Damn! She had to be referring to Jake. I tiptoed closer to the kitchen's entrance, wanting to know who was on the other end of the line. The way my luck had been running, it was probably the local newspaper's new gossip columnist. No one knew the identity of the writer, but "The Bend's Buzz" was a huge hit. It undoubtedly sold more papers than all the other articles combined—including the high school football scores and grocery store coupons.

Birdie had the telephone on speaker, so she could continue cooking as she spoke, and I was relieved to recognize Tony Del Vecchio's voice when he said, "Jake's boss let me know that she and Jake are undercover as boyfriend and girlfriend. She said they and the rest of their team probably wouldn't be able to risk being discovered by calling again. They don't even carry their private cell phones when they're on a case like that."

Ah-ha! I'd been right. Jake's boss was Meg, so that meant he was with his ex. And not just spending time with her, but spending time as a pretend couple.

"Jake and Dev together are as cute as a speckled pup in a red wagon under a Christmas tree," Tony said. "And that boy is plumb crazy about her, so I know he'd call her if he could."

My heart accelerated when Tony said that Jake was crazy about me. Then I realized it was probably wishful thinking on his part. He and

Gran were on a mission to see Jake and me together, and they wouldn't let a little thing like reality stand in their way.

"Humph." Birdie clearly didn't care what Jake's excuses were. She glanced around, and I eased back where she couldn't see me. "When you do finally speak to Jake, you better let him know that he's got some serious competition, so he needs to get on the ball. Dev isn't sitting around waiting for him."

"Son of a biscuit!" Tony's voice held a mixture of concern and disapproval. "It's only been a few days and she's already carrying on with someone else? What did she do, put an ad in the paper?"

"Of course not." Birdie sounded offended. "Besides, to be fair, Dev claims they're not dating." Gran heaved a sigh. "But she's seen him every day since Saturday." She took a pan of corn bread from the oven and set it on a wire rack. "And he's a sneaky bugger, so he's probably working on her each time they're together."

"Hmm." Tony paused. "I guarantee you that if Jake gets in touch with me, I'll light the fuse on that rocket and let him know that there's a rooster in his henhouse."

"You do that." Birdie put the potholders in the drawer. "Tell him my daddy always said that your fences needed to be horse-high, pig-tight, and bull-strong. And Noah Underwood talks a lot of BS."

Birdie said good-bye, hung up the phone, and yelled, "I heard you come in the door, so you might as well show your face."

"Good for you." I stepped into the kitchen and grabbed a bottle of wine from the fridge. "It didn't stop you from practically offering a dowry for me." I poured a glass of the zinfandel and admonished, "You and Tony need to back off. Jake and I are fine."

"Humph!" Birdie stirred a pot on the stove, and the heavenly aroma of homemade chili wafted through the air. Waving the wooden spoon in my direction, she demanded, "Did you see that man today?"

"No." Which was true. She hadn't asked if he sent me a message or bought me lunch.

"Do you plan on seeing him again?" She pushed me out of the way and started to set the table.

"Yes, I do plan on seeing Noah." I took the silverware out of the drawer and grabbed the napkin holder from on top of the fridge.

"Why?" She transferred the chili from its pot to a serving bowl.

"Well, for one thing, because he's helping us prove that Boone is innocent." I gave her the lone reason that she couldn't debate. "He's got a lot of connections that Poppy, Boone, and I don't have."

Gran grunted, unable to argue with that; then a

nanosecond later, she regrouped and demanded, "Did you at least do what I told you to about nipping the uh . . ."

"Rumors," I supplied

"Right." She nodded. "The rumors about you and him in the bud?"

"No." I fetched the butter dish and corn bread. "Did you really expect me to tell people that stuff about Jake?"

"Yes, I did." She grabbed the bottle of Jack Daniel's from the cabinet above the stove and poured a healthy slug into a tumbler.

We both sat down, and Gran spooned chili into her bowl, then heaped chopped onions and shredded cheddar cheese on top. I followed suit, and we ate in silence.

Finally Gran pushed away her empty dish and said with a phony quaver in her voice, "Lord knows that I don't ask you for much." She pretended to wipe away a teardrop, but I wasn't fooled. "So I thought you'd be willing to do the one thing I begged you to do for me. Especially since you know how very much it means to me."

"Sorry," I said. And I was sorry that I couldn't do what she wanted, but she was asking for something she didn't have the right to request. "Look, Gran. You've never tried to run my life before, and you can't start now."

"I'm not," she protested, her expression

stubborn. "It's just that I don't want you to make the same mistake that I made with Tony."

Birdie and Tony had dated when they were teenagers. He was a couple years older than she was, and she had refused to marry him before she graduated. So when he finished high school, he enlisted in the Marines. It was near the end of the Korean War, and when Tony ended up missing in action, Birdie married someone else—my grandfather.

"And what mistake was that?" I asked. Gran had never been willing to discuss the matter, but maybe now was the time to clear up the mystery.

"Missing out on the love of my life." She paused and patted my hand. "Not that I didn't love your grandfather, but in a different way."

"So why did you marry Grandpa so soon after Tony went MIA?" When Jake had first told me Birdie and Tony's history, there was a lot going on in my life—I'd been accused of murdering Noah's fiancée—and afterward I'd been reluctant to question Gran.

"That's not important." Birdie took a gulp of Jack Daniel's, then drained the rest of the whiskey and in a shaky voice whispered, "I don't want to discuss it. Some things are best left unsaid."

I was still deciding whether to press her for an answer when Gran roused herself and jumped up from the table. She immediately started clearing away the remains of our supper and shook her head when I tried to talk, so I stopped. If she wanted to practice better living through denial, that was her right.

Instead I got up to help, and while the sink was filling with hot, soapy water, she put the leftover chili and corn bread in Tupperware, and I returned the containers of onions, cheese, and butter to the fridge.

Once she started washing dishes, Gran seemed to recover from her emotional upheaval. After a few minutes, she said, "Just promise me one thing."

"What?" I asked cautiously, wiping a bowl dry and returning it to the cupboard.

"That you'll wait to hear from Jake before doing something you might regret with Noah." Gran put a handful of silverware into the basket and rinsed it.

"Okay." I could do that. I planned to take things extremely slowly with Noah, anyway. If we could be friends and if he had really changed, then maybe he and I could move forward, but I wasn't counting on it. "I promise."

"That's all I ask." Gran dried her hands on the crochet-topped kitchen towel hanging from the drawer's handle, then hugged me. "Now you can have dessert."

I was forking a bite of strawberry shortcake into my mouth when Banshee wandered into the kitchen. The cat rubbed against Gran's leg, purring, and she fed him a bit of the whipped cream. As I watched the ancient Siamese pretending to be a sweet kitty, I remembered Elise's Russian Blue.

What with Noah's sushi delivery, and my busy day at the store, I'd forgotten about the poor little creature. Tonight I would call Colin and see if he had the animal. That is, as soon as I figured out an excuse for my interest. And if he didn't have the cat, tomorrow I would get up early and go look for it.

CHAPTER 17

After supper, Gran and I settled in to watch television. Well, she watched until she fell asleep, and I stared at the screen while I tried to figure out how to ask Colin Whitmore about his cat. It was eight thirty before I came up with a semi-plausible reason.

I had briefly considered having Boone contact Whitmore, acting as his wife's attorney, but I quickly rejected that notion on the grounds that Colin probably hated Boone for representing Elise. Unless, of course, Whitmore believed Boone had killed her, and then I had no idea how Elise's husband would feel about him.

My next thought was to have Poppy go over to

Whitmore's house to ask him in person. She was so insanely beautiful, most men didn't question her motives and were more than willing to give her whatever she wanted—whether it was information or a new car. But what if Colin was the murderer? Sending my BFF alone into a possible killer's home didn't seem like something a friend should do.

That left me with only one idea, ludicrous as it seemed. Since Gran was asleep on her recliner with Banshee curled up on her lap, I went into my bedroom and closed the door. I didn't want to disturb her or take the chance that Colin would overhear her snores.

Whitmore answered on the first ring, and I said in a businesslike tone, "This is Ms. Jones from the Shadow Bend Department of Animal Control. May I speak to Mr. or Mrs. Colin Whitmore?"

"This is Mr. Whitmore." Colin sounded puzzled. "How can I help you?"

"Do you have a medium-size gray cat with green eyes?" I had researched Russian Blues online, so I would know what Tsar looked like.

"Uh. Well, uh," Colin stuttered. "It's really my wife's pet."

"So you are not the legal owner?" I was hoping he'd say no, but that he had taken the animal for safekeeping since his wife had passed away.

"Why do you ask?" Colin's tone held a tinge of distrust.

"This evening at approximately eight twenty-seven, a cat was rescued by one of our officers. He got your number from the tag on its collar, but, unfortunately, soon afterward the animal escaped."

"My cell number was on the cat's tag?" The suspicion in Colin's voice increased. "Why would Elise put my number there?"

"I'm sure I have no idea." I tried to sound as officious as possible. "Perhaps there were several numbers listed and our officer was only able to remember yours." It was time to ask what I really wanted to know before he figured out I wasn't legit. "Which is why I'm calling. We're hoping that the animal went home."

"Sorry." Colin's voice indicated that he had lost all interest in the discussion. "As I said before, the cat was my wife's pet, and she's dead. If that worthless piece of crap went anywhere, it would be back to her house. And since that woman was bound and determined to strip me of every possession I had ever worked hard to attain, I am no longer living at that residence." He paused, then muttered, "At least not until the cops release it as a crime scene."

"So you don't have the animal in your custody?" I figured I could ask one, maybe two questions before he ended our conversation.

"No." I heard him take a drink of something and then belch loudly before adding, "And if you find the little bugger, get rid of it. I always hated cats, and that one in particular, which is why that bitch I was married to loved him." Then Colin hung up.

That had gone better than I'd hoped. Not only had I confirmed that Whitmore didn't have Tsar, but I had also heard firsthand the animosity he had for his wife. The only downside was that the animal was still missing. But, hey, you win some and you lose some.

I had a few more calls to make in my quest for the cat, and I lucked out with the first one. The dispatcher who answered the police department's nonemergency line was an old high school classmate of mine. She and I had been on the speech team and in the drama club together, and she was willing to check the reports. She put me on hold, and when she came back on the line, she informed me that there was no record that the police had found a pet in Elise's house during the murder investigation.

My second call was to the real Animal Control. Again, the gods were smiling on me, because although the office was officially closed, one of the employees was working late and picked up the phone. He told me that they hadn't picked up any stray cats in the past week or so, which meant I'd be kitty hunting the next day. After thanking the Animal Control guy, I went to tell Gran that I needed to get up early and would be skipping breakfast.

Since she and Banshee were still sleeping in front of the TV, I left her a note. Once I checked my phone one last time to see if Noah had called or texted—he hadn't—I set my alarm for six a.m. and went to bed.

Wednesday morning, my eyes popped open to the sound of Pink singing "Raise Your Glass." Fighting the urge to turn off the radio, forget about finding Tsar, and go back to sleep, I forced myself upright. Once I had showered, I hurriedly dressed and grabbed a can of Full Throttle Blue Demon energy drink from the fridge. I figured I'd need the caffeine boost and I actually liked the agave flavor. Thus fortified, I set out to find Elise's missing cat.

I wasn't sure why it had become so important to me to find Tsar, but my conscience wouldn't allow me to rest until I had made every effort to locate the AWOL kitty and make sure he was okay.

Since Colin had been crystal clear about his loathing for the animal, what I would do with the cat when I found him was another question entirely. Banshee would never allow another feline in his domain. And I didn't want Tsar to become a midnight snack for the old Siamese, like my aforementioned gerbil.

A quick call to Boone the night before had confirmed that he was okay and spending the evening with Tryg. Before we hung up, I'd asked Boone for Elise's address. My plan was to start at her house and search outward from there. I'd go as far as I could before I had to open the store at nine. If I hadn't found the cat by then, I'd have to try again the next day, because on Wednesdays the shop didn't close until nine p.m.

Armed with a bag of Banshee's Temptations kitty treats, his seldom-used Pet Taxi, and a can of Fancy Feast, I drove to Elise's place. Her subdivision was only fourteen years old, new by Shadow Bend standards. It had been built on a forty-five-acre apple orchard a couple of miles outside of town.

When the parcel's previous owner passed away, a Kansas City developer had offered the heirs four times more money than any of the local farmers were able to bid. Since his kids weren't interested in keeping up the family tradition of working the land, they persuaded the city council to rezone the tract from agricultural to residential, and the sale went through without a hitch.

Now there were 250 houses instead of rows of trees laden with Red Delicious and Jonathan apples. Which was why I hated housing developments. The hypocrisy of tearing out a stand of trees and then naming the streets after them made me want to scream.

My GPS led me right to Juniper Lane and Elise's door. I parked my Z4 in her driveway, then grabbed the pet paraphernalia. Since I already had enough to handle with the cat gear, I locked my purse in the BMW. As I pocketed the keys and adjusted my load, I looked over the Whitmores' property.

The nondescript ranch-style house with beige vinyl siding and an attached garage took up three-quarters of the lot. There was no porch and only a small concrete front step. The three scrawny shrubs under the picture window offered no place for a cat to hide.

I circled around to the rear of the structure. There was a single tree in the tiny backyard and some kind of evergreen hedge growing against a wooden fence. The bushes' branches poked me as I edged past them, checking for Tsar, but all I found was a flattened Budweiser can, a deflated balloon, and two plastic grocery bags.

With no sign of the feline in the Whitmores' yard, I widened my search. Making my way down the length of the fence, I repeatedly shook the treat bag and called, "Here, kitty, kitty."

As I walked, I hoped that no overvigilant homeowner got the idea to shoot me for trespassing. Elise's street was only two blocks long and she lived on the corner, so when I got to the other end, I crossed the road and headed back down the opposite side.

Making my way through the neighborhood, I noticed that three basic house models alternated up and down the street: Elise's ranch, a boxy two-story, and a trilevel. All of them had meager lawns, neutral siding, and a mind-numbing uniformity.

No one was outside, which wasn't surprising at a few minutes before seven. Most of the nine-to-five folks would still be eating breakfast, and those who worked eight to four or attended school would already be gone. But the silence and sense of abandonment was a little eerie, almost as if everyone else had been sucked up into the mother ship and I was the only one left on earth.

Deciding to try the next block over, the one in back of the Whitmores' place, I strolled down the side street. So far, I hadn't seen any outdoor animals and very few spots where a cat might find shelter. Had Tsar already left the neighborhood for greener pastures?

The home directly behind the Whitmores' had a miniature Cotswold cottage playhouse in its backyard. The diminutive Tudor bungalow boasted imitation stucco siding, a green asphalt-shingle roof, and window boxes brimming with bright red silk geraniums.

I was peering into the upper half of the playhouse's cute little Dutch door, admiring the simulated antique plank flooring, faux fireplace, toy grand piano, and sleep loft, when a thirtysomething-year-old man wearing crisply pressed jeans, a snow-white button-down shirt, and a sky-blue crewneck sweater appeared beside me.

"What are you doing?" His voice was tinged with hostility. He pointed to what I had been assuming was a playhouse—although it appeared to be nicer than any of the *real* houses I'd seen on the block—and said, "If you're another neighbor intent on meddling, I cleared this with the homeowners' association."

Before I could respond, he continued. "If I'd had any idea how narrow-minded and nosy all of you were, I'd never have bought this place."

When he took a breath, I quickly explained, "I don't live around here." I reached in my pocket and handed him my business card. "My name's Devereaux Sinclair and I own the local dime store. I apologize for trespassing. I'm looking for a lost cat." I showed him the Pet Taxi, can of food, and bag of treats I was holding.

"Oh." He smoothed back his short brown hair. "Sorry. It's just . . ."

"No problem," I assured him. "I take it your family has recently moved here and you haven't had a very friendly welcome."

"Precisely." He stuck out his hand. "I'm Bryce Grantham."

"I'm sorry to hear that." I shifted the stuff I was carrying into my left hand and shook Bryce's hand with my right.

"I guess I should have investigated a little more thoroughly." He shrugged. "But the price was so much lower than the Kansas City suburbs, and the school has a good rating. . . ." He trailed off again, then said, "Would you like me to help look for your pet? What's its name?"

"If you have time, that would be terrific. This is taking longer than I thought. His name is Tsar and he's gray." I paused, considering whether to admit I wasn't the owner. When I couldn't think of a good reason not to, I added, "Actually, he's not my cat."

"Then he belongs to a friend?" Bryce bent over to examine a pile of wood stacked near the house's sliding glass doors.

"Not exactly." I checked a humongous bird feeder mounted on a platform near the deck. "Did you hear what happened Saturday night?"

"You mean the murder?" Bryce asked as he walked toward the next yard.

"Uh-huh." I followed him. "Tsar belongs to the woman who was killed."

"It was all anyone could talk about at the neighborhood watch meeting Monday night." Bryce hooked his thumbs in his back pockets. "Everyone is scared to death and talking about getting guns and pit bulls."

"Damn!" I hadn't thought about that when I worried earlier about somebody shooting me. Bryce walked with me toward the next yard. How could I not realize that the neighbors would have a right to be fearful after a murder occurred nearby? "I guess I'm lucky no one set their dog on me this morning while I've been poking around their yards."

"I think you'd be all right if they did." Bryce grinned. "The association rules currently have a weight restriction on pets. No animals over twenty pounds." He pursed his lips. "I had to cut back on the Beggin' Strips or my daughter's poodle, Sweetie, would have failed the weigh-in."

I chuckled at the image of a fluffy little dog on a *Biggest Loser*–type scale; then, as I looked under a parked car, I asked, "Why is there a neighborhood watch? We don't generally have a lot of crime in Shadow Bend. Heck, a lot of folks don't even lock their doors."

"They tell me there's been some vandalism and a few bikes have been stolen." Bryce's expression was skeptical. "But my guess is the guy who runs the patrol just wants an excuse to spy on everyone."

"Do you know if the police talked to the neighborhood watch?" I asked.

"Yes." Bryce moved the leaves of a hydrangea bush to check behind it. "As a matter of fact, Chief Kincaid was at the meeting. He questioned both guys who had been on patrol that evening."

"Did they see anything?" I stepped onto a concrete bench and scrutinized the nearby roofs.

I wasn't sure how a cat would get up that high, but since they were able to climb trees, they might.

"The block captain said he noticed a guy skulking around Elise Whitmore's street about half an hour before the body was discovered."

"Was he able to give a description of the man?" I asked, holding my breath, hoping that information could clear Boone.

"Yeah. But it was pretty vague." Bryce shook his head. "He said the guy was average height and maybe a little on the paunchy side."

"What made him suspicious?" I asked. Boone was tall and thin, so the police couldn't say he was the skulker. "I mean, even if you all know everyone who lives around here, couldn't he have been visiting someone? Or had a business appointment?"

"The guy was wearing a baseball cap with a suit and had on dark glasses even though the sun had gone down a couple of hours ago."

"Okay, that is definitely odd," I agreed. "Someone dressed like that would have certainly caught my attention." I wondered what Colin Whitmore looked like. "Did the block captain do anything about him?"

"No." Bryce shook his head. "Too bad they didn't report him to the cops." Bryce straightened from peering into a hollow log and smirked. "But I guess he was afraid to."

"Why?"

"Because the neighborhood watch has gotten into trouble for crying wolf one too many times." Bryce narrowed his eyes. "Sort of like when they called the building inspector about my daughter's 'unsafe' playhouse—which turned out to be just fine."

I glanced at my watch, then said, "It's quarter to nine, so I'll have to leave and try again tomorrow." We'd searched all the yards on Bryce's street and I started back toward the Whitmores' house. "I can't thank you enough for helping me."

"I'm happy to." Bryce smiled. "I'll keep an eye out for Tsar when I walk Sweetie."

"That would be great." I smiled back. "Give me a call if you see him." Before I turned to walk away, I asked, "What's the name of the guy in charge of the neighborhood watch?"

"He goes by Captain Ingram," Bryce answered. "I never heard his first name."

"Thanks again." I waved. "Bring your daughter to the dime store sometime, and the hot fudge sundaes are on me."

"I'll take you up on that." Bryce gave me a considering look, then waved back and disappeared down the street.

CHAPTER 18

I hated leaving Gran alone for the twelve hours that my shop was open on Wednesday, but the supplies and refreshments I sold to the Blood, Sweat, and Shears sewing group that met at six p.m. helped keep the dime store in the black. So I compromised and called home every few hours to monitor how Gran was doing and to see if she needed anything.

After another busy morning, I finally got a breather around one. I'd heard my cell phone chirp several times but hadn't had time to look at my messages. So once I checked in with Gran, I scrolled through my missed texts as I ate the leftover sushi that I had stowed in the mini fridge in my storeroom.

The first was from Noah. He apologized for not calling the night before, explaining he hadn't left the clinic until nearly ten o'clock. He was hoping to be less busy today, and he would get in touch with me when he had a break between patients.

The other texts were from vendors and auction sites, and I answered queries and made bids between bites of spicy tuna roll. Once I was finished with lunch, I cleaned up my worktable and got busy creating the nostalgia basket that the high school class of '78 had ordered to raffle off at their reunion.

Before I made much headway, I saw Poppy's Hummer pull in to the parking spot in front of the display window. I was surprised to see Boone get out of the backseat and Tryg get out of the driver's side. The attorney walked around and opened the passenger door for Poppy, and as she took his arm I spotted a new diamond bracelet on her wrist.

When the trio entered the store, Poppy and Tryg were holding hands. Bringing up the rear, Boone caught my eye, shot a look at their joined fingers, and raised his brows. I shrugged. What could I say? Girls like diamonds and guys like chrome.

Boone and I both knew there was nothing we could do except hope that Poppy's affair would run its course and neither she nor Tryg would get hurt. It was harder for Boone, since he was friends with both of them, but my concern was for my BFF.

Boone took a seat on a stool at the soda fountain and the happy couple followed suit. I put down the Atari 2600 video game system that I had been trying to stand on edge against the silver spangled disco cape and came out from behind the register.

As I went to the soda-fountain counter, Boone said, "I need a dark chocolate malt. Hell, after what I've been through, make it a double."

"Coming right up, Boone." I started to scoop

the ice cream. "What can I get for you guys?" I asked, nodding to Poppy and Tryg.

"The usual," Poppy ordered. "And Tryg will have the same."

"Two turtle sundaes with extra whipped cream and nuts," I confirmed.

"How long have you owned this place?" Tryg asked, twisting around to study the store. "Has it been in your family for generations?"

"Nope. My people were farmers." I slid a tall fluted glass brimming with chocolaty goodness in front of Boone. "I bought it less than a year ago from the original owner's ninety-one-year-old twin granddaughters."

While I ladled caramel and hot fudge over vanilla ice cream, Tryg quizzed me about the business. As I answered him, I wondered what had brought the trio to my store in the middle of the workday.

I finished up the sundaes with a generous sprinkling of pecans and a tower of whipped cream and placed the dishes in front of Poppy and Tryg, then leaned my elbows on the counter and asked, "So, what's up?"

Tryg ignored the sweet concoction in front of him and said, "I thought it best if we consulted regarding Boone's interview at the police station yesterday. We all need to be on the same page."

"That sounds good." I poured myself a cup of coffee. "Let's hear it."

"I don't know why we have to go over this again," Boone complained. "They mostly asked me exactly what they had before, again and again."

"Boone." Tryg's voice was firm. "You promised to cooperate."

"Fine." Boone played with his straw. "They wanted to hear about my relationship with Elise, why I was at her house, and what I did second by second from when I found her body to when I called nine-one-one." He took a sip of his milk shake. "See? Nothing new."

"You left out a couple of things," Tryg prodded, taking a notebook from the pocket of his polo shirt. "What else did they ask about?"

"They wanted to know if I had seen anyone lurking around Elise's house when I got there." Boone snorted. "Like that wouldn't have been the first thing I'd have mentioned when I was arrested that night."

"Hey." I raised my hand. "I think I know why they questioned you about that."

"Do tell," Boone drawled. "Is Chief Kincaid confiding in you now?"

"No." I swatted Boone's arm. Being a murder suspect was not bringing out the best in my friend. After explaining about my search for Tsar and the neighborhood watch, I concluded, "It looks as if they called you back into the station as soon as they heard about Baseball Cap Guy skulking around Elise's house."

"Interesting." Tryg narrowed his eyes. "Too bad Boone didn't see the man."

"What's really too bad is that Captain Ingram didn't call the cops," I said. "If he had, the murder might have been prevented, or at least the actual killer might have been caught."

"Did you say the head honcho is a Captain Ingram?" Poppy asked.

"Yes." I grabbed a leftover peanut butter cup cookie and munched.

"Wasn't the woman who blew the whistle on Colin Whitmore's affair named Lindsey Ingram?" Poppy licked caramel from her spoon.

"Maybe." I bit my thumbnail. "I'm not really sure. I didn't pay that much attention to *who* had exposed Colin's affair with the pet sitter. The rest of the story was the interesting part."

"Is Ingram a common last name in these parts?" Tryg asked.

"There aren't any Ingram families among the longtime residents around here," I said. "At least not that I'm aware of." I thought it over. "Nope. It doesn't ring a bell." I looked at my friends. "You?"

They both shook their heads. Then Poppy said, "I'll bet the captain is Lindsey's husband. Remember, Noah didn't know if she was local or not." Poppy pursed her mouth. "But if you think about it, if she was dropping off papers from work, it makes sense that she lives in the same neighborhood as Elise. If she were from Kansas City, would she drive two hours round-trip to deliver something to Shadow Bend? Isn't that what courier services are for?"

Boone tapped his fingers on the marble counter. "It sure would be odd if the woman who put the Whitmores' divorce in motion is married to the one man who saw someone loitering around Elise's house on the night of the murder. And I don't believe in coincidences. What if Captain Ingram made up this suspicious guy in order to draw attention away from his wife?"

"But why would Elise's colleague want to kill her?" Poppy asked.

"First we need to find out if Captain Ingram is married to Lindsey," Tryg cautioned. "Then we'll worry about a possible motive."

"You're right," I agreed. "Someone needs to investigate that."

"You can ask your new pal," Boone suggested. "Bryce Whatshisname."

"Grantham," I supplied. "I didn't get his phone number, but I can ask him tomorrow when I go look for Tsar again." I stared at my friends. "Anyone want to join me?"

None of them responded, and I narrowed my eyes. "Seriously, no one is willing to help?"

"Well," Boone refused to meet my gaze, "it's been five days."

"Actually, maybe longer," Poppy joined in.

"Boone said he didn't see him Saturday night, so maybe he ran away while Elise was still alive. He's probably long gone, or maybe someone adopted him."

"Thanks, pals." I grabbed the empty sundae dishes and slammed them into the water-filled sink.

Ignoring my displeasure, Poppy glanced at Tryg and said, "You mentioned there were a *couple* of things Boone left out about the police interrogation." She turned to Boone. "What's the other one?"

"It's not important." Boone slurped up the last of his drink.

"It's hard to tell what's important at this stage," Tryg countered.

"Well," Boone hedged, "I don't see how this could be significant."

"Boone." Tryg's voice held a hint of warning. "You promised to follow my advice, and I advise you to tell your friends everything."

"If you insist." He glared at his lawyer. "They found a jacket of mine at Elise's and wanted to know what it was doing there." Before anyone could ask, Boone continued. "It started raining one day while she was at my office and I didn't have a spare umbrella to loan her, so I gave her my old raincoat to wear home."

I glanced at Poppy, whose doubtful expression matched mine. Had Boone been having an affair with a client? And did we really want to know if he had been? If the police ever questioned us, it was probably best that we could honestly say we had no knowledge of his relationship with Elise—or with any other woman, for that matter.

Tryg broke the long silence that had fallen by asking me, "Did you discover anything when you talked to Whitmore's employer?"

"Noah had an emergency at his clinic yesterday so we haven't been able to talk to the bank president yet," I explained.

"What a surprise." Boone sneered, but his expression held a trace of disappointment. "I knew Dr. Deceiver's act was too good to be true."

"Boone." I laid my fingers on his arm. "I know you're stressed and that under normal circumstances you wouldn't be this obnoxious. . . ."

"What do you mean by that?" He shook off my hand. "I'm not acting any differently."

"Yes, you definitely are." I ignored his protest. "And you need to knock it off right now. We're all trying to help you." I gave him a hard look. "Including Noah. But we all have other commitments, as well."

"Yeah," Poppy chimed in. "Quit being a jerk." She gave him a one-armed hug. "I heard that there was too much chlorine in the high school pool, and most of the six a.m. senior water aerobics class had a bad reaction, so they were all rushed to Noah's clinic."

"A few extra patients that early in the morning shouldn't have kept Dr. Dutiful busy all day." Boone crossed his arms and pouted.

"Unfortunately, the aerobics instructor was so discombobulated when the seniors started dropping like flies, she failed to tell the school that there was a problem," Poppy explained. "Which resulted in the first-period swim class also having problems."

"Still," Boone objected. "How long could it take to hand out some salve and eye drops? If Dr. Devoted really wanted to help me, he would have."

"My source tells me that one of the seniors and several of the teens had severe asthma problems, which the overchlorinated water exacerbated." Poppy sighed. "Seriously, Boone, it's time to get over your grudge against Noah. He's doing the best he can."

I had kept silent, knowing that if I tried to defend Noah, Boone would be even less likely to see reason, but now I said, "Will you be mad at me because I can't go talk to the bank president today?"

"No." Boone shook his head. "I realize that the store is open late today and you don't have any help and can't afford to close it."

"Good." I patted his shoulder. "Just cut Noah the same slack. Okay?"

Boone nodded grudgingly, then said, "Shouldn't

someone be talking to Willow Macpherson? None of us has contacted her yet, right?"

We all shook our heads. Then Tryg said, "Yes, one of you should probably speak to her. Do any of you have an in with her?"

We all shook our heads again. Then Poppy said, "I'll check to see if any of my regulars at the bar have any kind of connection to her."

"I'll do the same with my customers," I offered, then added, "And I'll see if Birdie or her crowd has some kind of link to her."

"I can ask around, too," Boone said. "Unless I shouldn't?" He looked at Tryg.

"If you're extremely subtle," the attorney warned. "We don't want the police claiming that you're interfering with their investigation."

"Right," Poppy scoffed. "Like my dad will even hear about Willow unless we tell him." She paused. "Actually, shouldn't we tell the chief about the other people who have motives?"

"Let's wait until we have more facts." Tryg rubbed his chin. "Right now, I believe the authorities would brush off our information, thinking we're scrambling to clear Boone."

"Which we are," Poppy said. "Still, maybe we could make an anonymous tip."

"If Boone is called in for questioning again, we'll throw everything we have at them," Tryg said. "But until then, I believe our best move is to gather as much evidence as we can, because once the police get wind of the other suspects, we'll be closed out."

We all agreed to do what Tryg thought best, and the impromptu meeting ended. The attorney insisted on paying me for the soda-fountain treats they'd all consumed, and I admit my respect for him skyrocketed—at least for a second—until it crossed my mind that he'd turn around and bill Boone for the cost.

It was three by the time the trio departed, so I put my basket-making supplies away and braced for the afterschool onslaught. Then when the last of the kids left around five, I called Gran to touch base again. We had our standard conversation: She assured me she was fine and called me a worrywart.

Once I was sure Birdie was okay, I checked my messages to see if Noah had called. He had. There was a voice mail from him saying that he'd remembered the store was open until nine on Wednesdays, but that it closed at noon on Thursdays, so he'd gone ahead and arranged for us to have lunch with Max Robinson. He'd pick me up at twelve thirty and we could go together.

I texted back my agreement, then started setting up the craft corner for Blood, Sweat, and Shears. As usual, Winnie and Zizi were among the first arrivals. The mother-and-daughter duo exploded through the store's entrance, arguing about a book they'd both read.

Winnie marched up to me and demanded, "What did you think of that novel?" She shrugged out of her coat and winked at me. "Since you make erotic baskets, I bet you liked it."

"I haven't read it." The title she was referring to had been popular a while back, but I'd never gotten around to taking a look at it.

"It's nothing but mommy porn," Zizi insisted, crossing her arms.

"Lighten up, buttercup." Winnie poked her daughter, then turned serious. "Before I forget, I heard about Boone being a suspect in Elise Whitmore's murder, and I wanted to say that Zizi and I think the pigs are crazy to suspect him."

"Thanks." The quick change of subject left my head spinning, but I appreciated Winnie's support.

"Absolutely," Zizi said. "And if you ever need someone to run the store while you investigate— you are going to help clear him, right?" When I nodded, she continued. "Mom and I will be happy to come in and cover for you."

"Definitely." Winnie patted my arm. "This town wouldn't be the same without either you or Boone."

"Thanks again." The idea of Winnie in charge of my store scared me half to death, and I wasn't all too sure of Zizi, either. "It's so sweet of you guys to offer to help."

"Don't worry, kid." Winnie gave me a thumbs-up. "We've got your back."

Luckily, at that moment, several other members of Blood, Sweat, and Shears walked in and saved me from responding. The next three hours passed in a blur, and by the time the last of the sewing group left a little before nine, I was pooped. Although I wanted to forgo cleaning up, I knew that if I was cat hunting again the next morning, I'd better have the place ready for business before I left. So I lugged the folding tables, chairs, and sewing machines into the back room, then swept the floor.

Finally satisfied that the store was all set for the next day, I put the cash drawer into the safe and turned off the lights. I had already locked the front entrance when the last of the sewers left, and I had parked my Z4 in the rear lot, so I headed out through the back door.

Just as my hand touched the car door handle, a male voice behind me said, "Boo."

I screamed and jumped back, hitting my head against someone's hard chin. The last thing I saw was a pair of dull brown eyes peering down at me as my vision blurred and I passed out.

CHAPTER 19

Jake Del Vecchio, don't you ever sneak up on me like that again." Having recovered from my momentary swoon, I was now sitting inside a beat-up 1969 Dodge Charger, bawling out a man I barely recognized.

The guy I'd been dating for the past month was dazzlingly handsome. The dude in the driver's seat next to me looked like a cross between someone who had been sleeping on the streets and a member of a motorcycle gang. My Jake was clean-shaven with a lean, chiseled profile and bronzed skin that pulled taut over the elegant ridge of his cheekbones. This character hadn't been near a razor in several days, and his complexion was a pasty gray.

The man I'd been seriously considering sleeping with had gorgeous, silky black hair and striking sapphire-blue eyes. This guy was bald and his eyes were the color of a cow patty. He didn't even smell the same. Jake's scent reminded me of fresh air and newly mown fields of hay, while this dude stank of cigarettes, stale beer, and sweat.

Clearly, he was undercover, but the changes in him were stunning. How had he accomplished such a complete transformation in such a short time? Obviously, he'd started shaving his head and stopped shaving his face, but how had he changed his skin tone from suntanned to nearly dead white? Was he wearing makeup?

The different eye color could be contact lenses, and the odor was easily achieved by not bathing, but he didn't even appear to be six-four anymore, and his well-muscled body now seemed to be thicker and less toned. There was no way he'd gotten shorter and gained weight in the five days since I'd last seen him.

The only parts of him that were familiar were the strong column of his throat as it rose from the collar of his scuffed-up leather jacket, the hard thighs straining the fabric of his worn blue jeans, and the large calloused hands resting on the steering wheel.

I noticed all this while I continued to yell at him for scaring me half to death. Finally, once I'd calmed down enough to think, I demanded, "And why haven't I heard from you? Were you too busy getting reacquainted with Meg?"

Okay, I shouldn't have added that last sentence, but it just slipped out. My only excuse was that I was still freaked by how he'd crept up on me while looking like a serial killer.

"I'm sorry." Jake held up his palms in surrender. "I thought you saw me when you walked out of the store and that you were just ignoring me because you were mad I'd broken our date."

"I wasn't angry about that," I lied. "I knew you

were going back to the marshal service as soon as you were cleared." I pasted a fake smile on my face and added, "By the way, congratulations."

"Thanks." Jake's expression was cautious. "But you are upset that I haven't been in touch and am working with my ex-wife? Because, let me assure you, even though Meg and I are together constantly pretending to be a couple, we are not together in any other way."

"While it would have been nice to have heard from you sooner, I understand that you were too busy to make a call or send a text," I lied again, ignoring his comment about his nonrelationship with his ex-wife.

"As you've probably guessed," Jake gestured at himself, "I'm undercover."

"Really?" I widened my eyes in mock astonishment. "And here I thought you'd changed fashion stylists." I wrinkled my nose. "Or maybe just hadn't been able to complete your usual hygiene practices."

"Okay, if you're not annoyed about the broken date or because I haven't called, then why are you so pissed off?" Jake raised an eyebrow.

That was a good question. Why was I so furious at him? It wasn't as if he hadn't warned me that he'd be leaving Shadow Bend as soon as his leg healed. Or that I was unaware that his ex-wife was his boss. So what was my problem? Could it be guilt about Noah?

"I said I wasn't angry and I'm not," I insisted. "I'm just tired and confused. If you're working a covert case, why are you here?"

"Well," Jake drawled, "I had a chance to make a couple of personal calls this afternoon. And since I wanted to save the best for last, I decided to talk to Uncle Tony before I phoned you. But it turned out he had such a lot of interesting local news to tell me, I ran out of time."

"So you came in person. How sweet." Uh-oh. Tony must have done exactly what Gran had told him to do—ratted me out to Jake.

"Yeah. Wasn't it?" Jake angled toward me so he could look me in the eye. "Uncle Tony said you and Noah Underwood have been seen together all over town. As I understand it, you went to a dance with him, then had lunch, and you even took him to a party at Boone's. Tony is real concerned and he strongly suggested that I talk to you ASAP."

"You knew that Noah and I had resolved our differences and that we were attempting to resurrect our past *friendship*." I emphasized the last word and crossed my fingers that I was telling the truth.

"That's what I told Uncle Tony," Jake said, his expression unreadable. "But for some reason, he seemed to think it was more than that."

"I wonder where he got that idea," I hedged, unsure of how much Tony knew. "Gran doesn't like Noah, so she probably exaggerated."

"Then you didn't go to a dance with him Saturday night?" Jake asked. His voice was casual, but the muscles in his jaw were clenched.

"That was purely business—Noah introduced me to someone who was interested in placing a large gift basket order," I explained. "And in case you didn't hear, Boone is under suspicion for the murder of one of his clients." I gave Jake a quick summary of what had happened, ending with, "So both the lunch and meeting at Boone's house were about trying to help him."

"I'm sorry to hear that Boone is in trouble." Jake wrinkled his brow. "He's a nice guy. I wish I was around so I could help, too."

"Yes, he is." I sighed and massaged my temples. "I wish you were around, too, because I think the local PD is in way over their heads and have no idea how to investigate a murder like this one."

"You're probably right." Jake scrubbed his face with his fists. "It's quite a bit different from the crimes they usually solve."

"Exactly." I frowned. "I'm pretty sure that Shadow Bend's finest usually spend Saturday nights breaking up bar fights, responding to car crashes, and arresting kids playing mailbox baseball."

"What the hell is that?" Jake asked. "And why is it illegal?"

"Teenagers riding in the passenger seat of a car

use a bat to knock over roadside mailboxes," I clarified. "They keep score using a system similar to baseball—a point for each dent, and decapitating a mailbox is a home run. They get three strikes, and then the next guy is up to bat."

"Sounds like a lot of fun." Jake rolled his eyes, then slumped back in his seat. "I assume there is alcohol involved?"

I nodded, and we sat in silence. Apparently, we'd both run out of things to say. After several uncomfortable minutes, I was about to suggest we call it a night when Jake cleared his throat.

"Look, I know we never talked about not dating other people," Jake said, then muttered, "and I don't have any right to question you."

"No." I sat back, totally exhausted. "You don't. Just like I don't have any right to ask how things are between you and Meg."

"And, really, we've only known each other a month and a half." Jake stared out the Dodge's cracked windshield. "So it would be silly to even consider demanding exclusivity of each other."

"Right," I agreed cautiously, knowing he was correct but feeling a sudden ache in my chest. "That would be really foolish."

"I guess I wasn't thinking straight when I dropped everything to hightail it over here because Uncle Tony had a feeling," Jake admitted.

"Probably not." I examined the many gauges in the dashboard.

"I may have blown my cover," Jake mumbled. "I can't believe I did that."

"Oh." I wasn't sure how to respond. Part of me was thrilled that Jake had put our relationship ahead of his duty as a marshal. "So you drove all the way down from St. Louis to see me?"

"Uh," Jake hesitated. "Actually, the case I'm working is in KC."

"You never were in St. Louis, like your message said?" I fought to keep the anger out of my voice. Why did the fact that he was so damn close make it worse that he hadn't contacted me until now?

"Yes, I was." Jake leaned toward me, seeming to sense my resentment. "I went up there on Saturday, was briefed about the assignment, and then Meg, the team, and I came back down to Kansas City on Sunday." He looked at his watch. "And speaking of that, I need to get back before they discover that I'm not where I should be."

"By *they,* I take it you mean Meg?" Yes, I knew I was being bitchy and stupid, but I couldn't help myself. Blame it on fatigue.

"No." Jake gritted his teeth. "By *they,* I mean my new best friends—the scum-sucking drug pushers who I'm trying to get to lead me to one of the cartel bosses who skipped bail. He's the perp I'm trying to catch." Jake shook his head. "We have to apprehend this douche bag before he finds the witness against him and kills her."

"Sounds important." I reached for the door handle. "I'd better let you go."

"Wait." Jake grabbed both my hands and pulled me toward him.

"Why?" A shiver ran down my spine, and a flash of heat swept through my body. "You need to get back to work, and I need to get home."

"I just . . ." He trailed off, dropping my hands to cup my cheek.

The touch of his palm against my face sent another shiver through me, and my pulse began to pound in my ears. I had to suck in a much-needed breath before I could ask, "You just what?"

"I don't want to leave without settling something." He stared into my eyes, and I could almost see the sexual charge zipping between us.

"Something?" I knew I sounded inane repeating his words, but, once again, I was completely ambushed by the intense attraction I felt for this guy.

"Where we stand." He gave me a sinful smile that had doubtlessly annihilated the resistance of nearly all the other women he'd tried it on.

"I thought we had." Sensual images zoomed through my mind, and I closed my eyes.

"Not quite." Jake drew me into his lap—thank goodness the car was too old to have a console between the seats—and then with his lips inches from mine, he said huskily, "I want to make sure

233

the next time you see Underwood, all you can think about is me."

His voice washed over me like sugarcoated temptation, and my breath caught in my throat. "Oh." It took all the breath I had to utter that one-word response.

"Yes." His whisper was ragged, and he stroked my jaw with his thumb.

I could feel his uneven heartbeats against my palms. There was an unquestionable pull between us, and I knew I should stop this. But before I could force myself to move, Jake closed the gap between our mouths.

His kiss took my breath away, and as he licked into my mouth, I squirmed closer to him. He wrapped his arms around me, and I surrendered.

I knew that with him back on the job as a marshal and with my renewed feelings for Noah, we shouldn't be doing this, but he was a craving that I was compelled to satisfy. I had nearly given in to my lust when a banging on the window made me jerk my head upward.

It took me a long second to understand what the blindingly bright light was, and when I did, I groaned. We had just been caught necking by Chief Eldridge Kincaid.

CHAPTER 20

Chief Kincaid apologized for disturbing us and explained that he'd thought we were teenagers. But he couldn't hide a slight smirk, and I was afraid that our little indiscretion would be the hot topic around the squad room coffeepot the next morning.

The police intervention had shocked both Jake and me out of lust and into our senses. Soon after the chief returned to his patrol car, I mumbled a quick good-bye, scrambled out of the Charger, and crawled into my Z4. As I watched Jake drive away, presumably heading back to Kansas City, I realized that he hadn't said when he'd talk to me again or if he'd be coming back to Shadow Bend anytime soon. Then again, I hadn't asked.

It was a good thing that Birdie had already turned in for the night when I got home. I was upset that I had allowed myself to get carried away with Jake, and I might have been tempted to hold her responsible for the whole shebang. After all, she *was* the one who had pushed Tony to snitch on me, which was why Jake had shown up and surprised me into acting foolishly.

With Gran already asleep, instead of yelling at her—which, let's face it, was never a guilt-free option—I scarfed down the lasagna she'd left for me and went to bed. I blamed the pasta for causing me to toss and turn, and the restless night for causing me to oversleep the next morning. But I took full responsibility for choosing to shower, apply makeup, and do my hair rather than look for Tsar.

I paid the price for my self-indulgence at breakfast when Gran eyeballed me from head to foot, then demanded, "Why are you so gussied up? Aren't you working at the dime store today?"

"Uh." I took a gulp of coffee, both for the caffeine and for the time it gave me to think, then hedged, "I'm meeting Max Robinson for lunch. Remember I wanted to ask him about Elise Whitmore's crusade to get her husband fired?" When Gran nodded, I explained, "I figured he'll tell me more if I look attractive."

"Humph." Birdie raised a brow as she plopped a ladleful of oatmeal in my bowl.

I reached for the brown sugar, but she moved it from the table to the counter. Clearly, she wasn't convinced by my excuse. I got up and silently retrieved the box, then sat back down and started to eat.

Gran joined me, and just as I took a large bite, she said, "I suppose Noah will be at this lunch with Max Robinson, too?"

I nearly spit the hot cereal back out, but managed to swallow before I said, "How in the world did you come to that conclusion?" I knew that I hadn't mentioned Noah when I originally told her about Boone wanting me to talk to the bank president.

"I may be so old that I fart dust," Gran retorted, "but I'm not as senile as you or those fancy doctors think I am."

Before I could protest, Gran went on. "It took me a while to figure it out, but I remembered that Nadine Underwood recently stepped down from the bank's board and her son was appointed in her place."

"And from that you think Noah will be at the lunch?" I asked, astounded by her thinking. "There are other board members."

Gran continued as if I hadn't spoken. "And in the past, Max Robinson has not been a friend of our family." She pursed her lips and slitted her eyes. "He was definitely part of the witch hunt when your father was accused of uh . . ."

"Embezzlement," I supplied.

"Right." Gran nodded.

"Okay." I hadn't known that. Then again, the adults had made every effort to keep me out if it when my dad was being investigated.

"So, I put two and two together." Gran smiled triumphantly. "Who has influence with the bank president and wants to get on your good side?"

"Noah." I conceded defeat and admitted, "Yes, he'll be at lunch, too."

"Which is why you're all dressed up." Gran's voice was smug, daring me to deny it.

"Of course it isn't," I vowed, unsure whether I was telling the truth or not. "Like I said, it's to make a good impression on Max."

Gran narrowed her eyes but thankfully didn't challenge my statement.

After a few seconds, I asked, "By the way, you wouldn't know a Willow Macpherson or a Bryce Grantham, would you?" I didn't truly think either of them hung out at bingo or was part of the crowd who went on the senior bus tours—Gran's usual haunts—but I was desperate for a change of subject.

"The first name doesn't ring a bell, but the second one sounds familiar." She tapped her chin. "Bryce Grantham. Where do I know him from?"

While she pondered, I took a sip of coffee.

"Now I remember where I heard that name." Gran nodded to herself, then said to me, "His little girl is in Frieda's catechism class."

"So he attends St. Saggy's?" I was referring to St. Sagar's Catholic Church. When I was seven or eight, I had asked the priest about the name, and although he'd explained who St. Sagar was, further questioning revealed he had no idea why Shadow Bend's Catholic church had been christened for a martyred bishop from Turkey. Not surprisingly, the parishioners called it St. Saggy.

"No." Gran shook her head sadly. "He doesn't come to Mass; just his daughter."

"So his wife is the churchgoer?"

"No. I don't think she's in the picture." Gran shrugged. "At least, I've never seen her or heard anyone mention her." She paused then tilted her head and questioned, "Why are you asking about him?"

"I met him when I was looking for Elise's cat." I got up and rinsed out my bowl. "He helped me search for Tsar."

"He does seem like a nice guy, and Frieda says his little girl is really sweet." Gran brightened. "If things don't work out with Jake, maybe you could go out with him. Then I'd have a ready-made great-granddaughter."

"Why are you suddenly so interested in my love life?" I demanded. "You've never shown any interest in who I dated before."

"You were never on speaking terms with Noah Underwood before."

Once I escaped from my recently turned match-maker grandmother, I hurried to work. Because the dime store was open for only three hours, the morning was busy with shoppers who needed to pick up a few things before we closed. When the crowd thinned a little around eleven, I slipped into the back room to make a call.

Paging through my seldom-used Shadow Bend

phonebook, I was happy to see a listing for Bryce Grantham. He picked up on the first ring and confirmed that Lindsey was married to Block Captain Ingram. He also reported that there had been no sign of Tsar. I thanked him for continuing to watch for the animal and vowed that I'd be back the next morning to continue the hunt.

After I said good-bye to Bryce, I texted Boone and Poppy the information that Lindsey did indeed live in town. Then, having completed my sleuthing responsibilities, I went back out front to resume my store-owner tasks.

Hannah left at noon, and I locked the door behind her. Next, I cashed out the register and took the drawer into the storeroom. Opening the safe, I saw the antique chocolate molds I'd bought from Elise and bit my lip. I was glad that I hadn't told anyone except Gran about them, since I still wasn't sure I had purchased them legally.

Easter was my favorite holiday. I always said that you could learn a lot from the Easter Bunny. He was a smart dude who didn't put all his eggs in one basket and knew that the best things in life are sweet and gooey. My admiration for Mr. Rabbit was why I had designed such an elaborate window display for the holiday. But considering that if the molds were Colin's, he might sue me, it was a good thing I hadn't included them in my window arrangement.

I ran my finger over the intricate designs, picturing the chocolate molds as the centerpieces of several of the Easter-themed baskets that Oakley Panigrahi had ordered for his high-end real estate clients. Normally, I'd never recoup my money putting something as expensive as these molds into a basket, but he'd agreed to pay as much as a thousand dollars apiece for a truly fabulous gift. And these antique chocolate molds would make a stunning presentation, one that I was sure would impress Oakley with the uniqueness and luxury of my concepts.

Still, I probably shouldn't use them. From everything I'd heard, it appeared that Colin Whitmore might be the true owner and that his wife had sold them without his permission. If I did give the molds back to him, it would have to be secretly, so that he never found out I ever had them. The last thing I needed was to be named in a lawsuit. Who could have anticipated that such wonderful objects would become such a problem?

I was torn. On one hand, restoring the collectibles to their true owner was presumably the decent thing to do. On the other, I knew my moral compass had grown a little wonky from working in the investment field for so long, and although I was trying to fix that, sometimes I wasn't sure what was right anymore.

If Colin was the legal owner, I should return them. But if he turned out to be the killer, he shouldn't gain from his crime, so maybe I ought to keep them. The fact that I'd be out eight hundred bucks that I could ill afford to lose made the decision even more difficult.

After several minutes of wavering, I pushed the molds to the rear of the safe, put away the day's receipts, and closed the door. I'd wait until Elise's murderer was caught before deciding what to do.

Checking my watch, I made a quick trip to the bathroom, where I hurriedly kicked off my Keds and exchanged them for black high-heeled ankle boots. Next, I put a pink tweed crop jacket on over my white long-sleeved T-shirt, then inspected my black jeans for lint. Satisfied, I applied lipstick and combed my hair.

A few seconds after I returned to the front of the store, I looked out the main window and spotted Noah's Jaguar pulling into a parking spot. I grabbed my purse and rushed outside, opening the passenger door before Noah could even get out of the car.

As I slid inside, I commented, "What great timing." I hoped things wouldn't be awkward between us, as this was the first time we'd been together since he'd kissed me in Boone's driveway.

"We were always on the same wavelength," Noah said as he refastened his seat belt.

"By the way, I don't think I ever thanked you for the sushi," I said, reaching for my own seat belt. "It was really sweet of you to send lunch to me when you couldn't call, but you didn't have to do that."

"I remembered you liked that place the last time we were there together." Noah smiled. "That date is one of my favorite high school memories."

"Mine, too." I impulsively touched his hand. "I'm so glad we've moved beyond the bad parts of our past and can enjoy the good times again."

"I always hoped we could." His gray eyes darkened, and he brought my palm to his lips. "I can't tell you how much I missed you."

Swallowing a lump in my throat, I murmured, "I know. I missed you, too."

Noah continued to hold my hand, caressing it with his thumb. We sat there gazing at each other until I realized we were parked on Shadow Bend's main drag, clearly visible to anyone driving or walking by. All I needed was to have Chief Kincaid pull up in his squad car and catch me with another guy or, worse, have one of Gran's cronies see us and report back to her.

"Uh." I cleared my throat and pulled my hand out of his. "We probably should get going. We don't want to be late. Which restaurant are we meeting Max at?" There weren't many choices in Shadow Bend—the new Chinese place, the pulled-pork wagon, and a family diner were about it.

"I know Max likes nice things, so I figured

we'd take him to the Manor." Noah started the Jag. "We might as well butter him up with a fancy meal."

The Manor was located on a man-made lake midway between Shadow Bend and the neighboring town of Sparkville. It attracted diners from as far away as Kansas City, catering to the affluent for both a fine dining experience and elaborate parties. I had never eaten at the restaurant, but I had been there not too long ago when Jake and I had wanted to talk to Noah, who had been attending a committee meeting being held in one of the banquet rooms.

The restaurant was both elegant and intimidating, so I was glad that I had dressed up. My usual Devereaux's Dime Store sweatshirt, baggy jeans, and tennis shoes would have been out of place. And ever since my father's incarceration and my previous boss's high-profile fraudulent activity, my goal in life was to blend in.

Noah and I chatted about Boone's case as he drove the fifteen miles to the restaurant. It was a sunny day and I was enjoying the scenery. We crossed a creek bubbling cheerfully over shiny rocks and then zoomed past a stubble-studded field with a trio of deer munching the stray corncobs that the combine had missed.

As we turned into the Manor's long driveway, Noah said, "Oh, I almost forgot to tell you. Geoffrey Eggers claims that Elise's colleague,

Lindsey Ingram, had a strong motive to get rid of her. He said that Lindsey and Elise were competing for the same job and that Lindsey claimed she'd do anything to get the promotion." Noah repeated his conversation with the mayor and finished with, "So someone should probably talk to Lindsey and see if she has an alibi for the time of the murder."

"Definitely," I agreed. Then after Noah handed his car keys to a valet and we climbed one of the twin marble staircases into the Manor's imposing brick building, I brought him up to speed on what I had discovered regarding Lindsey and her husband.

As we stepped into the stunning lobby, I once again admired the Thomas Moser chairs and the sideboard displaying a collection of Murano glass. I smiled when I heard the sound of a harpsichord playing Scarlatti's Sonata in B minor, because, unlike last time, I knew that it was a live performance and not a recording.

As Noah approached the hostess, I studied a pair of large gilt-framed paintings on the side-wall. On my previous visit, I hadn't been sure if they were original works of art, but since then I had asked around and now knew that they were indeed genuine.

I hadn't been surprised, since I had been fairly sure that the portraits were authentic. I had a good eye for spotting the real thing, which had served me well in my previous occupation, in which I had been required to have a working knowledge of the value and authenticity of artwork, antiques, and the other trappings of wealth. It was an odd job qualification to insist on, but Mr. Stramp had wanted his employees to be able to judge a client's bank account by his or her possessions. It was only after his Ponzi scheme was revealed that I realized why he really wanted that kind of information.

Interrupting my thoughts, Noah informed me that Max was already seated. A striking woman wearing an exquisite black wrap dress and red high heels led us past generously spaced tables filled with well-dressed diners having thoughtful discussions.

She showed us to a booth tucked into a corner away from the other patrons. It was obviously one of the best locations in the restaurant, and when she put her hand on Noah's arm and purred, "I hope this is satisfactory, Dr. Underwood," I shot Noah a knowing look. Clearly, he was on good terms with this hostess, as well as the one at the Golden Dragon.

"Perfect." Noah shrugged at me, then smiled at the woman. "Thank you, Anne."

Once the hostess had departed, Max stood and greeted us. I couldn't recall having met him before, which wasn't all that surprising. I did most of my banking electronically and went to the building only to deposit the store's receipts in the night drop-off slot. Heck, I'd even gotten my business loan online.

Noah and Max shook hands; then Noah introduced me to the bank president. Max assured Noah that he and I knew each other, which was a revelation to me, but I kept quiet and nodded pleasantly. As I studied the bank president, I saw that we were nearly the same height. His hair was unnaturally brown and along his side part I could see gray roots. He wore a gray Turnbull & Asser suit—a brand my father had favored—with a light-blue pinpoint oxford shirt and a burgundy tie.

Once the formalities were over, Noah and I slid onto one of the padded bench seats, and Max took the other.

Noah said, "Thank you for agreeing to have lunch with us, Max. We have a rather delicate matter to discuss and thought it would be best if we talked away from the bank."

"No problem at all," Max assured Noah. "I'm always happy to make myself available to one of the board members. As I said when we spoke on the phone last weekend, I feel strongly that my position is not a nine-to-five job and I'm at your service day or night."

"Nonetheless." Noah's tone was businesslike and his expression was impassive. "I appreciate your cooperation."

Before Max could respond, a server appeared at Noah's side and said, "Dr. Underwood, would you like your usual drink or are you in the mood for something new?" She gave him a suggestive look.

"The usual is fine, Mitzi." Noah smiled at the young woman. "Thanks."

She beamed back at him, then, with a show of reluctance, turned to me and asked, "May I bring you something from the bar, ma'am?"

"I can recommend the Concha y Toro Don Melchor Cabernet Sauvignon 2001," Max advised, holding up his glass. "It has a dazzling nose of black currant and roasted coffee, with a powerful but still smooth palate of cassis, plum, blackberry, loam, and dark chocolate. It glides down the throat through a superlong finish."

"Uh." I was still fuming about being called ma'am, but I realized that the wine Max was talking about was extremely expensive. Squirming, I said, "I'd better stick to iced tea—lots of ice and extra lemon, please."

How much cash did I have in my purse? Since I was on such a tight budget and didn't want to be tempted into an impulse purchase, I didn't carry a credit card. I did have one for emergencies, but it was in the store safe. While I was sure Noah would try to pay for this lunch, I couldn't let him. Boone was my friend and it was his problem we were trying to solve.

"Super," Mitzi bubbled. "Two iced teas coming up. I'll be right back."

For some reason, which made no sense at all, it delighted me that I had chosen the same drink as Noah. He must have been pleased, as well, because he squeezed my hand as it lay on my lap.

The three of us spent the next several minutes reviewing the menu. I silently gulped at the prices. When Mitzi returned with our drinks and we ordered, I again worried about how much cash I had with me. Noah and I selected two of the more modestly priced entrées, but Max chose the costliest item on the list: lobster pasta with truffle oil. Noah hadn't exaggerated when he said that the bank president liked nice things.

Once Mitzi left, Noah straightened and said, "Max, I'm sure you heard that someone killed Elise Whitmore last Saturday night."

"Yes." Max took a sip of his wine and said in a detached voice, "What a horrible thing to happen in our little town." He shook his head. "Most alarming."

"It sure is," I agreed. "And almost more disturbing is that the police suspect Boone St. Onge." I paused, trying to gauge Max's reaction. "Of course, there's no way Boone could ever be a murderer."

"I'll grant you, St. Onge doesn't seem the type." Max's gaze was flinty. "However, can you or anyone really say with absolute certainty that under no circumstances could St. Onge ever kill someone? Think of all the people who claim their neighbor the serial killer was such a nice, quiet fellow."

I opened my mouth to defend Boone, but Noah leaned back and said casually, "True. None of us can really say what someone else is capable of." He chuckled. "We probably don't know what we're capable of doing ourselves. But Dev and Boone have been friends since they were children, so of all people, she probably knows him best."

"Ah." Max murmured. "But what about all the wives and girlfriends who claim their husbands or lovers could never be guilty?"

He started to add something else, but he was interrupted by the server, who placed our salads in front of us and asked, "Does anyone want fresh ground pepper?" We all nodded, and when she was finished twisting the long wooden mill, she said, "Is there anything else I can get for you right now?"

We all murmured "No, thank you," and when the waitress left, Max said, "You do have a point, Noah. Dev doubtlessly has had more experience judging people's guilt or innocence than most people."

Hmm. Had he just suggested something about my father or maybe my previous boss? I wasn't sure how to respond and decided silence was my best option, since I didn't want to alienate the guy.

"Did you know that Elise Whitmore's husband works at the bank?" Max commented, then was silent as he devoured his salad.

"Actually, we did," I answered, then realized I should let Noah take the lead. Glancing at him, I indicated he should go on.

"That's why we wanted to talk to you." Noah squeezed lemon into his iced tea. "Rumor has it that Elise was trying to get Colin fired."

"Really?" Max asked, pokerfaced. "How do they say she was trying to accomplish that?"

"We're hoping you can tell us." Noah smiled blandly. "Since I assume the only way she could cause his dismissal would be through you."

The server reappeared and replaced our empty salad plates with our entrées. Once she left, Max said, "I suppose that's true." He forked a huge bite of pasta into his mouth, then took his time chewing and swallowing before he added, "I am the boss."

I continued eating as if I wasn't all that interested in the conversation, and Noah did the same. He silently telegraphed to me that we should let Max take matters at his own pace. The man obviously enjoyed having the power to make us wait, and pressing him would do no good.

Finally, when he was nearly finished with his

food, Max paused, took a gulp of wine, and remarked, "Now that I think about it, Elise did stop by my office a week or two ago for a little chat about her husband's morals." Max patted his lips with his napkin. "I believe she mentioned that he'd been having an affair with the help."

"Did she tell you the woman's name?" I asked, finding it semi-amazing that Willow's identity had remained such a secret.

"No." Max wrinkled his brow. "At least not that I can recall."

"Were you considering Elise's request to get rid of Whitmore?" Noah asked.

"Well." Max twirled the stem of his wineglass. "She did make a good point. She said that a place of business such as a privately held bank shouldn't employ people who behave unethically, but . . ."

"But?" I prodded. Seriously, could this guy take any longer to answer?

"The problem was that although I was fairly certain that the bank owner, Mr. Bourne, wouldn't approve of Whitmore's philandering"— Max heaved a sigh—"I also knew that he valued the young man's unique skills."

"Ah." Noah nodded. "You were between a rock and a hard place."

"Exactly." Max laughed, sounding like the bleat of a telephone receiver left off the hook for too long.

"So what did you do?" I was running out of patience and wondered what we'd have to do to get this guy to finish his story.

"I decided the correct procedure was to allow Mr. Bourne to make that call." Max picked up his fork and polished off the rest of his meal.

"So you passed the problem up to the top." I wasn't surprised. I was sure Max Robinson hadn't gotten where he was by acting rashly.

"It seemed the prudent course of action." Max patted his little potbelly—something his expensive suit couldn't hide. "That was a delicious lunch."

"Did you inform Mr. Whitmore about his wife's visit?" Noah asked.

"I thought it only fair to apprise him of the situation." Max reeked of pomposity. "That way he could update his resumé should Mr. Bourne instruct me to dismiss him."

Something about Max's statement didn't sound right to me, but before I could figure out what it was, the server approached our table and cleared the empty plates. She stowed the dirty dishes on a tray behind her, then offered us dessert menus. Noah and I declined, but Max grabbed the card, studied the selections, and ordered coffee and truffe framboise—fresh raspberries and kirsch-moistened chocolate cake layers surrounded by bittersweet chocolate mousse.

As we waited for Max's dessert and he and Noah chatted, I pondered what we'd learned.

There was a question I was forgetting to ask, but what was it?

A few minutes later, just before the server slid the confection in front of Max, it dawned on me, and I said, "How did Whitmore react to the news that his soon-to-be ex-wife was trying to get him canned?"

Before Max could answer, the waitress approached us, carrying a tray holding a cup of coffee. She must have tripped on something on the floor, because I watched in stunned silence as she stumbled and the cup slid off the tray and bounced against Max's knee, and the scalding liquid soaked the entire lower leg of his pants. He jumped to his feet, cursing, and pulled up the leg of his trousers.

The hostess rushed over, and she and the server mopped up Max, gave him a cloth full of ice to apply to the burn, apologized profusely, and offered him a gift card for his next visit. Once the commotion died down and Noah had examined Max's leg and pronounced it a minor injury, we all settled back in our seats.

As Max dug into his dessert, I said to him, "I noticed that your leg was already injured. What happened?" I'd seen several scabbed-over gashes on his left calf when he exposed his leg.

Max paused, took another mouthful of truffe framboise, chewed, and swallowed; then he looked at me and with a show of reluctance he said, "You asked how Whitmore reacted to the news that Elise was trying to get him dismissed from his job. This is the result." Max shuddered. "He kicked over the coffee table in my office. The glass top shattered and the shards flew everywhere, cutting my leg. I'm lucky one didn't take out my eye."

"And he's still employed by you?" Noah questioned.

"I notified Mr. Bourne about his outburst. Truth be told, I'm a little afraid to fire Whitmore at this point." Max blinked. "After all, look what happened to poor Elise."

CHAPTER 21

As the valet assisted me into the passenger seat of Noah's Jag, I was still mulling over what Max had told us about Whitmore's violent tendencies. I had barely buckled up when my cell chirped, indicating that I had a text. Since Noah was still in the process of tipping the attendant, I checked the phone and saw that I had a message from Tryg.

My stomach clenched as I read: BOONE'S BN ARESTD. I'M @ 5-O ST8N W HIM. LET'S MEET 2NITE @ POPPY'S APARTMNT N TLK. Why had they arrested Boone again? Did they find some new evidence that implicated him? I sure hoped that Tryg would let Chief Kincaid know that there were several other people who were better suspects than Boone. I especially couldn't wait to tell the attorney what we'd just heard about Colin Whitmore.

As soon as Noah got behind the wheel and I'd filled him in on this latest development, he asked, "Do you want to go to the PD?"

"No." I forced myself to be sensible. "Tryg's with Boone, and there's nothing I can do there." I tapped my fingers on the dashboard. "What I'd really like to do is talk to Willow, Lindsey, and Colin."

"Colin will be at the bank." Noah turned the Jag out of the driveway. "And Lindsey will probably be at work in Kansas City."

"I wonder where Willow lives and whether she works from home," I mused. "And another thing no one's mentioned: Does she still pet sit, or did she quit after she got the big book deal?"

"She lives with her parents," Noah said, not taking his eyes from the road. "Their house is a couple doors down from mine."

"So you know her?" Had he mentioned that when he first told us that Willow was the woman with whom Colin had been having an affair? I didn't think so. But, then again, why would he?

"Not really." Noah shook his head. "I've run into her a couple of times when I've been out with Lucky—she has a neighborhood dog-walking business—and we stopped and talked for a few minutes."

"Hey, that's more of an acquaintance than the others in our little investigative team have with her." I smiled at him encouragingly. "None of the rest of us has even met her."

"So what you're saying is that you want *me* to speak to Willow," Noah translated. "And see if she has an alibi for the time of the murder."

"Actually, I want you to introduce me to her and see if she'll talk to me," I corrected, figuring that Noah wouldn't be a tough enough interrogator.

"Well. Uh." Noah's face flushed. "The thing is, I get the feeling she might be more open to telling me what we want to know."

"Why is that?" Was there a reason Noah didn't want me to talk to her? Then, before he could answer, it dawned on me what he was trying to avoid saying. "I get it. Willow's been flirting with you, so if you show up with another woman, especially one she may have heard you used to date, she wouldn't be as likely to cooperate."

"I guess that's it," Noah admitted, looking a bit uncomfortable. "I've never encouraged her; she's too young for me both in age and maturity." He twitched his shoulders. "But you know how it is. I'm the only single guy under seventy in the neighborhood."

"I understand." And I did. Noah always had,

and probably always would, attract female attention. He was like catnip. What heterosexual woman didn't want a guy who was tall, handsome, successful, rich, and, best of all, nice? *Uh-oh.* Did that include me? Was I falling under his spell for all the wrong reasons?

"Thanks." He beamed at me. "You know, since we both have the afternoon off and we can't do anything for Boone until we talk to Tryg this evening, we could go to a movie or take a hike or—"

"Is it possible you could find Willow and talk to her before we meet with Tryg tonight?" I interrupted him. Spending more alone time with Noah was not a good idea, and we really did need to keep our efforts focused on helping Boone, especially since he was back in jail. "Do you have any idea where she might be?"

Noah gave me a disappointed look, but admitted, "I've seen Willow working on her laptop at Brewfully Yours a few times." He shrugged. "I think she uses the coffee shop as a sort of writing office. Since she lives with her folks, she probably doesn't have much privacy. I guess I could drop by and see if she's there."

"That would be great." I squeezed his arm affectionately. "Now, if I could only think of a way to make Lindsey and Colin talk to me."

"Why don't you call and request a meeting with Lindsey?" Noah suggested as he drove around to the back of the dime store and pulled his Jaguar to a stop next to my Z4. "You could tell her you want to discuss the possibility of an ad campaign for your business."

"That's not a bad idea." I thought about it for a few seconds, then asked, "Do you know the name of the agency she works for?"

"I don't think I ever heard it, but I'm sure Vaughn Yager could tell you." Noah put the car in park and turned to face me. "Remember, he dealt with her company regarding advertising for his factory. That's how he met Elise in the first place."

"Right." I nodded. "You know, I really can't thank you enough for everything you've already done and are about to do to help Boone. And I'm sorry you were stuck with the check at the restaurant. Let me run inside the store and get some money to pay you back."

"Don't worry about it. It's no big deal. Consider it my contribution to the Get Boone Out of Jail Fund." Noah cupped my cheek with his palm. "Investigating with you these past few days has been fun." He lightly brushed his thumb back and forth across my earlobe. "It's been a long time since I did anything that wasn't expected of me." He frowned. "Even when I was engaged, we mostly went to charity functions and business dinners."

"I know what you mean." My heart was thudding so loudly, I could barely hear myself think. "It seems like I work all the time, too, and when I do have some time off, I'm too exhausted to enjoy it."

Which wasn't exactly true. The past month with Jake, I had actually relaxed a little and we'd gone out on some dates, but now didn't seem to be the ideal moment to bring up that exception.

"Maybe we should both try to add a little spice to our lives." Noah leaned closer. "We always had such a good time when we were together in high school."

"But that just made what happened more painful," I reminded him.

"I know and I'm sorry." His mouth hovered over mine. "But before that, it seemed like everything we did together was exciting and new and wonderful."

"True," I whispered. "Those couple of years we had together, before everything went to hell, were some of the best of my life."

"Mine, too." His voice was husky. "I'm so sorry they ended the way they did."

My mind kept telling me that I was making a big mistake; I wasn't the kind of woman who played the field. My few relationships had all been monogamous. Which guy did I want—Jake or Noah?

Before I could think, Noah pulled me against him and the heat from his body engulfed me. His fingers caressed my jaw, then dipped lower to touch the spot at the base of my throat. My pulse surged, beating frantically, and I made an urgent yearning sound. Cradling my chin, he lowered his head to cover my mouth with his.

In the moment before our lips met, I saw a hunger in his gray eyes that I'd never seen before. As his mouth touched mine, a shock wave soared through my body—an explosive rush that reminded me of closing a big investment deal, the split second after the client agreed but before he signed on the dotted line. Except instead of the satisfaction that usually followed that sensation, this one left a relentless need in its path.

An arrow of heat shot through me when Noah swept his tongue across my bottom lip, and I shuddered. It was all the invitation he needed, and he deepened his kiss, plunging his tongue into my mouth, allowing no shyness, no hesitation, and no second thoughts.

I tunneled under his suit coat and pulled his shirttail from the waistband of his pants. Once it was free, I wrapped my arms around him and caressed the muscles at the base of his spine. Noah's skin felt as smooth and supple as fine leather, and I wanted to stroke every velvety inch of him. His body was sleek and sinuous, and all I could think of was how much I wanted to be naked and pressed against him.

Flames of desire burned through my resolve not to get involved with Noah. As he pushed my jacket off my shoulders and started to peel my long-sleeved T-shirt over my head, I felt myself losing the last vestige of control. Then, like a bad case of déjà vu, I heard someone rapping on the passenger window.

It took only a moment to comprehend that I was about to be caught in a compromising position for the second time in less than twenty-four hours. I hastily pulled down my shirt and sprang apart from Noah, banging my thigh against the gearshift in the process. As I howled in pain, I tried to figure out why the console hadn't been an impediment when I was in lust but suddenly seemed to become such a huge obstacle when I tried to regain my seat.

Finally I turned to see who had witnessed my lack of self-control and discovered the grinning face of my best friend. Poppy was giggling like a schoolgirl while simultaneously giving me a thumbs-up. But if she was really that thrilled to see Noah and me together, why the heck had she interrupted us?

CHAPTER 22

Noah felt like snarling but pasted a genial expression on his face. As Dev ejected herself from his car, he shouted after her that he would call her as soon as he talked to Willow. She nodded and waved, clearly wanting him to leave. Accepting defeat, he drove away, extremely ticked off at himself for losing every damn bit of his famous willpower whenever he was around Dev.

It was a good thing Poppy had showed up when she did, because he knew that kissing Dev would not be enough. He wasn't sure anything would ever be enough to stop the ache inside him. He now realized that taking things slow wasn't going to work, not when he completely lost his self-control anytime they were alone. He knew he had to have her. But not in the front seat of a car parked in broad daylight in the middle of Shadow Bend.

If he'd been able to think, he'd have driven her to his place, swept her into his arms, and carried her to his bedroom. Too bad his mind had ceased to function the instant his lips touched hers. At that moment, he was positive he couldn't have pulled away from her if he was threatened with losing his medical license. He certainly couldn't have waited long enough to get her to his house.

Taking a deep breath, Noah forced himself to put his desire for Dev aside and concentrate on the matter at hand. St. Onge was in real trouble, and having agreed to help the guy, Noah was honor bound to put forth his best effort to prove him innocent. Noah considered himself nothing if not a man of his word.

Still, as he entered Brewfully Yours, the memory of Dev's sea-green eyes and velvety skin interfered with his breathing, and, for a crazy moment, he wanted to return to his car, drive back to where he'd left her, and wrap his arms around her once more.

Noah took another deep breath; then, having regained his composure, he scanned the café. He was in luck. Willow Macpherson was sitting at a table in the back. Her laptop was open, and she was staring at the screen as she sipped from a mug. Every once in a while she'd put the drink down, type a word or two, but then she'd stop and take another mouthful.

As Noah recalled from previous meetings, Willow was as slender as her name implied. Previously, she'd always had her waist-length, mahogany hair in a ponytail or twisted into a bun, but today she wore it unfastened. She had an oval face with high cheekbones and full lips that might have been sexy if not for their twist of permanent dissatisfaction.

Noah pretended to walk toward the bathroom; then, as he passed by Willow, he did a double take and said, "Hey, fancy meeting you here."

"Dr. Underwood." Willow giggled. "You need to work on your pickup lines."

"I guess I'm out of practice." Noah flashed a rueful grin. "Are you busy? Would you like another cup of coffee or something?"

"Sure." Willow glanced at her computer, then lowered the screen. "I was just about to take a break, anyway. How about a mocha latte?"

"That sounds good to me, too." Noah turned toward the counter, then said over his shoulder, "I'll be right back."

"I'll be here." Willow waved.

Once he had ordered, gotten their drinks, and was settled across the table from the young woman, Noah said, "I haven't seen you walking any dogs lately. Are you too busy writing your book to do that anymore?"

"Sort of." Willow's expression was hard to read. "It's due in a couple of weeks."

"So have you put your pet-sitting business on hold, too?" Noah asked, thinking that might be a good lead in to the subject of the Whitmores. "Or did you get such a big advance, you can close up shop permanently?"

"Unfortunately, no." Willow's expression grew martyred. "Everyone thinks that authors are all rich. And if this book is successful, maybe I will be someday. But the advance was only seven thousand, which didn't even put a dent in my college loans, let alone my credit card bills."

"I'm sorry to hear that." Noah sipped his coffee. "I'll keep my fingers crossed for you that your book is a *New York Times* bestseller."

"Thanks." Willow twirled a piece of her hair, seeming at a loss for words.

Noah blinked. He'd never noticed her nail polish before, but he did now—maybe because she was sporting a pistachio-green manicure that reminded him of fungus.

Finally Willow continued. "If my book takes off, I can make a lot of money from speaking engagements and advertisers on my blog. There's even been some interest in having me host a TV show on the Trinity Broadcasting Network." She winked. "Not to mention that I can ask for a lot bigger advance and increased royalties for the next one."

"That would be great." Noah noted that Willow's brown eyes glowed with anticipation. "Are you nearly finished with the manuscript?"

"Yes." Willow's voice held a note of uncertainty. "But the last chapter is harder to write than I thought it would be."

"Why's that?" Noah used his best bedside manner. "Don't you know how it ends?"

"Well . . ." Willow sipped her latte. "I thought I did, but now I'm not sure."

Noah made a noncommittal sound to encourage her to continue.

"The thing is"—Willow wrinkled her nose—"I might have been just a teeny, tiny bit misguided in some of my beliefs and assumptions."

"In what way?" Noah asked, leaning forward. "If I recall from the newspaper article about you, you believe in chastity until marriage."

"That's been my philosophy." Willow's tongue traced her lips. "But I recently had an experience that made me rethink that stance to some extent."

"And you're wondering if you should modify the book's ending because of it?" Noah asked, figuring she had to be referring to her affair with Colin Whitmore. Were they still seeing each other?

"It depends." Willow put down her cup and grabbed both of Noah's hands with hers. "The thing is, I doubt my editor would be happy with a change."

"But . . . ?"

"But." She let go of his hands and slumped back in her chair. "I may have no choice."

"Because . . . ?" Noah was trying to remember his rotation on the psychiatric ward and the lecture on counseling he'd attended. Short responses and reflecting back what the patient said had been advised.

"Because something I did might come out." Willow licked her lips again. "I thought I had fixed it so it wouldn't, but then something else happened recently and now I'm afraid that it will."

"Maybe you'd feel better if you told me about it," Noah encouraged.

"I would like to have another opinion. . . ." She trailed off, then seemed to catch herself. "No. I better not. My dad always says two can't keep a secret." She glanced at him. "No offense, Dr. Underwood."

"None taken, but I am pretty good at keeping my mouth shut," Noah coaxed. "I can promise not to tell anyone, unless it's something criminal." He knew adding that qualifier might have been stupid, but his conscience wouldn't let him omit it. Besides, if she had committed the murder, he doubted she'd confess. "Just tell me what you're comfortable sharing." It was clear she was dying to talk to someone about her problem.

"Okay." Willow glanced around, evidently making sure there was no one in earshot, then said, "But if this gets out, it could ruin me."

"I understand." Noah made a note to himself to remind Dev, Poppy, Boone, and Tryg not to share the information about Willow's affair unless she was guilty of the murder.

"I, uh," Willow blushed and looked away, "fell in love with a married man—let's call him John." She glanced at Noah and he nodded nonjudgmentally. "Co—I mean, John—promised me that he was in the process of divorcing his wife and that he'd marry me. But it was taking a long time and we, uh, couldn't wait, if you know what I mean."

"I do," Noah assured her. "So you two consummated your love."

"Yes." Willow adjusted her watch so the dial was centered on her wrist, then looked at Noah from under her eyelashes. "Unfortunately, we got caught."

"Oh." Noah kept his expression sympathetic and understanding.

"The thing is," Willow gave a high-pitched, mirthless laugh, "despite the fact that Shadow Bend is the hub of all gossip in the known world, I was able to persuade the one person who saw me to keep quiet."

"The wife?" Noah felt he needed to maintain an air of ignorance.

"No." Willow shook her head. "Co—uh, John—took care of her. Someone else."

"How did John take care of her?" Noah asked.

"I don't know." Willow shrugged. "He just said that his wife knew it was in her best interest to keep her mouth shut, or he'd open his."

"But you said something happened recently that may alter that," Noah reminded her. "Did the wife or the other person change their mind?"

"Not that I know of."

"So what's the problem?"

"Well." Willow looked around again, then leaned forward and whispered, "The wife was murdered Saturday night, and I'm afraid the police will find out about her husband and me, and then I can kiss my book deal good-bye."

Noah pretended surprise. "Are you referring to Elise Whitmore?"

"I, uh," Willow stuttered, then narrowed her eyes. "Why do you think that?"

"Because I'm fairly certain that hers was the only murder in Shadow Bend this weekend." Noah added under his breath, "Or any other weekend for quite a while."

"Oh, yeah." Willow blinked. "That was dumb of me, wasn't it?"

"I'm sure no one would be thinking straight under the circumstances," Noah consoled her, then asked, "Do you have an alibi for Saturday night?"

"Oh, my God!" Willow squealed. "You don't think I killed her, do you?"

"No, of course not," Noah answered in a soothing tone. "But if you do have an alibi, then the best thing might be to ask to speak to Chief Kincaid privately. Tell him your story. That way the police won't stir up the rumor mill while tracking you down, since they are already aware that Colin was having an affair."

"How do you know that?" Willow's tone became defensive. "Have you been spying on me?"

"Absolutely not." Noah noticed that her attitude toward him had subtly changed from flirtatious to guarded. "It's common knowledge that his wife was divorcing him because he was playing around."

"Oh. Yeah. Right." Willow nodded. "Yeah. I did

hear that. I remember being relieved that no one seemed too interested in who the other woman was."

"So where were you Saturday evening?" Noah knew the time of death was between eight and eleven p.m.

"Reverend Orville took my bible study group to Kansas City to see *Joseph and the Amazing Technicolor Dreamcoat*." Willow dug in her purse and produced a ticket stub. "Look." She thrust it at Noah. "We had dinner before the show; then afterward we stopped for dessert and coffee before coming home."

"When was that?" Noah asked as he examined the rectangle of pasteboard Willow had produced, then handed it back to her.

"We left at four thirty and didn't get back until nearly midnight."

"Then it seems you're in the clear," Noah reassured her. "Do you think Colin might have killed Elise—to protect you?"

"Of course not," Willow snapped. "What an awful thing to say. You really aren't as nice a guy as I thought you were." She opened up her laptop. "Now, if you'll excuse me, I have work to do."

"Sure." Noah stood.

"I'll think about your advice regarding going to the police." Willow pinned him with a cold glare. "But I'm trusting you to keep your promise not to discuss this conversation with anyone."

"Certainly. I won't tell anyone anything they don't already know." As he walked away, he thought to himself, *Except that you have an alibi, so you can't be the killer.*

CHAPTER 23

I can't believe you and Noah were hooking up in public," Poppy chortled.

Pretending she didn't exist, I stalked past her, unlocked the rear entrance, and hurried into the store. She managed to slip inside before I could close the door in her face, but I continued to ignore her and walked over to the desk.

As Poppy dogged my steps, she snickered. "You guys must have been really into it, since you're both so uptight about public displays of affection."

Crap! She had me there. I recalled how vehemently I had lectured Poppy about that very subject when she'd been caught last summer skinny-dipping in a nearby pond with some guy she *barely* knew—pun intended.

"Is Noah as good as he used to be?" Poppy asked, not at all disturbed by my silence. "I remember in high school, you used to make my hair curl describing his kisses." She made a face. "It was a shame you never let him get much further than that."

I gave up and spoke to her. "Look. Can we talk about something more important than Noah's and my sex life—or lack of one? I take it you saw the text from Tryg that Boone is back in jail."

"That's why I came to find you," Poppy countered. "I was so upset and I figured you would be, too. But I guess you had Noah to comfort you."

"Enough!" I shouted. "I don't want to discuss Noah right now."

"Touchy, touchy." Poppy appeared undisturbed by my outburst. "Anyway, about twenty minutes ago, Mr. and Mrs. St. Onge showed up at the bar in hysterics, and after I finally calmed them down, Tryg called me. He said that the cops got an anonymous tip that the murder weapon was hidden in a drainage ditch a block from the crime scene."

"But wouldn't finding the gun be a good thing for Boone?" Before Poppy could answer, I begged, "Please tell me Boone's prints weren't on it." I knew from my own previous experience as a murder suspect that just because your fingerprints were on a murder weapon didn't mean you were guilty. Conversely, I also knew that the police didn't always see it that way.

"No prints," Poppy assured me. "The problem is that whoever told the cops where to find the gun also said that he saw the guy who hid it."

"Did he name Boone?" I sank into the desk

chair. "And why didn't he come forward sooner?" This was getting worse and worse. "It's been more than five days since Elise was killed, and I refuse to believe the informant just now heard about the crime."

"The tipster didn't say it was Boone, but he described him to a T." Poppy pulled up a rolling stool and sat down next to me. "And I have no idea why the guy waited so long."

"Fu—" I'd given up dropping the F bomb when I quit my previous job, but remembering that vow during times of stress was still a challenge. "Did Tryg say if the police charged Boone?"

"He said they hadn't filed charges yet." Poppy shook her head. "Remember when Boone was arrested on Saturday, Tryg told us that the cops can hold him twenty-four hours without a case being filed against him?" I nodded and Poppy added, "At least this time, Tryg was able to be there within minutes of Boone being taken into custody, and he forced the cops to formally arrest Boone, so the twenty-four hours started at twelve fifty p.m. today."

"Which means there's nothing we can do until tomorrow," I said to myself. Then I asked Poppy, "Does Tryg still want to meet with us tonight?"

"No." She shook her head. "He said he needs to research some point in the law. Instead, he wants us to e-mail him a report on everything we've learned by noon tomorrow. That way, if the prosecutor indicates that she'll file a case against Boone, he'll present our findings to her before she does."

"Okay." I pulled the desk phone toward me. "Noah's going to try to locate Willow this afternoon and talk to her." I explained how he knew her, then added, "And we need to talk to Lindsey and Colin."

"How are we going to do that?" Poppy asked. "We don't know either of them."

While I dialed the Yager Factory, I told Poppy about Noah's suggestion for seeing Elise's coworker. And once I got the ad agency's number from Vaughn, I phoned Lindsey and set up an appointment to discuss a possible PR campaign for the dime store. When I told her that I would be consulting with a rival firm the next day, she agreed to meet me at seven p.m. at the store.

As I hung up, Poppy said, "That leaves Colin." She leaned her elbows on the desk. "Any ideas?"

"Nope." I filled in Poppy on what Max had said about Elise's husband. "I'm thinking that our best chance might be to catch him somewhere outside of work but in public." I raised my brows. "We don't want him to throw another fit at the bank, but we also don't want to be alone with him."

"Hmm." Poppy moved her mouth back and forth for a few seconds, then said, "How about the health club? Someone at the bar mentioned that they were surprised to see him working out there the day after his wife was killed." She crossed her arms. "Then someone else said that Colin works out at the club every morning from seven to eight, rain or shine, seven days a week."

"That alone should get him arrested. Who exercises every single day?" Which reminded me, I really needed to get back to doing yoga, even if I couldn't afford the classes anymore.

"Maybe he's OCD." Poppy shrugged. "Or has nothing better to do with his time."

"Maybe." Or maybe he was normal, and Poppy and I were lazy. "Anyway. Here's the plan. I'll go home and have supper with Gran. Can you meet me back here at a little before seven to help interrogate Lindsey?"

"Definitely. I'll call in a sub to bartend for me." Poppy jumped off her stool. "And then we'll both corner Colin tomorrow morning at the health club. Wear your cutest workout clothes," she ordered. "He obviously likes the ladies, so we might as well soften him up with our girlish charms."

"Right, like I have tights and a sexy sports bra in my wardrobe." I rolled my eyes. "Besides, no one gives me a second look when you're around."

"Except Noah and Jake," Poppy reminded me. "I get the sleazes," she threw over her shoulder as she flounced out the door, "and you get all the good guys."

Gran was looking forward to the evening—Tony and Frieda were coming over to play poker. Happy that she would have company, I helped her get the food on the table.

While we were cleaning up after our meal, I jokingly asked her if Tony could handle two women, and she retorted, "The older the ram, the stiffer the horn."

Shuddering at that image, I headed back to town. As I drove, Noah called to give me the bad news that Willow had an alibi. He had phoned Reverend Orville, and the minister had confirmed Willow's story. Before hanging up, Noah also pointed out that since she wasn't the murderer, we all needed to keep her identity as the other women secret, and I agreed that there was no reason to ruin her life by gossiping about her.

Noah and I said good-bye just as I parked my car at the store. And while I was letting myself in the back entrance, I realized that since Willow was in the clear, we really needed either Lindsey or Colin to be the killer. We had to find a good suspect to present to the prosecutor or Boone wouldn't have a chance of avoiding some serious jail time while he waited for his day in court. And if it went as far as a trial, who knew what a jury might decide?

I figured the soda fountain would be the best place to meet with Lindsey, so I made sure it was well stocked with ingredients. My plan was to lull her into a false sense of security by plying her with sweet treats, then sock her with the tough questions.

When Poppy arrived, I told her what Noah had conveyed to me about Willow; then, a few minutes later, Lindsey knocked on the front door and I let her inside. I introduced her to Poppy, explaining that my friend was also interested in a PR campaign for her bar.

Once the formalities were over, I invited Lindsey to take a seat on one of the soda fountain stools. Poppy hopped up on the one next to her and I went behind the counter.

Gesturing to the menu posted behind me, I asked, "What can I get you two?"

Poppy asked for a banana split and Lindsey requested a single scoop of frozen yogurt. As I worked on their orders, I studied Elise's coworker. My first impression of Lindsey had been that she was sporting a small white dog on the top of her head, but, upon further examination, I wondered who had convinced her that dyeing what appeared to be a platinum skullcap on top of her own dark brown hair would be a good look for her.

Once we all had our treats, I said, "Have you lived in Shadow Bend very long, Lindsey?"

"About a year." Her apologetic expression was unconvincing. "I'm sorry I haven't been in your store before, but now that I see how charming it is I'll be back soon."

"Don't worry about it." I sipped my root beer float. "I used to work in the city, too, and I know it's a lot easier to do your shopping there."

"Thanks for understanding." Lindsey took a tiny bite of yogurt. "You said Vaughn Yager recommended me, but I'm a little confused as to why, since he wasn't my client."

"Uh." I thought fast. I hadn't expected the opportunity to bring up Elise to come this soon in our conversation. "Vaughn said that with Ms. Whitmore being unavailable, you were definitely the person to talk to."

"How nice of him." I could tell by Lindsey's voice that she wasn't exactly pleased to have been second choice. "Actually, it was highly unusual for a client to prefer Elise's ideas over mine." She raised a brow. "So maybe he just preferred Elise."

"I did hear they were very close friends." Poppy's tone was full of innuendo.

"And she was getting a divorce." Lindsey beamed at Poppy. "I never believed her story that Colin had cheated on her. She always tried to make everyone else look bad."

What? Hadn't Lindsey been the one who told Elise that Colin's car was at the motel during a time when he was supposedly at the bank? "That must have been a rough situation, since you worked together," I murmured. Interesting how people rewrite history so quickly once someone is dead.

"Incredibly rough." Lindsey's brow furrowed. "Elise and I were up for the same promotion, and she was backstabbing me something terrible."

"How awful." I made sure my tone was sympathetic. Clearly, this woman had never heard the old saying about not speaking ill of the dead.

"Wow!" Poppy's angelic face shone with innocence. "That's sucky."

"Yes. Yes, it was." Lindsey leaned forward. "I'm just relieved that I have an alibi for the night she was killed, or the police would probably be knocking on my door."

"Why's that?" I asked, surprised that this was going so easily. "Had you threatened her?" Just because Lindsey claimed she had an alibi didn't mean she really did.

"Not in so many words." Lindsey chewed a thumbnail. "But I did make a sort of rash statement to the mayor." She looked between Poppy and me. "I really wanted to get the town of Shadow Bend as a client and I said I'd do anything to beat out Elise."

"I'm sure a lot of people make statements like that without ever meaning they'd kill for a job," I reassured her. Which was true; more often that sentiment led to bed, not dead.

"So what's your alibi?" Poppy asked.

"I was at an Herbal Choices party," Lindsey said. Then, at our confused looks, she explained, "It's an organic hair- and skin-care product line, as well as herbal dietary supplements." She shrugged. "A client's wife sells the stuff, and I had no choice but to attend. . . ."

"How did you find out what the time of death was?" I asked. As far as I was aware, that fact wasn't public knowledge. We only knew because Boone's attorney had a right to that information.

"My husband told me that Elise was found at eleven, and the officer who spoke with him said she hadn't been dead for more than three hours— something about the body still being warm to the touch and no rigor mortis," Lindsey answered. "And my friend Myrna Burnett and I left Shadow Bend in the early afternoon to do some shopping in Kansas City before the party. We didn't get back in town until nearly midnight."

"How fortunate for you." I smiled at her instead of gritting my teeth, which is what I wanted to do. Another suspect eliminated was not good news for Boone.

After the disappointing news that Lindsey couldn't have killed Elise, I pretended to get an emergency text from home and told the ad woman that we'd have to reschedule. Once I had hurried her out of the store, Poppy telephoned Myrna Burnett and asked about Lindsey's alibi. I'm not sure why Myrna was willing to talk to

Poppy, but she was, and she confirmed she'd been with Lindsey from two to midnight on Saturday.

Poppy and I commiserated that we hadn't found the murderer, deciding to postpone writing the report for Tryg until we'd talked to Colin Whitmore.

We agreed to meet at the health club at seven a.m., and I headed home. I waved at Gran and her poker buddies, who seemed to be involved in a cutthroat game of five-card stud, then closed myself in my bedroom to process the day's events. Just before I fell asleep, I realized that once again I wouldn't be able to search for Elise's cat the next morning and resolved to do so after work on Friday. I sure hoped that Tsar had found someone to take him in, or at least a place to stay warm.

The health club was on the outskirts of town in a tiny strip mall. Poppy and I arrived at the same time, and I admired her low-riding, skintight stretch capris and matching ruffled sports bra. She didn't seem quite as pleased to see my gray sweatpants and black T-shirt.

While we were signing in and paying for a day pass at the front desk, she hissed, "Are those clothes what you consider sexy?"

"Hey," I whispered back, "if I looked like Fairy Princess Barbie, I'd wear your outfit, but since

I'm more like a Jill doll, this is the best I can do. As a curvy girl, I firmly believe that wearing spandex is a mistake."

"Why? If you'd put on some lipstick, fix your hair, and wear some cute shoes, no one would notice the size of your ass," Poppy informed me as we walked down a short hallway. "And what in the hell is a Jill doll?"

"She was the teenage sister of an early 1950s chubby doll called Ginny," I explained. "Both Jill and Ginny were shaped like real people rather than the fashion dolls that appeared later that decade."

"Only you would know that." Poppy snorted, then glanced around the room and pointed at a man on an elliptical machine. "If that's Colin Whitmore, turns out I do know him after all. He comes to the bar's karaoke nights."

Since there was no one else present, I figured the guy had to be Elise's husband, but he sure didn't look like I had pictured him. The man on the machine was barely five foot six and maybe a 115 pounds soaking wet. He had a wispy mustache that drooped over plump pink lips. His brown hair made me think of a burlap bag, and a gold stud pierced his right nostril. It was hard to believe this was the guy who had succeeded in seducing Willow into giving up her vow of chastity.

As I approached him, his hostile hazel eyes

zeroed in on me, but his sour expression changed when he caught a glimpse of Poppy behind me. He puffed up his chest and started moving faster.

"Hi." Poppy waved. "I don't know if you remember me. I'm Poppy Kincaid. I own Gossip Central. You have a great singing voice."

Colin lurched to a stop. "Poppy, uh, what a surprise. Of course I know who you are. What man could forget someone so gorgeous?"

"Aw." Poppy fluttered her lashes. "How sweet. But I don't think I ever knew your name."

"Colin." He smoothed the sides of his short hair and tugged at neck of his faded T-shirt. "Colin Whitmore."

Either Colin was ignoring me or he'd forgotten I was there. I was used to fading away next to Poppy's exquisite beauty; it had been happening since first grade, when the bus driver was so enthralled by her that he missed my stop and didn't realize I was still on board until he parked back at the bus barn.

"Oh, my God!" Poppy pretended surprise. "Was it your wife who was murdered last Saturday?"

"Yes." Colin leaned awkwardly against the handles of the elliptical machine. "But we were in the process of getting a divorce."

"Still, I'm very sorry for your loss," Poppy said. "Do they have any idea who killed her?"

"I hear they think it's her lawyer." Colin's

284

expression was solemn. "I warned her about him."

"Really?" Poppy twirled a strand of her hair. "Why is that?"

"He was giving her bad advice." Colin licked his lips, his gaze on Poppy's breasts as they rose and fell under her skimpy top. "I told her that we could settle things amicably without involving attorneys, and save a lot of money, too."

"Now, Colin." Poppy wagged a finger at him. "Was that because you'd been a bad boy and she and her lawyer were going to take you for all you were worth?"

"I don't know what you're talking about." His voice rang with false sincerity.

"From what I heard, your wife caught you in a teeny bit of a compromising position." Poppy's tone was still playful.

"Well . . ." Colin winked. "When you're as awesome in bed as I am, it's hard to turn down a lady when she begs."

After I stopped myself from gagging, I joined the conversation in the role of bad cop and said, "So, when that lady begged you to kill your wife to protect her identity, you couldn't say no to that, either."

"No!" Colin opened his mouth, closed it, and repeated the process. "I would never have hurt Elise."

"Even though she was getting rid of all your

prized possessions?" Poppy prodded him. "Come on, Colin. Everyone in town knows how pissed you were."

"But—" His face had been ruddy with good health; now it was purple with outrage.

"You told anyone who would listen that she was selling or giving away items that had been in your family for years and were irreplaceable," I added to jog his memory. "Hell, you threatened to sue whoever bought your stuff from her for receiving stolen property."

"Okay." Knitting his heavy eyebrows together over his pug nose, Colin admitted, "I *was* mad. She was getting rid of heirlooms like my great-grandfather's set of golf clubs, signed baseballs that my dad had given me, and chocolate molds that had been a part of my mother's family business."

"That does seem mean." I felt a twinge of guilt at the mention of the molds and reminded myself to give them back if Colin turned out to be innocent.

"So you really must have been furious when Elise tried to get you fired," Poppy chimed in, her tone sympathetic.

"Sure." Colin shrugged. "But I knew Max would never get rid of me."

"Really?" I couldn't keep the cynicism from my voice. "That's not what I heard. I heard that when he told you he was turning the matter over to Mr.

Bourne, you became violent and broke a coffee table."

"That's a lie!" Colin yelped. "Who told you that?"

I shot Poppy a glance asking if she thought we should tell him. She gave a slight shake of her head, and I said, "I can't reveal my source."

"Well, whoever said it is a liar, and everyone at the bank will back me up." He swung his gaze to Poppy. "The front wall of Max's office is all glass, so if I did something like that, everyone in the place would have seen it or at least heard the noise."

"Interesting." As a matter of fact, now that I thought about it, the president's office was in full view of customers and tellers.

"Be that as it may . . ." Doubt curled Poppy's perfect rosebud mouth. "You still could have killed your wife."

"The police cleared me." Colin pasted on a satisfied smile. "I have an airtight alibi. I was in New York at a programmer's convention from Friday morning until Sunday afternoon. Every bit of my time the night Elise was killed is accounted for."

"How wonderful." Poppy recovered faster than I did.

"Why are you two so interested?" Colin narrowed his eyes. "Hey, I remember now. You're friends with Boone St. Onge. You're trying to pin

Elise's murder on me to help your friend wiggle off the hook." He advanced on Poppy and roared into her face, "Go to hell."

She raised a brow and said, "Sorry. I can't." Then she grabbed my hand and tugged me toward the door as she said over her shoulder, "Satan has a restraining order against me."

We hurried down that hall, glancing behind us to make sure Colin wasn't following us. He might have an alibi, but he also had a temper.

Once we were safely in Poppy's Hummer, she made a call to her source at the police station, and he confirmed that the cops had investigated Colin's alibi and it had checked out.

After she put away her cell, I said, "We are now officially out of suspects."

"Well, we'd better find some more." Poppy whacked me on the arm. "Boone will not look good in prison stripes."

CHAPTER 24

Poppy promised to e-mail Tryg our report regarding Willow, Colin, and Lindsey, then hugged me good-bye and drove away in her Hummer. We were both upset. Boone had been counting on us, and we had crapped out. Why did all of our suspects have to have alibis? What were the odds that three people could verify their whereabouts on any given Saturday night? When I was under investigation, I sure hadn't been able to prove where I'd been.

When I arrived at the dime store, the message on the store phone didn't improve my mood. It was the school secretary telling me that Hannah wouldn't be at work today. There was some sort of high-stakes achievement testing associated with the No Child Left Behind law that she was required to take with the rest of her class.

After quickly changing from my exercise clothes to my jeans and sweatshirt, I got the store ready for the day, then began creating a basket for one of Oakley Panigrahi's clients. I had already finished the other nineteen in his order and needed to deliver them on Monday morning.

As I chose the perfect luxury items and arranged them, I racked my brain trying to figure out who had murdered Elise. There had to be something we were all missing. I had been working on the basket for nearly an hour when there was a knock on the front entrance. It was still ten minutes to opening, so I normally would have ignored the early bird, but I saw that it was Bryce Grantham and he was holding a large plastic Pet Taxi.

As I let him into the store, he handed me the carrier and said, "Look who I found."

"Tsar, I presume?" A large gray cat with striking green eyes gazed at me through the wire mesh.

"That's the name on his collar," Bryce affirmed. "I found him this morning while I was walking Sweetie. I noticed him coming out of the half-open door of a neighbor's tool shed. When I investigated, I saw that he'd chewed open a bag of dry cat food that had been stored in the shed and had made himself a cozy little nest in a rag box."

"Was he hard to catch?" I asked, relieved that the cat had been warm and well fed the whole time that he was missing.

"Not at all." Bryce grinned. "I put a dish of tuna in Sweetie's Pet Taxi and Tsar strolled right in." He frowned. "Actually, he limped in. I think he hurt his foot."

"Poor baby," I crooned to him, then said to Bryce, "I'll take him to the vet's right now."

Normally, I hated closing the store, but with Hannah AWOL and an injured cat, I had no choice. I briefly considered calling Winnie but quickly decided against it. Better to lose business than to come back to the place in utter chaos.

"What will you do with him once the vet takes care of him?" Bryce asked.

"I have no idea." I shrugged. "I have it on good authority that Elise's husband doesn't want him. Would you like a cat?"

"Sorry." Bryce shook his head. "I'm more a dog person."

I thanked him and promised to return Sweetie's

Pet Taxi as soon as I could. Once Bryce left, I taped a note to the store's entrance saying that I'd be back in thirty minutes; then I took Tsar to Banshee's veterinarian.

There was already a waiting room full of patients and their humans when I arrived, but the receptionist assured me that the doctor would see Tsar as soon as there was an opening in the clinic's schedule. She said she'd call me with the results after the cat had been examined, so I left the cat there in the Pet Taxi and hurried back to my store.

Before resuming work, I sent Poppy and Noah each a hasty text that the cat had been found. Even though I knew they hadn't been as pre-occupied with finding the animal as I had, I thought they'd want to know that he was safe and being cared for by the vet.

My cell chirped a little after twelve and since I was alone—the store was deserted—I checked the message. My heart sank when I saw that it was from Tryg. The prosecutor had filed the case against Boone, and they were now waiting to go before a judge to see if Boone would be granted bail.

Sadness overwhelmed me. My BFF was in serious trouble and I hadn't been able to help him. According to the IQ tests I'd been given in school, I was supposed to be smart. So why couldn't I figure out who had really killed Elise?

While I was still castigating myself, the veterinarian called. Once we had established that I would foot the bill, he said, "Overall, Tsar is in good shape—well hydrated and with no sign of malnourishment."

"Thank goodness." I had figured the kitty was okay, but it was nice to hear it confirmed by a professional.

"However, there is one area of concern," the vet continued. "A claw on Tsar's right front foot is nearly torn off. The area between the nail and the footpad is jammed with something, and the only reason the claw was still attached is that he must have stepped in some type of resin and it acted as a sort of sealant."

"How could an injury like that have occurred?" I asked.

"He was probably in a fight," the vet guessed. "The claw will have to be removed. I'll perform the surgery after my regular hours and then call you in the morning to let you know when Tsar will be ready to go home."

As soon as I had thanked the vet and said good-bye, I headed for the safe. I would need my emergency credit card to pay Tsar's vet bill and didn't want to forget to put it in my wallet. The Visa was all the way in the back, and as I reached for it, I had to push aside Colin Whitmore's chocolate molds. *Shit!* Now that I knew he hadn't killed his wife, I needed to get the molds back to him.

I tucked the credit card into my purse, then checked the front of the store. Seeing that there were still no shoppers, I decided to package up the chocolate molds to send to Colin. Since I figured it was wiser to remain anonymous, I decided to drop them at the Kansas City FedEx when I delivered Oakley's baskets. I'd use a fake return address and send them to the bank, since I didn't know where Colin was living.

As I gathered the five molds from the safe, stacking them in my arms, the largest one slid from the pile and crashed to the floor. Hoping that I hadn't damaged it, I bent to pick up the foot-tall metal bunny.

It lay in two pieces, and for a minute, I was afraid it had broken. Then I realized it was supposed to open that way in order to unmold the chocolate. As I gently lifted the two halves, I saw that there was something taped inside each part of the mold. Actually, there were three somethings: an old-fashioned computer disk, a flash drive, and a tiny vial enclosed in a plastic bag.

I immediately guessed that the items belonged to Colin. After all, he was the computer wizard, and Elise wouldn't have sold me the molds if she knew there was stuff inside them. So what was the big secret?

Maybe if his wife hadn't been killed and my best friend hadn't been arrested for that murder, I might have given everything back to Colin without looking at the contents of the flash drive. But probably not. I had a nosy streak, and the mystery intrigued me.

My laptop wasn't equipped to play the disk, but the flash drive was no problem. Sliding the thumb-size white rectangle into the computer's port, I was half afraid it would be password protected. But, clearly, Colin didn't think anyone else would ever discover the items, because with one click, a list of files appeared. Another click and I was looking at a spreadsheet.

At first I didn't quite understand what I was seeing. The files were Shadow Bend Savings and Guaranty Bank records from fourteen years ago, but what was the big deal? Why tape them into a metal bunny's rear end? Finally the significance of that date hit me. These were the records from the period when my father was suspected of embezzling funds.

I sank into the desk chair and took a deep breath. This could very well be either proof of my dad's innocence or evidence of his guilt. My stomach sank. Since I had an MBA with a specialty in finance and had worked several years in the investment field, I was confident that I could interpret the data. But did I really want to?

Reluctantly I sat forward and began to study the figures. After a couple of hours, I pushed the laptop aside, leapt to my feet, and started to pace. Could I trust my conclusions, or was I too emotionally involved to be objective? A few more laps around the storeroom and I returned to the desk and rechecked the numbers.

Tears poured down my cheeks as I finally allowed myself to believe what I was seeing. There was no longer any doubt in my mind; my father was innocent of the embezzlement. Along with the relief came rage. Rage at all that my family had been through. Rage at the man who should have been in prison instead of my father. Rage at Max Robinson, the man who had really embezzled the money, thereby putting into motion the whole ugly sequence of events that had ended with my dad committing vehicular homicide.

I sat there stunned until I heard the sleigh bells above the front door ring. I glanced at my watch and saw that it was three o'clock. The after-school crowd was arriving. I quickly put both the molds and their contents back into my safe, locked it, then went out to feed my customers.

Ninety minutes later, the kids headed home for supper, and I sat down at the soda fountain to think. As I drank a cup of coffee, questions ping-ponged inside my head. Why did Colin have that computer flash drive? Did the disk contain the same material? Was it the original version, since flash drives weren't around fourteen years ago? Could the information I had just discovered help my father, or was it too late for him? Although I could now prove he didn't embezzle, he had still killed someone while driving drunk. And what was in the vial?

Setting aside my dad's situation, I thought about Elise's murder. If Colin hadn't broken the glass coffee table in Max's office, why had the bank president told us he had? If the table had never been broken, how did Max get those wounds on his leg? And, most important, did the answers to those first two questions have anything to do with Elise's death and Colin's possession of the flash drive?

While I was considering the possible answers to my questions, I heard someone enter the store. Swiveling to face the door, I was surprised to see Noah striding toward me.

As he took the stool next to me, he said, "Tryg texted me about Boone, and I came as soon as I finished with my patients for the day. How are you?"

"A few hours ago, I would have said frustrated, but now I'm not sure." A warm feeling washed over me from Noah's obvious concern.

"What happened?" He covered my hand with his.

I told him about what I had found in the chocolate molds, at the same time explaining how I had come to have the molds in my possession. Then I outlined the contents of the flash drive and the conflicting stories that Colin and Max had told us about the coffee table. I concluded with, "So my guess is that Colin was blackmailing Max."

"It does seem a distinct possibility," Noah agreed.

"But how does that fit in with Elise's death?" I asked. "Presumably, Colin has been blackmailing Max for many years, so what's changed now?"

Noah's forehead wrinkled in concentration; then he announced, "The divorce proceedings. Colin was suddenly in need of more money than usual, so he might have increased his blackmail demands."

"Okay." I narrowed my eyes. "Let's say that for all these years, Colin has been asking for a modest amount of money from Max. Maybe a monthly stipend or something. Then, suddenly, due to Elise's manipulations, Colin finds himself strapped for cash and significantly ups the amount."

"So, why wouldn't Max kill Colin?" Noah asked.

"Because . . ." I trailed off, thinking, then snapped my fingers. "Because Max must have been willing to pay more—like a lump sum—but only if Colin handed over the evidence."

"But computer disks and flash drives can be copied or even faked," Noah pointed out.

"Then those weren't what he wanted." I bit my lip. "It must be the vial. I bet it has his finger-prints on it."

"But what does a glass vial have to do with the embezzlement?" Noah asked.

"No clue," I admitted. "But I think that Colin must have told Max the evidence was in the chocolate molds and Elise had the molds and wouldn't give them back."

"So Max broke into the house to get them." Noah nodded to himself. "He probably thought no one was home, since St. Onge told us all the lights were off and it looked as if Elise had been napping in the back bedroom."

"She must have woken up and caught him."

"And he shot her." Noah shook his head. "Max couldn't allow himself to be arrested for breaking and entering. He could never explain that to the bank's owner or its board of trustees."

"So how do we prove it? All we have is a guess." I slumped forward, cradling my chin in my hands. "Even showing Chief Kincaid what I found in the molds doesn't tie Max to the murder."

Before Noah could answer, I shrieked, "The wounds on Max's leg."

"What about them?"

"If Colin didn't break the coffee table—and I believe that he's telling the truth about that, considering how public Max's office is and how easy it would be to check with the tellers—then how did Max get hurt?"

"How?"

"Tsar scratched him." I explained about the torn claw.

"But why would Max tell such an easily refuted lie?" Noah tapped his fingers on the counter.

"Several reasons," I answered slowly. "First, he had to come up with a fast explanation of his injury. Second, he's used to being the boss, and no one ever checks up on the boss—his word is law. But most important, he got away with one crime, and from what I've read about criminals, if they never experience consequences for their initial crime, they feel invincible."

"Then we'd better call the vet right now," Noah suggested. "Tell him to save the claw and the other stuff they remove from the foot pad. There's a good possibility that Max's DNA is on that material. And if it is, we've got him."

"In that case, we'd better contact Chief Kincaid and get him involved before the vet does the surgery."

"Why?" Noah asked.

"If the vet removes the material from Tsar's claw without a witness, it might break the chain of evidence." I flashed Noah a grin. "I knew watching all those TV crime shows would pay off someday."

After I contacted the veterinarian and told him not to operate on the cat until he heard from me, I reluctantly closed the dime store for the second time that day. Then I filled a shopping bag with what I would need for our talk with the chief, and Noah and I walked over to the police station.

Chief Kincaid was in his office and agreed to see us right away. I wondered how many more times I could play the friend-of-his-daughter card before I had used up all his goodwill toward me.

Once we were settled in chairs facing his desk, the chief said, "There's nothing I can do for Boone. The case is out of my hands."

"We understand," I assured him. "But if we have proof that someone else killed Elise, you'd reopen the investigation. Right?"

Frowning, he adjusted the leather blotter so that it lined up more perfectly with the edge of his desk. Then he stared at me, and when I didn't blink, he said, "It would have to be extremely compelling evidence for me to be willing to do that, since any new investigation might weaken the case against St. Onge."

Hmm. I hadn't considered that issue. I flicked a glance at Noah, and he smiled his encouragement. I took a moment to collect my thoughts. I wanted to present a concise and convincing account of what we believed had happened.

Laying the chocolate mold and its contents in front of the chief, I straightened my spine. "It all started fourteen years ago, when Max Robinson embezzled several hundred thousand dollars from the Shadow Bend Savings and Guaranty Bank. It ended last Saturday when he killed Elise Whitmore."

As I told him the rest of the story, Chief Kincaid fingered his shiny brass nameplate, then rubbed the mark his thumb had made off the surface with his handkerchief. When I was finished, he looked up and said, "How do I know you're telling me the truth?"

"Several points are easy to validate," Noah said, joining the conversation. "For instance, you know I wouldn't lie to save St. Onge, and I will swear to you that Robinson said that Whitmore broke his glass coffee table and that he showed us an injury he claimed was caused by the flying debris."

"Why would Robinson lie about something that can be readily checked?" The chief answered his own question before either of us could respond. "Because he's an arrogant twit who considers himself above the law."

"That's my guess," I said. "And he probably thinks no one will dare challenge him."

Chief Kincaid rose from his chair and said, "Wait here." He scooped up the flash drive and marched out of his office, closing the door behind him. I was glad that I had copied the drive onto my computer at the store and made a printout before we left.

"Do you think there's anyone at the station who can interpret the financial records on that drive?" Noah asked.

"I doubt it."

We sat silently for what seemed like hours, but was really closer to forty-five minutes. When the chief returned, he said, "The coffee table is intact, just as Whitmore told you, and none of the tellers remembers any kind of altercation between Robinson and the victim's husband."

"You walked over to the bank," I guessed. An advantage of a small town was how close by everything was located.

"Yes." Chief Kincaid smiled as if I had said something clever, then pointed a finger at me. "And on the way I dropped off your flash drive with a friend of mine. He just called to say that on the surface, your analysis of its content seems accurate. He'll need more time to be absolutely sure, but for now he'd say you're probably right."

"That's good, isn't it?" I felt so tightly coiled, I ached.

The chief took a small notebook from his breast pocket, flipped it open, and read something, then said, "Max Robinson matches the description of the man that the neighborhood watch captain reported seeing lingering near the Whitmore residence."

"I had forgotten about that," Noah murmured.

"Me, too." I turned to the chief. "So, what happens now?"

"We do a photo lineup for the watch captain and

see if he picks out Robinson," Chief Kincaid answered as he reached for the phone.

We were in luck; Captain Ingram was home and willing to come to the police station immediately. While we waited for him, the chief sent an officer to fetch a picture of Max from the local newspaper files, then assembled seven other photos of men in Max's age range.

While all this was happening, Noah had to return to his clinic to keep an appointment, but I waited. If Poppy were on better terms with her father, I would have texted her to come over and keep me company, but considering their current relationship, I was afraid she'd jeopardize the cooperation I was getting from the chief. I contemplated contacting Tryg but thought that his presence might also be detrimental.

An hour later, Chief Kincaid returned to his office and said, "Ingram identified Robinson as the man he saw skulking around the victim's house on Saturday night."

"Is that enough to get Boone released?" I crossed my fingers.

"No, but I spoke to the prosecutor." Chief Kincaid raised a brow. "She was not happy."

"Oh."

"I did talk her into getting a search warrant for Robinson's house and office, and one to examine his bank accounts."

"How about DNA?" I reminded him.

"And to get a court order for a sample of his DNA," Chief Kincaid confirmed. "Now I'm heading over to the veterinarian's office to witness the surgery on Elise Whitmore's cat and collect the material from the animal's claw."

"How long will DNA testing take?" I figured it was a lengthier process than the TV shows depicted.

"I'll pull in a favor or two, so if the samples are good, and barring any more urgent cases, I should be able to get the results by next Friday."

CHAPTER 25

To say it was a long weekend and an even longer week would be an understatement. There were a couple of bright spots. Oakley Panigrahi was thrilled with the baskets that I delivered to him on Monday morning, and Boone was granted bail that afternoon. On the downside, I'd mailed five of the chocolate molds back to Colin—the sixth was in the hands of the police— and thus was out eight hundred dollars.

Although Chief Kincaid refused to discuss what the cops were doing to investigate Max, he did tell me they had gotten the search warrants for Robinson's house and office and the court order for his DNA, and auditors were combing through his financial records.

I was afraid that Max would disappear during this time, but one of Poppy's inside sources at the PD told her that he was under twenty-four-hour police surveillance. Even Poppy grudgingly acknowledged that her father seemed to be doing everything right.

During all this, Noah's mother returned from her cruise. When he picked her up at the Kansas City airport, he had a talk with her before bringing her home, which he reported to me. He vowed that Nadine understood that if she did anything to upset me or tried to take any action against my family, my friends, or me, he would sever all ties with her. I, however, still had my doubts. Nadine Underwood was not a woman who was easily thwarted.

Finally, late Friday afternoon, I got the call I had been waiting for. The DNA matched. Tsar had indeed scratched Max Robinson. After my whoop of joy, Chief Kincaid stated that the search warrants had been fruitful—his words—and that the police were bringing the bank president in for questioning. I asked if I could watch and was astonished when the chief agreed.

After getting my weekend clerk in to run the store, I jogged over to the PD. According to the dispatcher, Max had just arrived with his attorney and they had been put in the interrogation room. When one of the cops led me to the area behind the one-way glass, a thirtysomething brunette was already there, and the officer introduced her as the county prosecutor.

She was wearing a severely tailored black suit as if it were armor. The frown on her face deepened when she heard who I was. Nodding silently, she turned her attention back the scene in the next room.

Chief Kincaid, seated across from the bank president, tapped the file in front of him. "It's all here. You might as well confess."

"I'm innocent." Max crossed his arms. "I have nothing to confess to."

"We have your DNA at the crime scene." Chief Kincaid pulled out a piece of paper and put it in front of Max.

"That's impossible." Max smirked. "Even if I had killed Elise Whitmore, from what I understand, she never touched her assailant."

"But her cat did." Chief Kincaid's expression was impassive.

"So a cat scratched me." Max shrugged. "That could have happened anytime."

Although Chief Kincaid didn't say it now, he'd told me earlier that Tsar's paw print in the dried varnish on the Whitmore kitchen floor acted like a time stamp. The feline had to have scratched Max, then almost immediately stepped in the resin, so the DNA they found in the cat's claw could only have been deposited there during a specific time period. The police could definitely prove that Max had been in Elise's house shortly before her death.

Moving on, the chief selected another page from the folder. "We also found shoes in your closet with traces of Elise Whitmore's blood."

The lawyer whispered furiously into Max's ear, and Max waved him off. "Maybe her husband planted them at my house."

I heard the prosecutor croon under her breath, "That's right, jerk, ignore your attorney and keep talking."

"They're your size and the wear pattern matches your other shoes." Chief Kincaid took a third sheet from the file. "And we also have proof of your embezzlement, which Colin Whitmore is willing to verify."

"The jury won't be impressed by the testimony of an extortionist." Max's lips curled. "He probably forged those computer records."

"So you admit he was blackmailing you?" the chief pounced. "And I never revealed that the proof was computer records."

The prosecutor muttered, "Strike one."

"Uh." Max seemed to belatedly realize what he'd said but again waved off his attorney's urgent whispers. "I don't know what you mean."

"Don't worry, the forensic accountants who traced the embezzled money to your accounts will explain everything when we're in court," Chief Kincaid assured him. "But let's put that all aside for a minute, because we also have a vial of Rohypnol with your fingerprints on it," Chief Kincaid stated. "Which poor innocent woman did you use that on?"

"None." Max's expression relaxed. "I've never drugged a woman."

My stomach clenched as the bank president grew more outwardly calm and whispered something to his lawyer. *Damn!* That couldn't be a good sign.

Max's attorney said, "We're done here." He sat back. "My client has nothing more to say."

Was Max about to weasel out of everything? My mind raced until something clicked and I knew how he'd used the roofies. Turning to the officer standing between the prosecutor and me, I said, "I need to talk to the chief right now."

He started to protest, but something in my eyes must have made him reconsider, because he said, "Wait here."

A few seconds later, Chief Kincaid stepped through the door and I hurriedly told him my theory. He nodded and returned to the interrogation room.

When the chief sat back down, he said in a conversational voice, "Did you know that Kern Sinclair is a friend of mine?"

"So?" Max's mouth tightened.

"And, as I said, we have proof you were the embezzler, not him."

"A white-collar crime." Max shrugged, but sweat was pouring off his forehead. "*If* I'm convicted, I'll go to Club Fed."

"You set up Kern Sinclair." Chief Kincaid pounded the table.

Max jumped.

"And when it looked as if he might not take the fall for the missing funds, you gave him Rohypnol, fed him drink after drink, and stashed a bottle of OxyContin in his glove compartment. Then you let him drive away," Chief Kincaid thundered. "You're as responsible for the death of the girl he hit with his car as he is."

"How could I know that would happen?" Max whined, as his lawyer tried to shut him up.

"Strike two." The prosecutor's smile was fierce.

"You're just a worm who should have never been anything more than a middle-management drone." Chief Kincaid's face was red. "And I'm going to make sure everyone in Shadow Bend knows what you did and who you really are."

I had never seen the chief like this before. Every word he uttered was like a knife carving away another layer of Max Robinson's ego.

"You're just like your father." Chief Kincaid sneered. "A nobody living off your betters."

I'd forgotten that Gran had said Max's dad was a drunk who barely eked out a living doing odd jobs for the town's wealthier citizens.

"That's not true!" Max's face was purple. "Unlike people like Kern Sinclair, who was handed everything on a silver platter, I clawed my way up the ladder." His voice was low and deathly quiet and he pushed away his lawyer, who was still begging him to shut up. "I earned the presidency of the bank, not him, but I needed a lot of money to be accepted into the right social circles. It takes a lot of cash to mix with the likes of Nadine Underwood and her crowd. I deserved the chance to be that person."

"And who is that person?" Chief Kincaid gripped the table edge, perhaps to stop himself from taking a punch at the man. "A murderer?"

"Someone important and powerful." Max grew more composed and his words held utter conviction. "Unlike my ineffectual father, I refused to drink myself to death. Instead I got rid of the people who thought they were better than I was, or were in my way. No entitled snob or blackmailer or blackmailer's wife was going to stop me."

"Strike three," the prosecutor crowed.

I could see that every cell in the chief's body was rigid with rage and dogged determination to bring Max Robinson to justice. Then he relaxed and smiled.

"Perhaps your victims couldn't stop you." Chief Kincaid gathered his papers and tapped them into a neat pile before inserting them into the folder. He stood up. "But I can. We have enough evidence to put you away for good."

"Surely we can talk about a deal." Max appeared to suddenly come out of a daze. "A reduced sentence, if I admit that I drugged Sinclair." He grabbed the chief's fingers. "Otherwise, there's no way to prove he was under the influence."

"That will be up the prosecutor." Chief Kincaid shook Max off, then opened the door to the interrogation room and said to the officer standing on the other side, "Lock up this piece of shit. I need to go wash my hands."

EPILOGUE

The prosecutor had assured me that she'd be looking into how the evidence against Max might affect my father, but she cautioned me about being too optimistic. Even if they agreed to a reduced sentence to get Max's testimony regarding the roofies, it might not be enough to free my dad.

Still, finally knowing for sure that he was innocent made me feel better than I had in a long time. And even though nothing had changed and Dad was still in prison, Gran was elated. I hadn't had the heart to tell her that securing his release from jail might be a long, hard fight. We didn't have the money to hire a private lawyer, so we'd have to rely on the public defender.

However, as I sat in Gossip Central, I couldn't help but smile. It was Saturday evening, and Poppy, Noah, Boone, Tryg, and I were celebrating the official dismissal of the case against Boone. Gossip Central had started out life as a cattle barn, and when Poppy had turned it into a club, she had decorated the place to reflect its origins. The center area contained the stage, dance floor, and bar, while the hayloft was available for private parties. She'd converted the stalls into secluded lounges with individually themed decor.

We were in our favorite alcove, the one we'd nicknamed The Stable. Poppy and Tryg were cuddled together on a brown leather love seat, while Boone and Noah had chosen the pair of saddle-stitched club chairs facing the couch. I had dragged in a stool from the bar and positioned it between the two men.

"Did they ever figure out who called in the false information about Boone hiding the gun?" Poppy asked.

"It was Robinson," Tryg answered. "They traced the call back to his phone, and he admitted that he had gotten nervous when Noah and Dev made the appointment to talk to him. So he called in the fake tip to turn the attention back on Boone."

I tilted forward to grab my margarita glass from the wood-and-wrought-iron feed box that served as a coffee table, then asked, "What I still don't understand is why Elise never told on Willow."

"Yeah," Poppy agreed. "You'd think she'd want to destroy the woman who screwed her husband."

"The only thing she would say to me about it was that her silence was golden on that matter," Boone said. "I assumed there was some monetary reward that Colin had bribed her with."

"However, now that we know Colin was a blackmailer, maybe he threatened her with something," I proposed.

"Now that you mention it," Boone wrinkled his nose, "Elise did say that she and Colin both had skeletons in their closets. And she was extremely worried about the promotion she was up for, so maybe he had something on her that would ruin her chances to be the one picked for the VP job."

"Willow said that Colin kept Elise quiet by threatening to reveal one of her secrets," Noah commented.

"So why wouldn't he use that threat to demand Elise give him back his possessions?" Tryg asked.

"Maybe Colin loved Willow more than his stuff," Noah suggested.

"Or it could be he was gambling that Willow's book would be a huge success and he wanted to be a part of the gravy train." I took a sip of my drink.

Then I asked Noah, "Didn't you say that she'd had some interest from the Trinity Broadcasting Network regarding hosting her own show?"

"Yeah." Poppy nodded. "That sounds more like Colin than true love."

"I have another question," I announced.

"Why am I not surprised?" Boone mocked.

"Clearly, there was something you were hiding about your relationship with Elise. What was it?" I demanded, a little surprised at myself for asking. Apparently, the alcohol was starting to affect me. Good thing Noah was the designated driver.

"Well . . ." Boone let out a huge sigh, then leaned forward and said in a low voice, "Since I got permission to share this from my client, I'll tell you. But you all have to promise not to tell anyone."

As we all promised, I wondered how he'd gotten permission from Elise. Had Boone attended a séance?

Boone shoot Poppy a look and asked, "You don't have the bugs in this room activated, right?"

"Of course not." Poppy's expression was hurt. "You know I always turn them off when we hang out in The Stable."

"Okay." Boone blew out a breath. "I was using Elise's place as a cover for visiting another client. He lives in back of her, and by going through her yard, I could enter his house without anyone seeing me."

"You mean Bryce Grantham," I guessed, realizing that that's why he'd been so nice about helping to find Tsar. He must have felt he owed Elise.

"Yes." Boone nodded. "His ex is attempting to get custody of their child, and he's trying to keep the whole matter confidential." Boone twitched his shoulders. "You know that if he came to my office or someone saw me going into his house, there'd be talk, and since his daughter has no idea that her mother is even alive, she's unaware of the custody battle."

"How in that hell did that happen?" Poppy asked.

"The woman deserted Bryce and the baby a few months after the birth," Boone explained.

"If she did that, no court would give her back to the mother. Would they?" I asked. "On the surface, Bryce seems like a great dad. What's the deal?"

"He's gay. His ex-wife waited until he'd moved to Shadow Bend and brought the case to the local court. If she'd done it when they lived in Kansas City, he wouldn't have been so worried about the outcome."

We all nodded. The county court was not exactly a bastion of liberal thinking.

"Does his partner live with him?" I asked.

"Bryce is not currently in a relationship," Boone explained, "and one of the things I was working on was to see if his ex-wife had any proof of his sexual orientation. Thank goodness Bryce has always been extremely discreet and never told his ex when he came out of the closet, which was after she left him."

"So the ex doesn't have anything to support her claim?" Poppy asked.

"It looks that way." Boone smiled. "And the court date is Monday. We should be fine."

"Speaking of Bryce," I said, "I've been thinking about poor Tsar. Since I can't keep him because of Banshee, who here is going to adopt him?"

"Sorry." Noah shook his head. "Lucky couldn't handle another animal in the house."

"And I can't take him," Tryg hurriedly said. "My condo has a no-pet rule."

"Not me." Poppy crossed her arms. "I'm allergic."

We all looked at Boone, who started to shake his head, then nodded. "Okay. I'll take the cat. After all, he did provide a key piece of the evidence that saved me." He shrugged. "Hey, maybe having a furry grandbaby will get my folks talking to each other again."

"They went back to not speaking?" I asked.

"Yep." Boone sighed. "The minute I was cleared, they resumed the cold war."

We all laughed; then Noah said, "I've been

wondering about why Robinson called me the afternoon before the murder. At first, I thought he might be interested in dating my mother. But after hearing what he said to the chief regarding being a part of the right social circles, I think he was just kissing up to me."

"Of course he was." I raised a brow. "Haven't you noticed that ninety percent of the town kisses up to you?"

"Right." Noah's tone was scornful. "Anyway, the only one I want kissing me is you."

"Gag me." Boone grimaced, and the conversation turned to other matters.

About a half hour later, I heard my phone chirp, excused myself, and headed to the ladies' room. Once I was in the bathroom stall, I checked the message. It was from Jake. He'd been at my house, looking for me, but couldn't stick around. He said his team was close to catching the bad guy and he and Meg were heading south. He warned that he'd be incommunicado until he returned.

In view of what had nearly transpired with Noah in his Jag a week ago, I was of two minds about Jake's departure. While I was worried about his safety and I would miss him, it would be nice to have some breathing room in that relationship. I needed to learn to trust myself and my feelings, or I'd never be able to trust a man and his feelings.

Then again, since Jake was now on a road trip with his ex-wife the decision about which man I preferred might be taken out of my hands. Jake might end up back with Meg, and I was positive that Nadine would do everything in her power to keep Noah away from me. So who knew what the future held?

Center Point Large Print
600 Brooks Road / PO Box 1
Thorndike ME 04986-0001 USA

(207) 568-3717

US & Canada:
1 800 929-9108
www.centerpointlargeprint.com